THE MENTOR'S DAUGHTER

ALSO BY STEVE HADDEN

The Sunset Conspiracy

Genetic Imperfections

Swimming Monkeys: Genesis

Swimming Monkeys: Revelation

Swimming Monkeys: Exodus

The Victim of the System

The Dark Side of Angels

The Secret That Killed You

THE MENTOR'S DAUGHTER

A PSYCHOLOGICAL SUSPENSE THRILLER

STEVE HADDEN

MahoganyRow
PRESS

THE MENTOR'S DAUGHTER

Edited by Julie Miller

Cover designed by Damonza

Published by Mahoghany Row Press

Visit the author website:
http://www.stevehadden.com

ISBN: 978-1-963584-06-6 (eBook)
ISBN: 978-1-963584-07-3 (Paperback)
ISBN: 978-1-963584-08-0 (Hardcover)

Category: Fiction / Thriller / Suspense

Version 2026.03.01

For Kelly and all the other therapists and counselors who change lives every day.

CHAPTER 1

SOMETIMES IN LIFE you just have to absorb the blow. Take it, then pick yourself up off the floor and fight. When Eli Scott spotted her entering the Tulsa restaurant, he knew this was one of those moments. Something was terribly wrong. After three unanswered calls, his mentor of sixteen years was a no-show. Now, in his stead, his mentor's daughter, a notorious lawyer and image consultant, had appeared unannounced. They'd never met, yet her history and public reputation built a wave of worry that surged through him. For the second time in his life, he knew he'd have to rely on a sociopath.

With every step she took, his mentor's uncharacteristic absence took on a more sinister meaning. Eli's body instinctively braced for fight or flight, but trapped by his obligations to her father, he could do neither. Whatever lies she carried, Eli had to hear them. His adrenalin spiked, then he realized his past was the source of the anxious pressure building inside. He filled his lungs, reminded himself who he was today, and readied to face the woman marching toward him. Despite his hatred of liars, Eli decided to accept Hope Munro for who she was and where she was today: a woman who made her fortune by lying.

She smiled at the hostess, passing her with a dismissive wave. The brilliant noontime sunlight streamed through the plate-glass windows. Eli's trepidation grew as she made her way along the white quartz floor between the onyx tables and past the glistening brass rails. Without a word, she stopped across from him, grabbed the back of the opposing chair, sat, and faced him.

"Mr. Scott, thanks for waiting for my father," she said, her expression bright and optimistic, her tone confident and engaging. She seemed charming. Eli wanted to relax, expecting a simple explanation, but he knew not to be fooled. Still, he played along.

"Not a problem. I wouldn't be where I am today if not for your father. I was getting concerned."

Her million-dollar smile spread across her thin face. "Well, we have that in common." But the smile dissolved into a stare that felt like a predator locking on its prey. Her deep brown eyes bored into his as she reached across the table and covered his hand. "My father *is* the problem."

Eli's heart rate doubled, pounding in his ears. He embraced the warning that clawed in his gut, trying to dig its way out. His body quaked. His jaw felt locked in place. He narrowed is eyes on her. "Is he okay?" he said, not wanting to hear her next words.

Hope's eyes drew tight, and a tear drifted down her cheek. "He's been kidnapped."

He lunged toward her. "What!" A few heads from surrounding tables snapped in his direction. He didn't want to believe what she'd said. Jim was much more than his mentor. He'd filled the void Eli's father could never fill. Now, Eli envisioned life without him, the loss slicing him in half. He imagined Jim and his captors, and he forced himself back into his seat and gripped the arms on the chair until his knuckles whitened. He forced himself to take a breath.

Eli assumed she loved her father considering how Jim had stood by her. Yet a warning that she lied for a living—a particularly good living—rang out again somewhere deep inside. Eli wasn't an investigator; he was an oilman who had donned his armor and had fought his way from the oilfields into the executive ranks until he refused to follow in his father's deceptive footsteps.

Eli gritted his teeth and resisted the urge to throttle her. "How long has he been missing?"

"Since yesterday evening," she said, calmly.

"What about the police?" Eli asked, trying not to yell. She'd taken far too long to ask for help.

Hope pulled out a tissue and wiped her cheek. "I can't. They wouldn't believe me."

"Can't what?" This time Eli was loud enough to draw the attention of the two women seated next to them.

Hope eyed them, forcing them to look away, then she turned back to Eli. "There's a video," she whispered.

"What?" he asked, swallowing his frustration.

"It said not to go to the authorities, or he's done," she explained.

Eli checked the proximity of the ladies on either side and leaned forward on his forearms. "Show me."

Hope thrusted her hands out to the side. "It's gone. The video disappeared as soon as I looked at it."

Eli's microscopic speck of trust in anything she said evaporated. "How was it sent?"

"To my Signal account," she said as if Eli should have known that.

He knew the app was an encrypted messaging service that had the capability to automatically delete messages and videos. He wasn't surprised she used it with her high-profile clients. But considering her history of twisting the truth, the fact that the video disappeared and couldn't be verified was a problem. A big one.

"Describe the video," he said, doing his best to deliver a more pleasant smile.

"My father was in a nondescript gray room anchored to a metal chair. A garbled voice said that unless I gave them what they wanted, they'd kill him. His head was wagging no the entire time. They said they'd be in touch with further instructions."

It sounded like every TV ransom setup. Too rote. She let the description hang in the air between them, like bait on a hook. She kept her eyes glued to his.

"And they didn't say what it was they wanted?" he said. He watched her for any signs of deception. She showed none, but still, he didn't trust her.

"No. I'm assuming that comes next," she said.

Eli leaned forward on his elbows again and whispered. "Did you notice any other sounds in the background?"

Hope matched his lean. "No. It was silent other than the garbled voice."

Still leaning closer, he asked, "Could you tell if the camera was stationary or handheld?"

She leaned back again. "What difference would that make?" Despite challenging his question, she remained oddly calm.

"It says something about the alleged kidnappers," Eli said, firmly.

She shrugged. "It was moving around. Like a video someone was posting."

"Did it look like a home or an industrial setting?"

Hope folded her arms and smiled. "Don't you think I would have mentioned that?"

Still unsure about her answers, Eli had a choice. Believe her, freely giving her his trust, and help her save the man who'd helped him navigate the worst times of his life, or Eli could assume she'd lied, taking the risk that she hadn't. But deep down, he wanted to believe some of her lies because they were Jim's only hope.

Jim Munro was also the father who'd said he'd recognized Hope's condition after he'd witnessed a soccer game where she was more interested in kicking the other girls than the ball. In retaliation, two opposing team members had beaten and kicked her as her teammates stood and watched until the coaches ended the melee, the faded scar on her neck a result of those injuries. A few years later, when she'd confessed to stealing her mother's friends' jewelry from their unoccupied homes and keeping her loot hidden in the garage, her mother gave up, leaving her father with the carnage.

Jim had said he'd guided Hope through a gauntlet of run-ins with the local police in high school until he'd helped her discover where she could best survive. She had the grades, and her father's connections led to the University of Tulsa law school. Passing the bar on the first try, she had become a defense attorney. Then, based on her ability to rehabilitate her clients' images in the courtroom, she'd added image consultancy to her services. A parade of disgraced tech giants, politicians, and oilmen had followed, and her reputation and bank account had swelled.

Eli shifted in his chair. He didn't want to trust a liar. It was a recipe for disaster. But he didn't have a choice. As much as he hated lies, he'd have to find a way to sort through Hope's.

Hope's expression said she'd recognized his doubt. "My father said to come to you if anything happened to him. You'd know what to do. He said you'd help me because you were the best friend he ever had."

Eli imagined he was playing a deadly game of truth or consequences, where the wrong answer could destroy everything he'd painstakingly rebuilt. But while Hope hadn't earned the benefit of the doubt, James Munro had. And then some.

"I'll look into it and get back to you," Eli said, knowing he had little choice.

"I need an answer now. He's in trouble. I know you know that feeling." Another tear ran down her cheek.

Eli wanted to jump in with both feet. But he felt triggered. He felt himself shifting into crisis mode, something he was very good at. He reminded himself of her very public reputation. Better to think about it. "Give me a few hours. I'll call the number tied to your text."

She skidded her chair back and stood. "I'll be waiting."

As he watched her confidently stride from the restaurant and slip on her dark Bottega Veneta sunglasses, his suspicions still begged for his attention. There was something about their conversation. It seemed to go just the way she wanted. And there was something about her behavior. Not that it had felt scripted. That was the wrong word. Every word, every expression had been driven, confident, and measured. It had been as if she were on autopilot. It was compulsive. Then it hit him. It had been *pathological.*

Eli got the attention of his server and asked for the bill. The last time he'd delt with a sociopath, he was seven years old. He knew he needed professional help to better manage this one. He pulled out his phone and selected a number from the most recent calls. He called Lizzy Beauregard's number.

She answered on the first ring. "Eli?"

"I need to see you this afternoon."

CHAPTER 2

ELI KNEW THE trip to Lizzy Beauregard's practice would take only a few minutes. It felt like a lifetime. He gripped the steering wheel and wrestled the dilemma tearing at his heart. The weighty certainty of his obligation to Jim Munro was clear, but so were the warning flares ignited by his mistrust of Jim's sociopathic daughter. He needed Lizzy's help to untangle this mess. He took in a slow deep breath and eased it out just as she had taught him. He regained his focus on the present moment.

As he drove past Utica Square, the upscale outdoor shopping mall, the cold winter day limited the number of well-dressed shoppers. Still, he sensed the old money power of the area. Those powerful oil families had built stately homes with long winding drives among the one-hundred-year-old trees guarding stone-and-brick mansions that peered over the area from their hilltop perches. Throughout the last century, they'd built Tulsa into the more cosmopolitan of the two major cities in Oklahoma. While Oklahoma City was the capital, scratched from the red flat plains of the western part of the state, Tulsa had been cultivated on the rolling green hills of northeastern Oklahoma by the oil barons who'd made Tulsa the oil capital of the world in the first half of the twentieth century. They'd continually enhanced the city's cultural pedigree. While it had taken too long for some, they'd also come to recognize the contributions to its culture from Native Americans and Black men and women—far too many of whom had paid with their lives in the city's worst moments.

Eli turned into the small, shaded parking lot facing the converted home just after 1 p.m. Built in 1910, the Craftsman-style home featured red brick accented by natural stone topped by a dark-gray slate roof. A low brick wall bordered the front porch that welcomed visitors to the rounded wooden entry door of NorthStar Counseling. Eli remembered how the comfort of the place scrubbed the tension from his body. This place had saved his life. But it was all he could do to contain the energy ricochetting through his head.

Inside, Eli was greeted by the gentle sound of trickling water from the pebbled fountain in the corner. Soft natural light fed the deep green plants placed atop the natural wood furnishings, giving him the sense of the magic of life. The familiar scent of sandalwood filled the air. Two sofas, upholstered in gentle gray-and-blue woven fabric, provided a brief respite for those who waited for their sessions. The four parlors had entrances off the foyer. The waiting area was empty, a function of the late lunch break for the practice. Lizzy's door was open.

"Eli?" Lizzy said.

Eli walked to the open double doors and took a calming breath. "Hey, Lizzy."

"I didn't know you were here already. You practicing your cat burglar skills? Your session won't go any better if you sneak up on it."

Eli smiled as he always did when she greeted him with her quips. "It took me a while to clear your security."

She grinned. "You know what I say. More security builds suspicion, and suspicion is the mother of insecurity."

He had known Lizzy for over a year, but Eli felt she knew him as if she'd been a lifelong companion. Together they'd plumbed the depths of his deepest fears and sorrows and continued to rebuild his thinking about his life. That had grown into what Lizzy called a *professional* relationship neither had expected.

He stepped into the parlor and took the familiar king chair facing her. She placed her pad of paper on the small table next to her. She'd told him she'd never believed in desks. She said they were too much like a barrier or a throne. Her bright green eyes found Eli's and she smiled.

At fifty-eight, she'd reached the point where she could manage the practice and take on a limited number of clients. She'd come to Oklahoma from Charleston, South Carolina, thirty years ago with her now ex-husband and toddler son so her husband could take the chief counsel position in a small but growing pipeline company. After his multiple affairs, she'd left him and returned to school, graduating with a master's in psychology from Oklahoma State. After working as a school counselor until her son, Brady, was out of grade school, she'd begun her private practice.

Lizzy sighed and a look of concern swept across her face. She looked down at his foot, and Eli realized he was tapping it. He stopped. "What's the emergency? You sounded out of sorts on the phone, and you seem unsettled now. What gives?" Lizzy asked.

Eli wanted to be careful. He didn't want to pull Lizzy into something and didn't know what her legal obligations might be. "I need to run something by you. Just to check my thinking. But start the *consulting* clock." He wanted to make a distinction between Lizzy's consulting and his counseling sessions, always respecting the red lines of their professional relationship. "I also have a question to start. Theoretically, if someone tells you about a crime, do you have to report it?"

Her eyebrows shot up, one higher than the other. Her face twisting with concern. "Are you in trouble?"

Eli shook his head. "No. Let's say it's not me."

Lizzy tilted her head. "Is it a credible threat to someone else?"

Eli didn't want to answer. He thought for a moment, then it hit him. "No. Not credible." *Yet*, he thought.

"Then no." She grabbed the notepad from the table. "Tell me what's going on."

Eli leaned forward. "I had a visit from Jim Munro's daughter at lunch."

Lizzy seemed surprised. "Wow. That's a blast from the past. How is he?"

"That's what she wanted to talk about."

Lizzy furrowed her brow again. "Oh no. Is he okay? I know you two were close."

Eli swallowed hard. "That's just it. I don't know. Jim had told me years ago his daughter was a sociopath."

As she looked down and wrote a note, she said, "Must have been a while back. We don't use that term anymore. We use *antisocial personality disorder*."

Lizzy's definition made him feel worse. "Okay then. He said she lies all the time. And that's the problem."

"How so?" Lizzy asked.

"She said she received a Signal video that showed him kidnapped."

Lizzy looked up from her notes. "Did she call the cops?"

"No. She said they wouldn't believe her, and they threatened to kill him if she did."

Lizzy shrugged. "Just show them the video."

Eli shook his head, showing his disappointment. "It was one of those that immediately delete themselves once viewed."

Eli could see her connecting the dots. She jotted something down. The more she wrote, the drier his mouth became. "I see." She looked up from the pad. "You don't believe her?"

Eli carefully thought about his reply. Eli and Lizzy had uncovered a few trust issues he had. Mistrust came much easier to him, and Lizzy knew it. In this case, he felt justified, but the irony wasn't lost on him. He needed to find a way to trust a liar. "I called and texted him before she showed up and after she left and didn't hear back. So, it fits... but you know what she does for a living?"

Lizzy nodded. "I do. She's quite famous."

"Notorious," Eli said. "Jim had told me she also had juvenile problems with the cops involving violence, missing neighborhood pets, and stealing when she was growing up."

A look of concern returned to her face. "I remember you talked about Jim being upset about her."

Eli locked his eyes on hers. "Here's the question. How can I trust her? Jim told me she'd been diagnosed as a sociopath on her eighteenth birthday. When I met her, I got the sense I was being manipulated and everything she did was rehearsed."

Lizzy tapped the top of the pen against her lower lip. "Did Jim ever talk about her problems in detail?"

Eli wasn't sure where Lizzy was going. He felt like this was going backward. He needed an answer to his question, now. He took a breath. He trusted Lizzy. "Only about his need to stay close to her and his frustration with her behavior. And the fact that Hope's stash of stolen items from his wife's friends' houses was the thing that broke their marriage."

Lizzy paused and looked at her notes. "Did he talk about her remorse? Did she apologize either to him or to them?"

Eli still wondered where Lizzy was going with this. He was getting impatient. "He just said she apologized but didn't seem to mean it. She didn't seem as guilty or ashamed as he would have liked."

"Is she single?"

"What?"

"Is she alone?"

Eli gave her an exaggerated nod. "Yes. I think so."

Lizzy ignored his frustration. "Did she seem nervous?"

"No. Not nervous. But here's the thing. She did seem genuinely worried. Like she needed to get him back."

Lizzy wrote a few more things down. She stared at the page for a few seconds.

"What is it?" Eli asked a bit more loudly than he'd planned.

Lizzy drew in a breath and let it out. "Look. I can't diagnose anyone without meeting with them—getting to know them. But if I'm"—she made air quotes— "'consulting,' I can give you some advice."

Eli glanced at his watch.

"Are you pressed for time?" Lizzy asked.

Eli realized he'd been keeping her in the dark about his urgency. "I forgot to tell you, Hope said the kidnappers gave her a deadline to come up with what they want. I only have seventy-two hours, and the clock started yesterday."

"Good God," she said, staring.

Eli stared right back. "I know, right?"

"What do they want?"

"That's yet to come."

Lizzy slowly shook her head and looked down at the pad in her lap. "Now I know why you were asking those questions."

"I can't get the authorities involved. Please. They'll kill him if it's true."

Lizzy held her gaze on him for a few seconds. Finally, she sighed, wagged her head, and turned her attention back to her notepad. "Look," she said, tersely. "Here's my professional take. She checks the boxes on some of the traits and behaviors that are used to assess psychopathy or antisocial personality disorder."

Eli's heart jumped into his throat. "I'm dealing with a psychopath, not a sociopath?"

Lizzy looked up from her notes. "Wait a second. Don't jump into the pool until I fill it with water."

Eli chuckled to himself, then settled and patiently waited for Lizzy to finish.

She looked back down at her pad. "From what you've told me,

she has a history of being capable of violence. She lacks empathy and remorse. She's deceitful, manipulative, and superficially charming. She's repeatedly broken the law. And she seems to be a loner, perhaps pointing to a limited ability to demonstrate and connect with emotions."

"That captures what I know. She also gets paid to lie."

"That brings up one of the mitigating factors. She apparently can manage money."

"Or she makes so much, it doesn't matter."

"A valid point. But what I'm trying to say is she may be somewhere on the scale. I doubt she's a full-blown psychopath. I'd agree with the diagnosis of ASPD. If she's sociopathic, it's more common than you'd think, as many as one in twenty-five people."

Eli turned his head, curiously. "I feel like you're trying to tell me something that I'm missing."

"I am. I'm trying to tell you to be careful. She may be a *highly functioning* sociopath. That would mean she doesn't experience emotions like we do. It's their absence that's the problem. She appears to be very intelligent. She hides her condition very well in social situations. It's a dangerous combination."

Eli still looked for the bottom line. "I shouldn't trust anything she says?"

"You'll have to make that assessment yourself. Sociopaths can experience strong, painful urges to act out. And acting out can be some type of antisocial behavior, like lying, hurting others, or breaking social norms by stealing. But here is the thing. If they can't do those things to alleviate the painful pressure building inside, a few of them can give in to their violent impulses."

"They snap?"

"I wouldn't use that term professionally, but yes, they can snap."

"That's why you want me to be careful."

"That and I value our relationship." Lizzy crossed her legs, rested her pad on her knee, and leaned back. "Look. You need to know a couple of things." She started a count on her fingers. "First, you have to understand the person she is."

"What do you mean?"

Lizzy closed her pad. "I mean she has no conscience. None whatsoever. She won't feel shame, guilt, or remorse for anything she does. She is a predator. She only wants to win. And that winning is defined by dominance through control or manipulation of those of us with a conscience. That's why she's so good at what she does for a living."

It wasn't the answer Eli had hoped for. His pulse slowed and he sighed. As usual, Lizzy could read him well.

"What are you thinking?" she asked.

"I'm thinking, what about Jim? I have to do *something.* I owe Jim a lot. He sent me home to sit with my mother while she was in hospice. Four weeks. He went against the rules—made sure I was paid, didn't dock my vacation. He showed me the ropes in the oilfields. He gave me opportunities, and those opportunities and his advice got me through the worst times in my life."

Lizzy put her pad on her table and settled. "I'm going to switch hats for a moment and do some of that therapist stuff. You ready?"

Eli relaxed. "I'm ready."

"Do you remember our work on self-worth? How you were very confident in your abilities, but you had that voice driving you to always improve. To be better."

Eli remembered the sessions. "Yes. Those were tough sessions."

"Yes, they were. My point is, a sociopath can spot that need a mile away and exploit it."

"Really?"

"Yes. Number two is to always approach all matters with her intellectually. Keep your emotions out of it."

"Okay."

"It is your superpower. She'll feed off your emotions if you let her. They will fuel her. Luckily, hiding your emotions is one of your strengths."

Eli wanted to laugh. "You mean the thing we've been working to fix all this time is an asset?"

Lizzy grinned. "Don't get carried away. I said hide your emotions, not suppress them." She held up three fingers. "Third. Change the game but don't tell her."

"What?"

"Her game is to win. Dominate through manipulation and control. Pick your objective and stick to it. Intellectually. Don't get swept up in her game."

"My goal is simple. Find and rescue Jim."

"Fine. Stick to it." Lizzy made sure of her eye contact with him. "Now. Be patient. You'll feel the fight-or-flight response when she targets you. It will cloud your judgment. You need to let it go."

Eli opened his eyes wide. "Uh oh."

"What is it?"

"Already felt it. When I was talking to her."

"Let it go. It will wear you out. Play the intellectual game instead."

"Got it."

"Four. Don't confront her head-on. It will escalate her impulsiveness. She's already shown a tendency for violence, like we discussed. Be patient. Remember that she's better at her game than you'll ever be. Think before you do anything."

Eli nodded.

"Last but not least, try to enlist someone else to help."

Eli knew that was a nonstarter. "Help. I can't. I can't tell anyone."

"You'll find someone. I have confidence that you'll find a way. There is safety in numbers. Two heads and all that stuff."

Eli was always surprised by her confidence in him. "I'm not sure I understand that therapist lingo."

"Very funny," Lizzy said, folding her hands in her lap. "Let me ask you: Are you trying to save Hope?"

The question cut straight through to the dark dungeon he hid from everyone. Lizzy had found it—again. His recent work with Lizzy had uncovered a pattern. He'd subconsciously find women who were flawed in some way, who even treated him poorly. He then spent his time trying to change *himself* to cause them to fix themselves and fix their relationship with him. It was a product of the buried sense of not being enough that he'd adopted as a kid. It had been a strength in his run up the corporate ladder, as he constantly sought to improve himself. It was also self-destructive behavior that had made him a sucker for someone in distress. Someone like Hope.

"Eli? What are you feeling?"

He ran through the list of emotions they'd been working on. He struggled a bit identifying the emotion tied to experiencing Hope. "I felt as if I wasn't good enough to deal with her. I also felt like I *had* to help her. I *had* to believe her. I wanted to say that I would. But I felt triggered."

"Good," she said. She gently smiled. "Now. Think back to our EMDR session a few months ago. Did it feel like that?" Eli remembered the session where they'd worked on a feeling that he'd been experiencing since the day he'd been fired from his executive job because he refused to go along with a lie. "I think that's it. Not quite as intense, but it's there."

"Do you remember the root of that feeling?"

Eli recalled the EMDR light sliding side to side. It was hypnotic. As he'd held the sensation inside him, a string of events from his past arose and Lizzy captured them all. Their follow-up work took them to the oldest memory. It was the night he had watched his mother, strapped to a gurney, being loaded into a waiting ambulance. Her body and mind failing under the weight of his father's trail of soul-crushing lies. Eli was alone and seven years old.

"I remember." The sinking, raw shame of not being enough for her—to save her, reached up from the darkness inside. Then, it hit him. "I do want to save her. I also want to save Jim." When he'd remembered what they'd just talked about regarding changing the game, he sat up in the chair and pulled his shoulders back. His determination intensified. He was ready to save the man who had saved him.

"Find Jim and save him," he said again.

"Good," Lizzy said. "Be careful about that first one. If she is a sociopath, she's a predator. Like I said before, they can find a weakness in anyone with a conscience and manipulate it."

Eli's confidence grew. "I'll focus on Jim. Banish the shame gremlins."

She reached over and touched his forearm.

"You and I have been through that hell together. And you've battled through it. You've worked harder than most. I think you know what to do. I'm here if you need me." She leaned back in her chair. "Back to consulting. With Hope, I'm telling you to move with caution."

Lizzy was right. He knew what he needed to do. Whether he could do it was another thing.

"Back to my question. How can I tell for sure if she's lying or telling the truth?"

Lizzy picked up her notebook and stood. "You can't."

CHAPTER 3

ELI SQUIRMED IN the seat of his idling Explorer, tapped his finger on the steering wheel, and stared at the screen of his phone. At six-foot-three and 220 pounds, one reason he'd bought the Ford was because of its comfort, but he found little comfort in the deep bucket seat. It was just before 2 p.m. and he needed to make his decision. Hope's text stared back at him. He looked up at NorthStar Counseling, then closed his eyes, stepping back from his tangle of racing thoughts. Jim Munro could be in trouble. Even if Hope was unreliable and sent him on a mission into harm's way, it was probably worth the risk. Maybe.

Eli remembered the most concerning story Jim had told him. It was a fall afternoon, and Jim received a call from Hope's high school counselor.

"This is Claire Roberts. Unfortunately, we have a situation regarding the school's homecoming court that involves your daughter."

Jim made his disappointment clear with his tone. "Are you sure it involved Hope? She's done so well this year."

"Not sure, Mr. Munro. The top three vote getters in the court have reported a series of thefts. Hope, as you may know, is fourth in the voting, but has not experienced any such thefts. I hate to ask, but she's been accused and with her history…"

"Accused by whom?"

"Mr. Munro, I'd like you to come to a meeting this afternoon with Hope if you're available. I'd also ask that you check to ensure you don't have evidence of any of the stolen items at your home."

"What items?" Jim said, making no effort to hide his disgust with her question.

"Lipstick, makeup, single earrings, one Apple earbud, and three blouses, and three USB thumb drives."

"I haven't seen her with any of that, other than what she owns."

"Please check and then join us at four in my office."

Jim slammed the phone down and forty-five minutes later he was sitting across the desk from Mrs. Roberts with Hope at his side.

"Hope, I called in you and your father to discuss some very serious allegations of theft by your fellow homecoming queen candidates."

Hope smiled sympathetically, slowly wagged her head, and locked eyes with Mrs. Roberts. "I'm so sorry you've been put in that position. Sorry they've done that to you. Especially considering all the help you've given me."

"So, you deny taking any of the items we discussed before your father arrived?"

"I know what the girls are saying about my past, but you know that's all behind me. It hurts that they would bring up things that happened back in junior high." Hope began to sob. "It hurts. They've spread it all over the school with their rumors."

Mrs. Roberts turned to Jim. He thought he saw tears welling in her eyes. "Mr. Munro, do you have any evidence to the contrary?"

He hugged Hope. "No. I think you know what's going on here. She's had no problems all year. Those girls are mean."

Mrs. Roberts stood and handed a tissue to Hope. "Thank you both for coming in. I needed to clear this up."

Hope left the office sobbing in Jim's arms.

Six days later, he discovered the stolen items when replacing an air-conditioning vent. But the most concerning thing wasn't the stolen items. He also found a thick journal from years ago, before Hope's mother had left, that contained plans to kill her mother. He tore the pages out and wrote them off to preteen angsts. Her mother was fine and living in Houston. He'd also told Eli that he'd begun to hide critical, private, and confidential information from her in a cold war, spy-like fashion.

Eli stared at Lizzy's office. If Hope's lies led to his demise, well, he couldn't think about that outcome. Still, Jim Munro was a mentor and friend, and *his* daughter had asked for help. If the shoe was on the other foot, Jim Munro wouldn't hesitate.

He opened his eyes, selected her number, and called Hope. She answered on the first ring.

"Glad you're on board," she said.

Eli took a beat. He realized this was who she was. He wasn't going to change that. He ignored his ire and her comment that triggered it. He'd play the intellectual game.

"Meet me at your father's house off Utica."

"I'm already here."

Eli had visions of her staging a scene. He'd have to live with his mistrust.

"I'm just a few blocks away. Be there in a few," he said.

She hung up on him.

Eli shook his head, dropped the phone in its cradle, and turned right out of the parking lot. He headed toward the Munro home. Once on Utica Avenue, he cleared the outdoor mall and turned left. As he drove south, the houses, lots, and trees grew larger. Turning onto Grayson Way, he spotted the familiar black iron gates guarding the light-gray granite home. Jim had built the home after his retirement from the oil business. The lot was two acres, split off from a larger estate by the children's trust of one of the original oil families. Because his wealth and public profile had grown due to his focus on green energy in the middle of the oil patch, he'd decided some security was necessary.

Eli pulled to the gates and pressed the button on the call box. A camera mounted on one of the stone pillars stared back at him. There was no response. Only a high-pitched tone as the gates parted.

"Thanks," he said to the call box, chuckling to himself.

He pulled down the circular driveway and parked in front of the main entrance to the house. The thick black front door opened, and Hope stepped into the threshold. She smiled as if welcoming him to an open house. Eli exited the car and walked to the door.

"Come in, Mr. Scott," she said, showing the way with an open hand.

Eli would normally be thrilled with such a cordial welcome to someone's home. But equipped with Lizzy's warning about Hope's proclivity for charm, he felt like he needed a shower. He decided to treat this like a business transaction and shoved his emotions aside.

"Thanks." He pushed past her and she shut the door.

"The office is down the hallway," she said as if he'd never been here. In all the times he'd visited Jim, he'd never seen her. Maybe she didn't know, but Jim would have mentioned at least one of his visits. She started through the great room with a towering timber-lined ceiling. Eli didn't follow.

When Hope recognized she was alone, she looked over her shoulder and stopped. "Aren't you coming?"

He stood firm. "When you first got here did you notice anything unusual?"

Hope's eyebrows shot up. "Of course not. I would have led with that if I had."

"Are his cars in the garage?"

"Yes. Both of them."

"Does he have a housekeeper?"

Hope folded her arms and strolled back toward Eli. "Yes. He does."

"What day does she work?"

Hope stopped a few feet from him. "You don't believe me. Do you?" Her smile didn't waver.

He refused to take the bait. "I'm just looking for anything that can help."

"Wednesdays," she said curtly.

"And you got the message yesterday evening—Wednesday night?

"That's what I told you."

Eli could see that his rapid-fire questions were frustrating her. "Any idea what he might have that someone would kidnap him for?"

"No. Nothing. Other than money."

Eli turned away from her and surveyed the great room. Everything was in its place in the kitchen, living room, even in the pool area visible through the towering plate-glass windows. It was all spotless, as if no one lived there. Too much so.

Eli scanned the room one last time, then faced her and nodded toward the hallway. "On to the office."

She spun and led him down the hallway lined with white wainscoting and mill work adorning the barreled ceiling. Beautifully framed western art Eli had admired with Jim at the Philbrook Museum lined the walls.

Reaching the office, she opened the oak double doors and stepped inside. *Office* was a misnomer. The well-finished room looked like a library with two-story bookcases, thick mahogany paneling, and smart brass lighting fixtures and rails. The second level of bookcases circled the room above, with a small walkway and brass rail in front of them.

Eli examined the room and again and noted the impeccable order and cleanliness. Even the large wooden desk, blotter, and wooden in and out baskets were empty. A tablet computer sat perched on the blotter. It was tied to a large monitor facing the black leather office chair.

Eli walked to the desk and reached for the top drawer. "May I?"

"Certainly, but you'll need this." She produced a key from her pocket.

Eli did his best to hide his suspicion. He realized that if she was indeed a sociopath, she'd probably be a walking lie detector. He decided the effort to hide his displeasure would be futile. "You've already gone through it?"

She read him instantly. "Oh. No. I just wanted to be ready for you." Her expression looked genuine, but flares ignited in his chest.

He took the key and unlocked the desk. The top drawers contained supplies. The file drawer on the right held well-organized personal files: investments, taxes, medical, and travel.

The right drawer contained a couple of accordion folders and a copy of *Building the Life You Want* by Oprah and Arthur Brooks. It was one of Jim's favorites. The book had handwritten notes on the pages but no loose papers. Eli returned the book, closed the drawers, locked the desk, and handed the key back to Hope.

He pulled out the lap tray holding a keyboard and mouse and shook the mouse. The computer wasn't on.

"Do you happen to have access to this, too?"

"No. Sorry." Hope appeared to be sincere.

"What about his phone? Have you looked for it?"

"First thing I did. Didn't find it."

Eli remembered the camera at the entrance. "What about the security cameras?"

"There's a control pad in the mudroom."

"Let's go," he said.

Eli followed Hope back through the great room and down a short hallway to the mudroom. The room had cubbies for shoes, a few coat hooks—one holding Jim's favorite winter coat—and a long cabinet topped by a thick black countertop. Eli spotted the small tablet on its stand next to a door at the other end of the room.

"Where's that door go?"

"To the garage."

Eli walked to the tablet and touched the screen. It came to life. He touched the button marked *Activity* and prayed Jim had left it logged in. He had.

There were several video clips of Jim entering and leaving the garage in his cars over the last week. A number of FedEx and UPS trucks had dropped off packages into a box at the gate, the morning paper had been delivered every day, and the yard maintenance crew had made their rounds on Wednesday. Each day had activity. Usually, Jim left and came back, including the last time he returned Wednesday evening. But Thursday showed no activity during daylight. Not even the morning paper. There was one clip at 7:04 p.m. An older, dark-blue Toyota Corolla pulled to the gate. It was difficult to see the driver, but an arm reached for the box. It was definitely a dark-skinned person. They pressed the box five times within the sixty seconds of the clip, then backed onto the street and raced away. The next clips were Hope and Eli arriving.

Eli set the tablet back in its cradle. "Did you delete anything from the system?"

She looked surprised. "Me. No. I haven't seen those before." Hope seemed credible if that meant anything.

Eli's suspicion was growing. "It's possible someone did."

He reached down and picked up the tablet and played the clip of the dark-skinned person at the gate again for Hope. "Do you know who that is?"

Hope bent closer, then pulled back. "Never seen that car before. Have no idea. You think they're involved?"

"Exactly what time did you get the video?"

"I don't know. It was about the same time."

Eli hesitated, trying to get a read. Nothing in Hope's face swayed him one way or the other. He now understood how she'd gotten all those dirt bags' reputations rehabbed. He replaced the tablet on the counter. Something stirred in his gut.

He put his hand on the doorknob on the door leading to the garage. "Shall we?"

Hope nodded and he opened the door. Both cars were in the garage, just as Hope had said. A newer Ford Bronco, in British racing green, filled the near bay, and a white Lexus sedan filled the other. Eli walked around both cars, inspecting the floor and the cars' exteriors. Hope stood and watched. Most every time he'd ridden with Jim or met him for lunch, Jim had driven the Bronco. Eli went to the driver's side door and looked inside. The graphite-colored dash shone like it had been recently wiped down. The seats were graphite with a brown trim. Nothing looked out of place.

He opened the door with his shirttail in case they pulled in the authorities or they just showed up. Carefully, he leaned in and inspected each area of the driver's interior. Then he froze.

It was barely visible inside the well holding the shifter. It looked dark brown on the graphite finish. Eli thought it could be dried blood.

"What is it?"

He turned to look at Hope. "I'm not sure. Could be a speck of dried blood."

Hope's eyes flashed wide and her face reddened. "I told you he was taken!"

Eli's muscles tensed and he felt his adrenaline ramp up his defenses. She had turned from host to banshee in a split second. Then she seemed to catch herself and return to her softer demeanor.

She seemed to immediately read his mind. "Look," she said, fondling the large starlike pendant on her necklace, "I had problems. Still do. But my dad was the only one who stuck with me. He's the only one who kept me safe and taught me how to stay that way. He helped me survive. Someone took him. Whether or not you help me, I don't care. That's the thing. I never care. I don't care now. But I know if you do help me, there's a greater chance of finding him." She kept toying with the pendant. She noticed him looking at it.

"My father just gave this to me," she said, holding it away from her neck. "He said it was made from a meteorite. Stardust, he called it. When I was young, he'd told me stardust is the one thing I have in common with everyone. We all came from stardust." She began to sob. "Now he's gone."

"Sounds like he really cares," Eli said, keeping his emotions in check.

The story sounded like Jim. Maybe an effort to give his daughter some connection with others, despite her condition. Eli liked the metaphor. *We're all connected.*

But then Eli thought about the little things that didn't add up. The immaculate conditions in the home, the security clips and lack thereof, and maybe the dried blood on the shifter. He knew threatening Hope about honesty was not the right thing to do here. He'd have to trust but verify everything Hope told him. He'd have to watch her closely in case she snapped.

He looked at Hope. Tears in her eyes. *No safe choices.* Eli knew he was about to find out what it cost to trust a liar.

"I'll do what I can," he said, and headed for the door.

CHAPTER 4

AS HE DROVE west toward his home, the piercing sun was low in the winter sky. Eli lowered his visor. It was 3 p.m. and he needed to change clothes. This was the one appointment he couldn't miss. The rest could be moved or canceled. But this one meant too much to him. Despite his tough façade he'd developed to deal with the brutal realities of the corporate world, this served his core purpose in life.

Eli had left Hope at Jim's to search the home for any remaining clues. The list of questions was growing, and Eli needed answers. He considered just calling the cops and reporting Jim missing. But he'd confirmed that Hope had told the truth about her father's absence. He'd again called and texted Jim who had always answered right away. He hadn't, and his house was vacant with both his cars still in the garage. *Trust but verify.* He wanted to proceed with caution, but he couldn't. If she was telling the truth about the video, he couldn't risk Jim's life by his own inaction.

Eli needed specialized tech help. Maybe he could get a clue from Jim's digital life. He commanded the voice assistant to call Butch Dalton. He'd met Butch over fifteen years ago, during his first year in Tulsa after moving in from Ravenel Energy's field office in Hominy. They'd bonded over a beer one night sitting around the apartment complex pool. They'd become close friends, sharing their love of sports, their foray into motorcycles, and their love of no-money fun.

A few years older than Eli, Butch had started in the oilfields after graduating from high school in Miami, Oklahoma. He'd quickly learned he had great mechanical competency and returned to the University of Oklahoma to get his mechanical engineering degree. He'd gone to work for an international pipeline company based in Tulsa. He'd traveled the world on projects. His mother was a descendant of the Miami Tribe of Oklahoma. His father was a small-town banker. Eli had been the best man at Butch's first wedding. Butch and his wife had moved to Houston, and he'd started his oilfield technology company. His specialized drilling equipment and data-management business took off in the shale boom, but his marriage faded, and he'd moved his company to Tulsa after their divorce. Three years later, he'd remarried.

Butch answered on the first ring.

"Hey pardner! How you doing?" Butch said in his slight Okie accent that had been shaved by his world travels.

"Catching them faster than I can string 'em."

"Better to be wanted than dead," Butch said.

Eli loved their banter. It lightened any mood any time. "Hey, I need your help with something, kind of off book as they say."

"Shoot."

"Just between us, Jim Munro may be missing."

"Missing? Did you call the cops or the FBI?"

"No. Can't do that. I'll fill you in later, but I need your help. I need to see if I can get access to his computer. His emails and his files, too."

Butch paused for a few seconds. "Okay. I have his email address. I'll start there. Is his house empty?

"No. His daughter is there."

"I remember her. Still has trouble with the truth. Can you get her out for at least a couple of hours?"

"Why?"

"Not asked and not answered. You don't want to know."

"Okay. I'll get her out."

"That works."

"Great. Ping me when you have something."

"Will do. If he's using the cloud for backup, I'll try to get in there too. You know what service he uses?"

Eli gave him the name just as his phone vibrated. He looked at the screen. "Hey Butch, I gotta go. Got another call coming in."

"Copy that. Adios."

"Thanks, man."

Eli saw the call was from Hudson Walker. Hudson had worked with Eli up in Hominy. When Eli was a green engineer, Hudson had shown him how the oilfield really worked. He was tough, gnarly, and colorful. As a result of a short stint in state prison for stealing his stepfather's car to go see his biological father in Texas, he'd solved most problems with his knuckles in his youth. That is, until he'd met Sherry. She was as tough as he was but one of the most beautiful women Eli had ever met. Even now, in her sixties, that still was the case. Like a lion tamer, she'd settled Hudson down. They'd taken Eli in and showed him the ropes, and Hudson had regaled him with fantastic stories of the people and situations he'd encountered or heard about in his rowdy life in the oilfield. They'd stayed in touch during Eli's ascent to the executive ranks. They'd kept him grounded.

"Hey, Hudson. Nice to hear from you."

"I ain't said nothin' yet." Hudson chuckled.

"You got me there. How's it going up there in God's country?"

"Don't know what's happening in God's country, but up here it's raining like a cow pissin' on a flat rock."

Eli laughed and shook his head. "How's Sherry?"

"She's staring at me right now. Probably something I said. So she's doing well. How you hangin'?"

"Up to my ears in it right now. What's up?" Eli asked.

"Have you heard from Jimmy M?"

Eli's throat tried to choke off his reply. "No." He cleared his throat. "No. Why?"

"Well, he'd called Wednesday and asked if I had anyone to provide some muscle and security for him. I got Sonny and a few NLBs lined up. But I can't get ahold of that boy."

The answer cut straight through Eli. He had lived in the next trailer over from Sonny in Hominy. An oilfield pumper, he was a six-three and 280-pound Osage Indian. Kind and fun, but tough. He'd broken the legs off Eli's sofa one Friday night showing him how Hulk Hogan had body-slammed Andre the Giant in 1987 after they'd tested a bottle of tequila Sonny had bought. If Jerry had gotten Sonny involved, this was serious.

He, Hudson, and Sonny had a friendship that had lasted since those early years in the oilfields. That bond had grown into the Nine Line Bind Society, a group Eli had started, named after drillers' slang for when the thick cables that lifted the heavy drawworks on a drilling rig got so tangled they shut down the operation. In the oilfield, Nine Line Bind became a metaphor for any intractable problem.

The NLBS had started when Sonny's first child needed specialized cancer treatment. Jim had used his contacts in Houston to get the toddler into MD Anderson, and Eli had raised money to help with out-of-pocket costs. It had grown into a tight but powerful group of committed friends who helped each other and other oilfield families in need. They provided money, connections, and, when necessary, muscle, to solve life's most difficult problems. The group included Eli, Jim, Hudson, Sonny, and Butch, pulling in a few others when necessary.

Eli pulled over and stopped his SUV.

"He's missing, Hudson. I'm looking for him, too."

"Dadgum it. Blow my dress up! I took too long."

"What time did you talk to him on Wednesday?"

"Hang on," Hudson said. "Oh, what, honey? Nine-thirty?"

Hudson asked Sherry. "Nine-thirty. Just before bed," he said back into his phone.

"Okay. That helps. Look, I'll keep looking here in Tulsa, and I'll let you know what I find."

"Tulsa? Whoa. He said he was headed this way on Thursday."

"To Hominy?"

"Yeah, man."

"Why?"

"Don't know. I thought he was either bringing something up or getting it here."

Eli's mind was spinning. Why to Hominy? Jim hadn't lived there since he was area engineer when Eli had arrived sixteen years ago. What could be in Hominy? Was he meeting someone? Picking something up? Or bringing something valuable up there?

"Okay, Hudson. Sit tight until I get back to you. I've got someone looking at his computer. I'll let you know what we find."

"Hang on there, hombre. If you're trying to do what I think you are, it's going to be harder than trying to screw standing up in a hammock. Don't go it alone."

"I won't, Hudson. I promise. I'll call you back in a bit."

"Sherry says be careful. And she's ready too."

"Thanks, guys."

Eli ended the call. Hope was telling the truth. At least a half truth. He signaled, then did a U-turn and headed back to Jim's house. He needed Hope's help. She was a lot of things. But she was connected and got things done. Hard things. Things as hard as trying to screw standing up in a hammock.

CHAPTER 5

AFTER LETTING ELI through the gate again, Hope stood in the front doorway. The January winds had kicked up, and she crossed her arms, rubbing her shoulders, probably to stay warm. Her Audi sedan still sat in one of the guest spaces to the right of the garage. The expression on her face was identical to the one earlier. She'd said she didn't care. Never cared. Lizzy had suggested the same. He guessed she may be telling the truth, at least about that.

Eli left the car and with each step closer to her, his unease and annoyance frayed his nerves a little more, as if he were fighting to keep his balance on a high wire while approaching a wasp's nest.

She threw her shoulders back and blocked the doorway. "Back so soon?"

Eli took a beat and let the primitive need to crush her challenge crest and roll through him. "I have some new information. I need to ask you a few more questions." He turned sideways and extended his hand past her. "Inside, if you will."

She took the hint and led him inside. He closed the door and turned to face her.

"Did you find anything else here?"

"No."

He wasn't sure how she'd react to the news. Lizzy had advised that she could access anger well. Lizzy's warning about Hope snapping made him carefully choose his words.

"I just received a call from a friend of your father."

"Which friend?" she asked as if she didn't really care.

"Do you know anything about your father asking for security on Wednesday?"

"No. The video was the first I'd heard from him in a while."

"So, you don't know anything about a meeting he may have been setting up?"

Her eyes narrowed on him. "I'm not going to play twenty questions with you. Who called you?"

Eli decided her insolence needed to stop. He kept his emotions out of it. "Look. If you're going to be this way, I'm not sure my desire to help you will remain."

Instantly her demeanor softened. "I'm so sorry. Please excuse me. I'm just upset about my father." She reached out and touched his arm. "Please, continue."

She was good. If Eli had an Oscar, he'd give it to her. "Hudson Walker called."

"Don't know him," she said. Her calm smile returning. "Who's he with?"

"Retired from Ravenel Energy. In Hominy."

"Hominy?" Her face twisted. "Who would want to go to Hominy? Besides, I remember Dad saying they closed that area office a long time ago."

"That's true."

"So what gives? Why did Walker call?"

Eli wondered why he had that feeling like he was jumping out of a plane.

"Your father called him on Wednesday and asked for help."

"What kind of help?"

"Security and protection."

Both of Hope's perfect eyebrows rose. "Protection? From whom? The asses who sent the video?"

"We have to assume so."

Hope looked away in thought.

"That brings us back to the question *What do they want*?" he said.

She snapped her attention back to Eli. "I still don't know. They haven't contacted me again."

Eli tried to read her body language. Again, it looked as if she was telling the truth. She believed it at her core. She always *looked* like she was telling the truth. He wondered if that was an indication of the degree of sociopathy—where someone was on the spectrum. He'd have to check back in with Lizzy. He didn't want to leave Hope alone, especially if another video came in.

Eli checked his watch. It was 3:40 p.m. "I need to get home. There's nothing to do here, and I need to do something. Can you come with me? I'd like to stay close in case another video comes in. I have a friend checking your father's digital footprint. Maybe that will give us some direction."

Now Hope was reading him. Probably better at it. After a few seconds, she said, "Let me get my bag?"

Hope's preparedness fueled his suspicion. "You have a bag here?"

"In my car. I always carry a go bag in my line of work."

He knew she still had a house in Tulsa. Jim had said somewhere in the haughty Woody Crest neighborhood. He said she was always on the road. It made sense. Eli guessed her clients popped up at all hours in Tulsa, Houston, DC, or Hollywood.

She led Eli to the front door, opened it, and faced him. "Let's go."

He slipped past her as she eyed him like a hawk, her frigid stare tracking him. Heading to his car, his watch vibrated. He read the text. It was from Butch.

Making good progress. Not good. Come by after five. Alone.

He glanced back at Hope pulling the bag from her trunk and wondered what Butch meant.

CHAPTER 6

ELI CHECKED THE time as he headed to his home in the Maple Ridge neighborhood of Tulsa and felt his obligations tearing him in half. It was just after four and Friday rush hour clogged the streets. He glanced at Hope, thumbing through her phone in the passenger's seat. He didn't want to let her out of his sight. If another video came in, he'd be able to verify it and experience Hope when she told the truth. Butch's message was clear. But first, there was another appointment. One that couldn't be missed. It gave him that rarefied sensation he loved.

He searched for the right words to convince Hope to go with him. Then, afterward, he'd need to find a way to ditch her while he heard what Butch had to say.

"We'll stop by my home, but then I would like you to come with me for a short meeting at the Y."

Hope looked up from her phone and wrinkled her nose. "Why?"

"I meet a young boy and his mother every Friday on the basketball courts to help him learn the game. His father died from an oxy overdose, and he struggles with that. I know a little bit what that feels like. It only takes less than an hour."

"Why do that now? My father is missing."

Eli watched Hope's anger simmer. "He needs it. I made a commitment."

"If that's what you have to do. But I don't have to go." She resumed her scrolling.

He decided to tell her the truth. He slowed the car and looked at her. "I want to be together if you get another video."

She straightened up in the seat and grinned at him. "You don't trust me. That's why."

"I want to be able to verify it if we end up getting the authorities involved."

Hope wagged her head and chuckled, once. "You don't lie very well."

She was right. Now he was the liar. He returned his attention to the road and accelerated.

She sat back in the seat and watched the traffic ahead. "You need to know some things about me."

"Okay," he said. His frustration sounded too much like sarcasm.

She seemed to ignore his tone. "When I was little, about four, I had this painful pressure. Nothing helped it until I took a pen from my father's desk and kept it. I immediately felt better. So I continued to steal. Just little things, mind you. Then I started to lie. That helped too. When I started school, I had these urges to steal from other kids. When one of my classmates aggravated me, the pressure became unbearable unless I hit them. I never cared. Even when I knew something was wrong, I didn't care. I just did it, and the pressure went away. I really wasn't aware of what was going on at first. My mother would lecture me about right and wrong. But I just didn't care.

"Then after I stole from her precious book club friends and showed her my collection of items I'd snatched, she gave up. Her yelling and lectures didn't work. So she left. My dad was the only person who tried to help me instead of judging me. He went with me to see a therapist and helped me understand I wasn't bad—I simply had a personality disorder. We developed a mantra I still use today."

"Mantra?" Eli asked.

"Yes. Cues that help me."

"What are they?"

"Safety before truth and survival before violence."

"So, you lie," Eli said.

Hope turned to face Eli.

"I lie if it keeps me safe, and I avoid violence to survive. I learned very early that violence could get me hurt or killed or take my freedom away in jail. I still didn't care about something being wrong, but I wanted to live." She turned back to the traffic ahead. "Anyway, my father figured out how I could do those things. It took me to law school where twisting the facts to your advantage was rewarded. Then, after doing so well for my clients, they started to ask me to help them with their public images. I was even better at that."

"Can *you* tell when you're lying?"

She wagged her head again. "Yes. But I don't care. If the truth threatens my safety, I'll tell a lie. If I need to lie to avoid that urge to be violent, I'll tell a lie." She eyed him again. This time an air of superiority swept over her. "Here's the kicker. I don't feel shame, or guilt, or regret like you do. I don't feel empathy. All the things other people wish they didn't feel. I watched people all my life to be able to mimic the behaviors that look like I'm experiencing those emotions. So trust me. Don't trust me." She raised her voice. "I don't care."

Eli didn't feel any better. He felt worse.

She looked out the side window. "I *will* tell you that I know my father is very important to my survival, and I'll do anything to get him back."

Eli pulled into his driveway, stopped the car, and thought for a moment. "All right. Thanks for telling me. I'll accept you for who you are, but you'll have to do the same."

"No, I won't. But would you feel better if I said yes?"

Eli didn't answer.

Hope shrugged. "I'll go with you. Not because I care about you, that boy, or his mother. But because it's the only way to have you help me find my father."

CHAPTER 7

ELI WATCHED HOPE as she roamed through his living room, picking up each item and inspecting it as if she were at a garage sale. As he left to change into his sweats and Nikes, he wondered which personal items would disappear. When he returned to the living room, Hope was sitting on his couch talking on the phone.

"Yes. He's on the spectrum," she said. "Always has been. You can understand how that sometimes manifests itself." While listening to the caller's response, she looked up and grinned at Eli. "Of course. He'll make a sizable donation. Ten million sound okay? All we ask is that you'll join him to accept the check at your largest shelter. I'll coordinate the PR with your representatives."

She nodded. "Thanks so much. See you then."

Ending the call, she looked at Eli. "Damage control for some misogynistic techie."

She appeared much more relaxed than usual, as if she'd had a drink or two. Eli assumed what he heard was mostly lies.

"Ready?"

"If I must," she said, rising.

They headed to the car, drove past the municipal golf course, and turned into the Bandy YMCA, one of several Ys in Tulsa. Eli had a long-standing relationship with the Y. He volunteered his time and donated when he could to programs geared toward children. He'd always loved kids but had never found the right woman to share his dream of having a family. His past was a trail of failed relationships with stunning but caustic women. The few wonderful women he'd found, he'd pushed away once their kindness made him uncomfortable. Lizzy had helped him see that those choices were purely a result of his own thinking, his reasoning unconsciously hamstrung by his childhood experiences.

As he entered the Y, Nathan greeted him just inside the double doors. "Mr. Eli! I'm ready."

Nathan was a little taller than his classmates and his thick dark-brown hair was brushed forward and swept with a low taper fade. He had a basketball tucked under one arm. Eli noticed Nathan had become all arms and legs in the time since they'd met seven months ago. Nathan hugged Eli, then noticed Hope standing behind him. She was staring at him, expressionless. His eyes widened, and he looked at Eli then at his mom.

Eli recognized his unease. It was something they had talked about during their practices. Eli put his hand on Nathan's shoulder, and together they faced Hope. "Nathan, this is my friend Hope. Hope this is my friend, Nathan." Nathan glanced up at Eli, and Eli nodded.

"Hi… hi, Miss Hope," Nathan said. "Nice to meet you."

At first, Hope didn't respond. Then Eli moved his eyes from Hope to Nathan, suggesting she respond.

She plastered a smile on her face. "Nice to meet you." The smile immediately disappeared.

Then Nathan's mother stepped up. She was a pleasant-looking young woman, dressed in scrubs with her blonde hair pulled back efficiently into a ponytail. Her eyes were marked by the black circles of a single working mother. She offered her hand to Hope. "I'm Aurora. Nathan's mother."

Hope shook it and turned on the charm. "What a beautiful name. Hope Munro."

"I've heard of you," Aurora said.

"All good, I trust?" Hope said.

"How do you know Eli?"

Eli's body braced for Hope's reply. He had no idea what she'd say.

Hope thought for a moment, then said, "He and my father are friends."

Eli relaxed. "Let's get to it, shall we, Nathan?"

They headed into the gym. While Eli dumped his sweats, Nathan found an empty court. Hope and Aurora stood next to each other against the wall beside the door. Silent.

Eli and Nathan worked on their drills. Passing, dribbling, defensive stances, and lay-ups. While they were working on rebounding and boxing out, Nathan asked, "Are you coming next week?"

Eli recognized the smothering self-doubt from being abandoned by a parent. He turned the ball under his arm and bent down to look Nathan in the eyes. "I am. If for some reason I can't, I'd call your mom. Why do you ask?"

Nathan cut his eyes to Hope. "Miss Hope doesn't like me."

"I don't think that's the case. But remember what we talked about?"

Nathan looked up and to the right, accessing his memory. "Uh… yes. Everybody has a story."

"Remember, that never changes. And you can't read someone's mind. Until you know their story, you don't know what they may be thinking. Miss Hope has something on her mind. That's all." He pulled the ball from under his arm and held it in front of him. "Now, what are we?"

Nathan smiled and said, "Brave enough to try, good enough to succeed!"

Eli bounced the ball to Nathan. Nathan caught it, and Eli gave him a high-five.

As they finished the session with a fun game of one-on-one, Eli felt his watch vibrate. It was his home alarm system giving him a video alert. A car in the driveway. He looked closer and noticed it was the dark-blue Corolla. He noted what looked like a broom or mop handle visible above the backs of the front seats. A Black woman, who appeared to be around fifty or so, exited the car and made her way to the door. He got four doorbell ring alerts in rapid succession. Then, she rushed to the car and left. With no front plates required in Oklahoma, he couldn't get a plate number.

As he and Nathan approached Hope and Aurora, Hope asked, "What is it?"

Eli didn't want to inadvertently pull Aurora or Nathan into something. "Some delivery at my house."

He leaned down and hugged Nathan. "Great workout, dude." Nathan hugged his neck.

"See you next week," Nathan said.

"Will do," Eli said. He hugged Aurora.

"We're going to stay and shoot a little more before dinner," Aurora said. "Nice to meet you, Hope." Aurora nudged Nathan.

"Nice to meet you," Nathan said.

"Nice to meet both of you," Hope said. She seemed genuine.

Eli knew the drill. Nathan and his mother had a short walk to their one-bedroom apartment only a block away. Eli waved as he and Hope headed to the parking lot. "Have fun."

"See you next week!" Nathan hollered again.

"Wouldn't miss it for the world," Eli said over his shoulder.

When they got into the SUV, Eli looked at Hope. "You know that car that was on the security camera at your father's house?"

"The old blue one?"

"Yes. It was at my house just now."

"Geez."

"You have no idea who it may be?"

"No. But let's get going. It will take ten minutes to get there."

Eli's watch was alerted again. This time it was the back door alarm. "Someone's breaking in!"

Eli jammed the shifter into drive and raced out of the lot.

CHAPTER 8

WITH VISIBILITY DIMINISHING in the fading daylight, Eli raced down Riverside Drive, careful not to draw the attention of the police who regularly cruised the throughfare. Pedestrians, dog walkers, and the occasional bike rider made their way along the paved path that followed the Arkansas River on the left, while Eli dodged the cars emerging from the side streets on the right. He was certain that the break-in wasn't a coincidence, but he resisted the urge to floor it. The invasion of his personal space, perhaps by the very people holding his Jim, infuriated him. The urgency to catch the perpetrators fueled the focus and determination burning inside him. Catching them meant questioning them, getting critical information that just might save his friend.

He'd called the alarm company and canceled the alarm to prevent the cops from responding. He turned right before the Gathering Place, an expansive park across the street from his home and one of the biggest and best in the country. They reached his driveway, and Hope grabbed for the car door handle.

"Wait," Eli said.

"Because I'm a woman?"

He reached across and opened the glove box, pulling out his Glock 17.

"Aren't you full of surprises," Hope said.

"I'll clear the house, then you come in." Eli pulled his door handle and pushed the door open.

"Sure," she said without wavering.

Eli eyed Hope. She was either lying or telling the truth. He'd forgotten he couldn't read her. He shook his head and left the car, heading around the left side of his attached garage.

He eased open the gate to his six-foot privacy fence. It was clear. He slipped behind the garage in seconds. Leading with his gun, he crept onto the back porch. The back door was half-open. He quietly slipped inside.

He'd cleared many structures before, but that was with his Marine unit. This was his home, and he was alone. Gently, he eased the door shut and locked the deadbolt. He didn't need anyone coming up behind him. Moving quickly, he cleared the great room. Nothing had been disturbed. The only sound was the fan on the heat pump coming through the registers. It was bright daylight, and he knew every inch of his home, so he had the advantage.

He started down the hallway which led to the office, utility room, and garage. The office was first. The door was open, as it usually was, and light from the backyard streamed through the large windows. He targeted the doorway, pivoted inside, and cleared the room. All his books were still neatly slotted into the bookcases lining the walls. The cabinets and drawers were closed. His work papers were neatly stacked in the wooden box on his desk as he'd left them. He spotted the computer mouse. A frigid bolt froze his spine. The mouse sat atop his desk on the built-in leather blotter. He'd always left it on its pad next to the keyboard in the lap drawer. Anchored firmly where he stood, he held his breath and listened. He heard nothing except a dog barking in the distance.

He slid along the wall and stopped when he reached the supply closet. He aimed his gun at the door and grabbed the doorknob. The door burst open, and Eli fired, hitting the door and missing the masked intruder. They shoved him aside, and he grabbed their arm. They twisted, nearly snapping Eli's wrist, freed themselves, and raced down the hallway. Eli sprinted after them, aiming at the center of their back. He dropped his aim to their right leg. Just as he was ready to fire, Hope stepped in the way, blocking the intruder's path. She swung a pot, missing their head. Eli pulled up and held his fire. The intruder proficiently blocked her next swing and plowed her down as the pot crashed to the floor.

"Shit!" Eli hurdled her and followed the intruder through the open front door. Sprinting between the houses across the street, Eli chased them into the drainage ditch, then over the wooded berm that surrounded the back side of the park. He momentarily lost sight of the intruder. Eli crossed the bike path that split the top of the berm and pushed through the narrow woods onto the Gathering Place road. He scanned the concrete road that was flanked by parking spaces on either side. The cold wind cut through Eli's sweats. Most parking spaces were empty, and not a soul was in sight. He spun in the road, desperately searching for the intruder. They were gone. He dropped his head. "Shit!"

An approaching SUV with a young mother at the wheel, her child in a car seat in the back, slowed but then accelerated past him, giving him a terrified glance. He looked down and realized he was still holding his Glock. He covered it under his arm and headed back to his house. When he arrived, Hope was waiting in the driveway.

He marched up to her. "What the hell was that?"

"What?"

He pointed to the house with the Glock. "You could have been killed."

She shrugged.

"That doesn't register with you?"

"It registers. I'm just not afraid."

"Christ." Eli walked around her and entered the front door. She followed him and he stopped inside. "How did you get in, anyway?"

"Obviously you didn't listen." She produced a hair clip. "I used to break into my neighbors' houses, remember?"

Eli wanted to choke her. Instead, he turned away and went into his office. Glancing into the closet, he noticed nothing was missing. He closed the door, went to the desk, and dropped into his chair. He laid his gun on the desk and shook the mouse. The screen came to life. His email application was open and every message from Jim Munro was on the screen.

He leaned back in the high-back leather chair. Hope walked in the door and hovered over his shoulder.

"Looks like you have to believe me now," she said, sounding more arrogant that ever.

Eli turned and eyed her, still livid about her antics. But she was right. He had to believe her now. At least the part about her father being forcibly taken. Everything else was a crapshoot. Luckily, the emails didn't contain anything that would be helpful to anyone.

He closed the application, opened his security system, and replayed the clip of the Black woman. It clearly hadn't been her in his home. The person he grabbed was taller, muscular, and well trained. He paused the video a couple of times, captured screenshots, and printed them. He needed answers and he needed them now. He remembered Butch's warning. He went to his bedroom and changed, stuffing the Glock into its belt holster, and slipped on his jacket. He left and entered the living room. Hope was watching something on her phone. She looked up as he raced to her. Finally he'd get to verify what she saw.

"I just got another video," she said.

"Let me see."

"It's gone." She showed him the empty chat.

Eli shook his head in disgust. "You're kidding me."

Hope raised her free hand out to the side. "Wish I was."

"What did they say?" Eli said, his excitement drained by his disappointment.

"It was a video of my father again. He looked worse. Beaten and bloodied. They said I needed to give them the sample and the methodology of his invention by Sunday at seven or he's dead."

Eli wagged his head and looked around the room, then refocused on her. "What invention?"

"I don't know. Do you?"

"No. Where are we supposed to drop it?"

"They said 1.2 miles down a gravel road exactly 4.2 miles outside of Wynona."

Eli recalled the area from his time as a field engineer in Hominy while working for Ravenel Energy. The area was heavily wooded by blackjack oaks. He'd set stakes for the location of several wells to be drilled in the area. But that lease name wasn't one of Ravenel Energy's. "That's north of Hominy."

Hope shrugged.

Once again, he'd have to verify what Hope had said. He needed more than trust. He needed information. "I need to go somewhere."

"Again?" Hope protested.

"This has to do with your father."

"Let's go," she said, standing.

"You can't go."

"I'm going." She headed for the front door.

Eli followed. "You can't go. They will only talk to me. I can drop you at your house."

She kept walking. "I'm not doing that."

Eli could see he would get nowhere arguing with her. "Fine. Then you wait in the car when we get there."

Hope didn't stop to reply. She continued her march to the car. She raised her head, not stopping or turning. "Fine," she said into the air.

Eli wondered what the truth looked like from behind.

CHAPTER 9

THE SUN HAD set, and the darkness framed the Tulsa skyline ahead. While Eli sped toward downtown on the Broken Arrow Expressway, Hope had taken a call. The conversation made Eli want to puke. He discerned the call was with a politician somewhere in DC who'd been caught on a hot mic making a derogatory comment about the new African American Museum in Charleston. Hope spoke to him like a mother speaking to a child, instructing him on how to take responsibility, then spin his sizable donation to his advantage. Eli heard just how competent Hope was at her job, but he didn't know how she could stomach it. He ignored the remainder of the conversation and drove to the twenty-story office building near the center of downtown.

Hope got off the phone after she lost the signal when they entered the parking garage. Eli found a spot, parked, and killed the engine.

"I need you to wait here."

"I can't." Hope sounded like an impetuous child.

"We talked about this."

"No. I can't." She held up her phone. "I don't have cell service."

Eli looked around the garage. He pointed to the stairwell next to the elevators. "Okay. Go to that stairwell and up two flights. It will take you out to a courtyard between the buildings. You won't be seen from the street, so it should be safe. But don't leave. I'll stop and pick you up on my way back to the car."

They left the car and walked to the stairwell next to the elevators.

"See you in a few minutes," Eli said.

Hope was already checking her phone for a signal and silently nodded, paying no attention to Eli as she pushed through the steel door.

Eli took the elevator to the fourth floor. He had more questions than answers. He had no idea what invention the kidnappers were talking about. Hope said she didn't either. If Hope lied about that, she was probably lying about the last video. Eli reminded himself he'd verified that Jim was missing and he needed to stay focused on his mission.

He wondered why Jim had been planning a trip to Hominy, of all places. That made no sense. And the Black woman showing up, seemingly in a rush, to both their houses. He could explain it as a cleaning person looking for work, but her panic didn't fit with that theory. The elevator reached the fourth floor. The doors opened. He hoped Butch might have some answers.

The receptionist, seated in front of the modern backlit logo for BD Technologies, recognized him immediately. "Hi, Mr. Scott."

Eli didn't recognize the young woman. "You can call me Eli, please." Eli hadn't been called Mr. Scott since he'd been pushed out of Blackwood Energy three years ago.

"Okay. Eli, Butch is expecting you." She led Eli to a pair of thick glass doors and swiped her keycard against the black reader. The magnetic lock clicked, and she held one door open. She led him to Butch's corner office. "Mr.... oops . . ."—she smiled at Eli—"*Eli* is here."

Butch rose from his desk, flanked by two large floor-to-ceiling windows with a view of downtown, and walked to Eli. He was thick and stocky with tanned leathery skin. "Hi, my friend. Great to see you." The two embraced.

"Hey, Butch."

"Hey, Eli. How's the good life?"

"Not as good as I'd like."

"You need anything to drink?"

"Yes. But it's way too early for that."

"It's five o'clock somewhere."

Eli laughed. They'd painted the town regularly in their younger days.

"We're good, Susan. Please close the door on your way out. Thanks," Butch said. They took a seat at a round table stacked with papers and a few handwritten notes.

"I've done some digging with some help," he said.

"Help from whom?"

"You don't want to know." Butch pulled his notes from the top of the stack of papers. "By the way, where is the daughter?"

Eli nodded to the door, exhaling in disgust. "She's downstairs, waiting."

"Quite a handful, I'd imagine."

"You have no idea. She claims she got the ransom demand. It said to bring the invention to them."

"What invention?"

"They didn't say, according to her."

He looked down at his notes. "We may have a clue that ties to that. We got into his home computer and accessed a few online sources. Found a couple of interesting things. First, his digital activity just stops Wednesday night. It just disappeared. No activity. No phone, no computer, nothing."

"That fits with the timeline I'm working with. Taken Wednesday evening."

Butch looked back down at his notes. "The only number he

called was a New York-based cell phone. They exchanged calls three times before everything went dead."

"New York? Did you find out whose?"

"No. Couldn't. Called it, too. No answer and no voicemail," Butch said, looking up from his notes.

Eli drifted his thinking back to his previous executive life.

"You thinking what I'm thinking?" Butch said, eyeing him.

"Wall Street," Eli said. "Investment banker. They do shit like that if they want to keep something big quiet." Eli formed a timeline in his head. "When was the last call?"

"Ten after three Wednesday afternoon," Butch handed him the list of calls.

Eli stared at the six calls. "I know the firms he trusts. Had to be one of them."

Butch shook his head. "They won't talk."

"I know," Eli said. He knew they'd keep any deal confidential. They were good at that. But it fit with what Jim had said about their lunch. Something big. The bankers would be sure there was competition to run up the bidding. He immediately wondered who the other interested parties were and what they'd be after. "I'll see what I can find out. What else?"

Butch returned his attention to his notes. "He made two cash withdrawals last Tuesday and Wednesday. Each five thousand dollars. It's unusual because other than ATM withdrawals, he didn't pull out cash all last year."

"Any idea why? It certainly wouldn't be for the bankers."

"Nope. But it implies he had to pay someone in cash. He didn't want a digital trail to them." Butch looked up from his notes. "We also found that he had just added a Signal account last month."

That sent a quiver through Eli. "That's the same app where his daughter said she received the videos."

"Can we get a look at her phone?"

Eli shook his head. "Don't think that would be easy."

"If we did, we might be able to tell where they were coming from."

"Or if they ever existed?" Eli asked.

"Not sure about that."

Butch grabbed the next page and held a list of web sites in front of Eli. It covered the length of the page. "The last thing we found may hint at what that invention may be," Butch said. "His last searches in his web browser."

Eli reviewed the list. It contained seven websites. Two were technical papers about lithium batteries, one from the National Institutes of Health and the other from the American Chemical Society. The remaining five were from various start-ups, all trying to develop a modified lithium battery.

"It's not unusual for Jim to be investigating lithium batteries. After leaving Ravenel Energy, he focused on helping companies develop alternate energy sources."

"It could be just a coincidence," Butch said.

Eli looked closer at the links and saw the papers were focused on some organic materials being developed to replace some of the metals in the batteries. These were the last things Jim had done before being kidnapped, if indeed he was.

"It could be related to that invention his daughter was talking about. But why would someone kidnap him if the invention was someone else's?" Eli said.

"Have no idea. That's all we could get. You need me to dig further?"

Eli added the new information to his mental list. Jim's trail of activity stopped Wednesday evening. He'd withdrawn ten thousand dollars in two days, perhaps to hide who he was paying. If someone had discovered a reliable organic replacement for one or more of the rare earth metals in a lithium-ion battery it would be worth billions. The use of electric cars was ramping up around the world, and the demand was skyrocketing. Eli knew the batteries would be renewable, less prone to fires. The list of those competing for the rights to the new discovery would be long. The Chinese and the Democratic Republic of the Congo, the two major suppliers of such metals, would lose their grip on the supply, something they would do anything to prevent.

The last thing Jim had done was look at battery technology being developed by someone else. Was he involved in some form of corporate espionage gone bad? Maybe the payments were to an insider at one of the companies. If that was the case, who was he working for? It just didn't make sense. Jim's moral compass wouldn't allow him to participate in such nefarious activity. Then, Eli thought about the woman with cleaning supplies in the back seat of her car. She probably wasn't the inventor, but perhaps she was the person stealing secrets. With Jim gone, she could be panicking.

"I see those wheels grinding," Butch said. "I think I see the smoke coming out of your ears."

Eli didn't want to get his friend in any deeper than necessary. He folded the paper with the websites on it and held it up. "I'll run with this for now. No need to do anything else."

He stood, reached across the table, and gave Butch a fist bump. "I owe you one."

"Bullshit," Butch said, standing. "Let me know if we can do anything else."

CHAPTER 10

AFTER DRAGGING HOPE away from her phone and back to the Explorer, Eli pulled from the parking garage and headed out of downtown. Once again, he found himself having to lie to a sociopath. He needed to talk to Lizzy, and after he'd texted her from Butch's office, she'd agreed to meet him at 7 p.m. Everything hinged on Hope telling the truth at least some of the time. Before he waded deeper into this mess and risked the comfortable life he'd struggled to build, he needed to know when she was telling the truth. At least be able to estimate its likelihood. And Lizzy had answers. Answers Hope couldn't hear.

Eli figured he'd start with a half-truth. "I need you to do something for us. I need to pick up a few items at my locker at the gun club."

Hope didn't hesitate. "I can stop with you."

Eli was suddenly conscious of his breathing, facial expressions, and tone. "No. This will be a better use of time. We have to move quickly." Still, the truth.

Hope turned from her phone and eyed him as if he were her first meal in a week. Finally, she said, "What do you need?"

"If you can go back to your father's house and pull the video of the woman with the cleaning supplies, then get online and figure out the year of the Corolla, we can use that to see if we can find her."

Hope kept her eyes fixed on him. "What did your friend tell you?"

"Your father made large cash withdrawals. He never had done that before. It could be payments to someone or for something he was trying to hide."

"A cleaning lady?"

"We don't know. They were cash withdrawals. Last Tuesday and Wednesday. She's the only lead we have."

"All right, I'll do it."

"Thanks. I'll be quick. Don't do anything with the information until I get back."

Hope smiled at him. "Don't worry. I know you like to be thorough. I'll wait." Still smiling, she raised her eyebrows. "Where's your club?"

"On the other side of the river. Jenks."

Eli watched her check her phone. When she apparently confirmed the gun club's location, she relaxed.

After dropping her at Jim's house, he drove to the gun club on the south side of Jenks. Lizzy was waiting in her Cadillac SUV. Eli parked next to her and got in.

She grinned at him, feigning surprise. "We're meeting at your gun club? Must be getting serious."

"Sorry. There isn't much time, and I had to see you."

"You said it was an emergency. Hope you don't have to get your guns." Lizzy chuckled.

"I'll do that after we talk."

Lizzy's grin disappeared. "What?"

"Better if you don't ask. I need some advice again about Hope."

She turned in her seat to face him head-on. "Okay." She glanced at the lighted sign in front of the gun club and grinned again. "Shoot."

Eli wagged his head and smiled back. "I need to know more about when she's lying. She's telling me she's seen something, but I can't tell if it's the truth."

Lizzy furrowed her brow. "You probably can't. But you might be able to handicap it."

"Handicap it?"

"Yes. For example, if you can make her tell it in public, you might have a slightly greater chance that what she says is the truth."

Eli shook his head. "That's out. It's just her and me."

"Then ask yourself if you feel unduly complimented or praised just before she tells you something. That puts the odds a little greater that what follows may be a lie. An attempt to manipulate you."

Eli thought about his conversations with Hope. Several times she had praised him. But when she talked about the video, she went straight to it. Still, he didn't like handicapping the truth. If he was wrong, the cost would be disastrous. He had just recovered from getting pushed out of his job running operations for Blackwood Energy. Despite the large payout from his employment contract for being let go without cause, it had triggered a spiral of self-doubt that nearly killed him. Making the wrong choice here would either send him back into that spiral or get himself killed.

Lizzy watched him struggle. "Don't go there. Fight it," she said. She knew him well.

So did he. He allowed the doubt to flow over him, just like she'd taught him. He wasn't stuck in the past any longer. He was brave enough to succeed and certainly worthy of that success. He envisioned ripping the shameful black muck from his soul and putting it where it belonged.

He took a long breath. "Thanks, Lizzy. I'm good now."

"That was a quick trip." Her wry smile returned.

Eli agreed with a nod. "Thanks to your help. Anything else?"

"Yes. A couple of things I thought of after our last session. Watch for her pity play. They all do it to some extent. If she's trying to get you to feel sorry for her, be suspicious of what comes next."

"She already did that. A couple of times." Eli looked at Lizzy for her take on his miss.

"She's trying to keep you engaged for some reason. Be careful."

"What was the second thing?"

"Remember she's addicted to getting a reaction from you. Not giving her one is your best weapon. Above all, do not confront her. It could be dangerous—very dangerous. Trust your gut. Trust yourself. You'll make the right choice."

Eli saw the time on the dashboard clock. "I gotta get going. I'm permanently in your debt."

She waved him off. "Get out of here."

Eli left and watched Lizzy pull from the parking lot and disappear into the Friday night traffic. She'd saved his life more than once early on. Now, armed with her insights and the weapons in his locker, he'd see if he could save Jim's.

CHAPTER 11

NOW SUFFICIENTLY ARMED, Eli raced through Jenks and back across the river toward Jim's home. With his confidence fortified by Lizzy's insights, he shifted into crisis mode. It was a strength he'd had ever since he was a kid. Everything slowed down, any fear fell away, and he focused. He'd find Jim, but to do that he couldn't leave Hope alone.

Hope's task was simple, and something told him the lead she was working on may be the key. The trip took just minutes driving counter to the Friday night traffic. He reached Jim's house and turned into the entry. He slammed on the brakes, shocked by the open gates. Looking to the right, he saw that Hope's car was gone. He floored the SUV and screeched to a stop at the front door. He threw the driver's door open and jumped out. He barged through the unlocked door and scanned the room. He looked for any clue about where she might be.

Everything in the great room was as it was when he'd last left the house. He worked his way toward the hallway but then stopped and pulled out his Glock. He'd realized that nothing was ever as it appeared to be with Hope. She'd left the door unlocked and someone, including her, could be lying in wait.

He moved down the hallway and entered the office. He slowed

his breathing and listened. The wind rustled the leaves outside. Again, everything was as it was before. He decided he had two choices. Assume she'd lied, gotten the image, and somehow found an address for the woman in the Corolla, or she'd been surprised when she entered the house and had been taken. With no sign of a struggle, it was more likely she'd lied, gotten the address, and headed there.

"Shit," he said to himself.

He knew he had to hurry. If she'd gotten the image, she'd most likely found it using the computer on Jim's desk. He slipped into the desk chair and rattled the mouse. The screen came to life. Jim's ID was still logged in. She'd had his password all along. Eli knew Hope probably had contacts that could help her with the DMV information. They wouldn't want a digital trail, so she'd have to call on her phone. But once she had the information, she'd probably google the address.

He clicked on the browser and pulled up the history. He clicked on the last link. The map showed a route to an apartment complex in south Tulsa, not far from the mall. He put the address in his phone and sprinted through the house and out the front door, leaping back into his Explorer.

He raced from the driveway, swerved onto the street, and floored it. He knew he didn't have much time. If Hope had concluded that she'd found the person responsible for taking her father, she may have snapped. If that was the case, Lizzy had said her violent tendencies would take over. Luckily, at 7:40 p.m. on a Friday, the traffic wasn't bad, and he turned into the old apartment complex just before eight.

In the darkness, the three-story apartment complex, lit by a few landscaping lights, looked like a light-gray monster, hulking over the parking lot from the darkness. Eli drifted through the lot until he spotted Hope's car. He pulled into the spot next to her, facing the complex. Her car was empty.

He checked his phone for the apartment's number. It was 217. That meant the second floor. The complex looked like it had been built in the seventies: a wooden structure with second-floor balconies. Access to the second-floor apartment would be directly up a set of stairs to a shared landing. Eli left his car and scanned the apartment numbers illuminated by the small light fixtures at each apartment's door. When he spotted 217, he noticed the door was cracked open.

Pulling his Glock from its holster, he quietly trotted to the base of the stairs. He paused and listened. Someone was moving inside the apartment. He noticed the jamb had been splintered. He doubted Hope had done that kind of damage. Slowly, he crept up the stairs, stopping with his shoulder touching the broken jamb. The noise inside sounded as if someone was searching, opening and closing cabinets and drawers.

Eli raised his Glock, then spun into the doorway ready to fire. The two-bedroom apartment had been ransacked. Eli moved in toward the noise coming from one of the bedrooms. He spotted Hope shuffling through one of the dresser drawers on the floor. The mattress was sliced open and thrown against one wall, the floor cluttered with clothing.

Hope suddenly looked up and saw him. She didn't appear surprised.

"Oh. You found it," she said, matter-of-factly.

Eli waited for his anger to fade as he holstered his Glock. "You didn't wait. You said you would."

She shrugged her shoulders. "I couldn't."

Eli wanted to say *You've gotta stop doing this!* but then swallowed the words when he remembered Lizzy's warning about confronting Hope. He pointed to the mess on the floor. "Did you do this?"

"It was like this when I arrived. The door was busted open, and no one was here."

The damage to the door said that was not a lie. "Who lives here?"

Hope produced a folded piece of paper and stepped to Eli, handing it to him. It was a cable bill. The name on the bill was Abena Williams. Eli pulled out his phone and searched for the name and *Tulsa.* A half dozen names came up from the usual paid search sites. Several had the address correct and all of those showed Abena Williams was fifty years old. That fit the image on the security footage.

"She's gone," Hope said. "But I don't think she was taken."

"How do you know that?"

"No car keys, wallet, or purse. They aren't here. Kidnappers would have just taken her. Especially after tossing the place. They weren't looking to rob her, either."

"They wanted something they thought she had."

Eli thought about what that could be. Was the cleaning lady stealing secrets from where she worked? Or was there another tie to Jim Munro? Eli walked back into the main room of the apartment. Cushions were ripped open, the chairs overturned with their stuffing protruding from their seats. He spotted a toppled bookcase with books scattered around it, most face down and open, spines sticking up. A few were novels, a few were cookbooks… but then he spotted a thick blue book with a tan spine. *Handbook of Chemistry and Physics.* He went to the pile of books and pushed a few aside. Another book, *Rechargeable Organic Batteries*, was buried beneath the pile.

Eli began searching the floor for any photographs.

"What are you searching for?" Hope asked, emerging from the bedroom.

"Family photos."

She pointed to the far corner of the living room, next to the sliding doors to the balcony. "Over there."

He spotted the broken frames and picked up two eight-by-ten photographs that had been face down in the pile of debris. He flipped them over. One was a photograph of a younger Black woman with her husband and a child, maybe nine years old. They were dressed in colorful clothing Eli recognized from his travels to Africa for Blackwood Energy. The material looked like raffia, made from palm. The second was a graduation picture with the same woman, the woman from the security image, with a much taller young man in a graduation gown but no father. Eli held up the second photo.

"Looks like she has a son. Probably at least in college. Those science books must be his."

Hope walked over to the overturned books and examined them. "These probably aren't hers. I think she is a cleaning lady based on the supplies, the navy work pants, and the work shirts I found in there." She nodded toward the second bedroom.

"But why her?" Eli asked.

"She must know my dad."

"And she must know that he knows me."

"We've got to find her," Hope said.

Eli thought for a moment. Hope was right. There was something here. And if the woman hadn't been taken already, they needed to find her first. He looked down at the picture in his hand. "I think I know where to start."

He heard a siren in the distance. "We gotta get out of here. Now."

CHAPTER 12

ELI AND HOPE left the apartment together and stopped at Eli's car.

"I need a little bit of time," he said, "but I don't think we can stay at my home, yours, or your father's."

Hope looked at Eli, her eyes examining his face. He wasn't sure if she was preparing to lie again or if she was evaluating how much she could trust him. "What is it?"

"I have a place. No one knows about it. I frequently stash my clients there until things settle down."

"Here in Tulsa?"

She wagged her head. "No. Outskirts of Broken Arrow."

"That works. Can we go there?"

"Follow me." She headed for her car.

Eli got in his and followed her out of the apartment parking lot. He could hear the sirens getting closer. Like it or not, they might end up in the cops' crosshairs.

He followed her south through Tulsa on the back streets and into Broken Arrow. They passed subdivision after subdivision, until the well-lit cookie-cutter neighborhoods disappeared, and they were out into the rural land south of Broken Arrow. Darkness hugged the road, and Eli split his attention between the rearview mirror and

Hope's taillights up ahead to ensure they weren't followed. There were no streetlights to light their way. The only crossroads were on the section lines, a mile apart. Then two white brick monuments appeared up ahead, a black mailbox atop one, and Hope turned in. Eli followed onto a gravel road and passed between the columns. The road was lined with trees. Dust from the gravel in Eli's headlights gave the route a ghostly pallor. Ahead, Eli saw Hope's brake lights illuminating the dust cloud. He pulled beside her in front of a white brick ranch home.

Eli grabbed his pack from the back seat, went to the trunk, and opened it. He pulled out a rifle bag, tossed it over one shoulder, and closed the lid. He followed Hope to the front door. She entered a code into the digital deadbolt. The battery-powered lock rotated, and she opened the door, stopping and welcoming Eli inside. "You look prepared," she said.

Using her phone, she activated the lighting in the home. The interior was recently renovated. The smell of fresh paint still hung in the air. The decor was modern, with cold angles of black trim and glass. The upholstered furniture was bright white.

"You can set up over there. I'll arm the system." She pressed her phone and looked up, pointing to a rolltop desk in the alcove off the dining area. "The password for the Wi-Fi is Foolmeonce, no spaces, F capitalized, followed by a dollar sign and exclamation point."

Eli laughed to himself. *Figured.*

He pulled his tablet and keyboard from his pack, sat at the rolltop desk, and flicked on the small desk light.

Hope walked to the back of the house while Eli waited for the computer to boot up. It did and he linked it to the Wi-Fi. By that time, Hope had returned and stood next to him looking over his shoulder.

"Do you have a VPN?" he said. Eli knew the protection of a virtual private network would conceal his online activity.

"Built into the router. Why are you wasting time with this? We need to find that woman."

Ignoring her, Eli pulled out the graduation photograph and examined it closely.

"What are you looking for?" she said.

"The major shown on his diploma in this photo."

"That was college graduation?"

"Yes. See here." Eli pointed to the photo. "It's the University of Tulsa. I've seen hundreds of them over the years."

Eli spotted the line with the degree awarded. It was small and difficult to read. He held it closer. Hope leaned in over his shoulder. Normally it would aggravate him, but her younger eyes might see something his couldn't. He held it up for her to get a closer look.

"It starts with a P and it's two words," she said.

"Petroleum Engineering?"

"Yes. That's it. Why is that important?"

"Two things. Those books wouldn't be needed for a petroleum engineer. Second…" Eli opened another browser window, went to the Society of Petroleum Engineers website, and signed in.

"You're a petroleum engineer?"

"Chemical engineer but trained by my first company as a petroleum engineer. Joined a long time ago."

Eli opened the member directory and found the section with *Williams* as the last name. He pointed to the screen. "This is the other reason why." He found the Williams that matched the graduation date and university. *Darnell Williams.* He opened another window and searched for that name. A LinkedIn page came up. He opened the link and found the company that employed Darnell. "He works in Dallas. He's not here in Tulsa. And if his mother is hiding, she wouldn't risk jeopardizing her son."

Hope quit looking over his shoulder and stood up straight behind him. "I don't get it."

Eli looked over his shoulder at her. "We just eliminated him as the source. It has to be his mother."

"Again, that's what I said. She must be stealing it from somewhere. Where she works. Let's just call him."

Eli's temper rumbled inside. He waited a few seconds and reminded himself not to react. He weighed separating again but thought the better option was to stay together, especially with the rising likelihood of the video being real. If she got another one, better he were with her.

Eli stood, face to face with Hope. She held her ground in a clear effort to intimidate him. There was no sign of fear or anger in her eyes.

"No," Eli said. He measured each word carefully. "That will raise suspicion and maybe result in a call to the cops. We don't want to put him in harm's way. We need to go."

"Where?" she asked.

"I have a way to find out. But we have to do it in person. Can't—"

"I can make one call and get the answer," she interrupted, obviously frustrated.

"Call who?"

"I have a higher-up in the State Patrol that needed my services."

"Absolutely not. Don't do that. We can't risk exposing Abena Williams any further… or us for that matter." Eli moved around her and gathered his things.

"Where are we going?"

Eli headed toward the door. "I'll tell you when we get there."

CHAPTER 13

ELI SPED ALONG the Creek Turnpike heading east. The only sound was the wind whistling through the sideview mirrors at seventy-five miles an hour. Hope had stayed silent in the darkness, with her nose in her phone since they'd left the house. That was fine by Eli. The less she said, the less he had to handicap as a lie.

It was late and this visit was a risk, but he needed to see Butch again.

Butch lived east of Tulsa on the northeast side of Broken Arrow. He'd purchased the large ranch for himself and his second wife after they were married ten years ago. Butch had purchased a lake house a couple of hours northeast of the city on Grand Lake. The ranch was situated on a direct route to the lake, between the turnpike and his country club. Eli was betting that in January, Butch was home and not at the lake, but on a Friday, he couldn't be certain.

A few minutes later, he exited the turnpike and turned east toward the ranch. Leaving the lights of the interchange, Eli flipped on his brights. The road was straight down the section line with short blackjack oaks on either side still holding their dead leaves. Up ahead beyond the reach of the headlights, they disappeared into the darkness.

In the distance, he noticed a glint of light from what looked like a small reflector in the blackness. The high beams finally reached it, and he jammed the brake pedal to the floor. Hope's phone hit the floor, and she braced herself on the dashboard.

"Shit!" Eli yelled as his heart pounded out a warning.

"What the hell is—"

"A wreck." What looked like a long, white stock trailer had jackknifed and flipped across the road. A large dual-wheeled pickup had skidded onto the shoulder, its front tire shredded. Eli didn't see anyone in the truck and not a soul on either shoulder. The deep bar ditches on either side made the road impassable.

"I don't like this," he said, pulling his Glock out. He backed the car further away from the trailer and stopped.

"You think it's a trap," Hope said, absolutely no concern in her voice.

A bit stunned by her indifference, Eli glanced at her, then back at the trailer. He peered along the perimeter of the trailer. It was on its side, and he couldn't see beneath it or, therefore, behind it. Then, out of the corner of his eye, he saw movement in the bar ditch to his left.

"Get down!" He yanked Hope forward as he ducked. Two shots rang out and hit his door. "Go. Out your door. Hurry and stay down."

Two more shots shattered his window. Crawling across the console, he followed Hope out and onto the cold pavement. He pushed Hope behind the front wheel for protection. He needed a better angle on the shooter. He inched to the front bumper.

"Wait," Hope whispered.

There still wasn't any sign of fear. "Stay down. Don't move," Eli said.

"I'll draw him out," she said flatly. She took off for the trailer in front of them. Eli had no choice now. He stood to fire, but the shooter didn't fire at Hope. Another two shots rang out, one burning through high on Eli's left arm. He fired six shots around the flashes and heard metal clatter on the pavement. He paused, listening in silence, and swept the area with his gun. It was quiet, other than

Hope's footsteps approaching. He made his way around the front of his car and approached the shoulder. A pistol straddled the edge of the asphalt. Leading with his gun, he looked into the ditch. He saw a man in dark jeans and a mask lying motionless in the shallow water in the bottom.

Hope grabbed his arm, and he winced. He turned, wanting to punch her.

"You're bleeding."

Eli was certain that this time she wasn't lying. He holstered his Glock, reached around, and twisted his bicep to examine the wound. He was indeed bleeding, and a chunk of his skin was splayed open. He could see his breath but didn't feel the cold. He pulled out his shirttail and ripped a piece free. "Help me tie this off. It just nicked me."

Hope did. As she was finishing, Eli asked, "What was that all about over there?"

"What?"

"Running into the open."

She finished the knot. "I didn't have a gun and don't want one. That's your job. So I was the one who had to draw fire."

"You're not afraid of getting killed?"

She shrugged.

"You don't want a gun?"

"No. I told you, that's your job. Dad said my condition and guns would be a bad combination if I wanted to continue to be a free person."

That immediately made sense.

He re-examined his arm. "Thanks."

She shrugged. "We can't get through. Where are we going?"

"A friend's. But first we must find out how they knew where we were going. The cops will be here soon. We'll go around." Eli headed toward the Explorer and wondered how long he could keep Hope alive, or how long before *she* got *him* killed.

CHAPTER 14

ELI PULLED TO the roadside under the interchange. He needed the cover and the light from the tall halogen lights on either side of the overpass. He stepped out, brushed the glass from his seat, and shut the door. Earlier, he hadn't mentioned where they were going to Hope on purpose. Partly because he didn't trust Hope, but partly because he knew anyone could be listening. Whoever was after them had known where they were going because they'd tracked their location. He carefully inspected every inch of the Explorer's body, undercarriage, and engine compartment.

"Can we go?" Hope said through her open window.

Then Eli spotted it. Wedged up against the firewall of the engine compartment. He pulled the device out and crushed it under his heel. He checked the time. It was after nine. "Now we can go." Eli got back into his SUV.

"What was that?"

"A bug. They were tracking us."

"Who?"

"Great question." Eli jammed the shifter into drive, drove to the first section line road, and turned north. He'd discovered how they'd found them. Still, there was one question that badgered his mind: *Why didn't the thug shoot at Hope?* Maybe they wanted to keep her alive to find whatever she was supposed to deliver Sunday. But the other explanation churned in his stomach. She could be lying. She could be part of this. But why pull him into it only to kill him?

As he approached the next section line road and turned east toward Butch's ranch, his body went taut. He tightened his grip on the steering wheel and accelerated. While he reminded himself that Butch could defend himself, he worried about what he might find. He hoped he'd only find answers.

As he pulled through the gate, Hope asked, "Who lives here?"

"My friend, Butch."

"Is this the guy you saw earlier?"

"Yes."

"Why are we here? You already talked to him."

Ignoring her question, Eli parked the SUV in front of the large stone home and got out.

Butch met him at the door with his Colt Defender pistol in his hand.

"Thought that might be you," Butch said.

Hope joined Eli on the front steps. "You have a problem here?" Eli asked.

Butch pushed the door wide open. Jennifer, his wife, stood holding a shotgun.

"No problem here." Butch looked around Eli at Hope, then at the shattered window of the Explorer. "You all right?"

"We're good, my friend." Eli stepped past Butch and went inside. "Hi, Jen."

Jennifer lowered the shotgun and hugged Eli.

"You must be Hope?" Butch said as she passed. "I'm Butch." He extended his hand.

Hope stopped, looked at his hand, then shook it. "Not sure why we're here." She walked inside and scanned the interior of the home like a real estate agent on a caravan.

Butch glanced at Eli and shook his head.

Jennifer led them into the massive great room with a huge, vaulted ceiling. Eli noticed a blood smear on the tile in the kitchen next to a bucket.

"You did have a problem," Eli said.

"A little one," Butch said, still holding the Colt. "That is until they underestimated my wife. The asshole took Jen hostage. But she surprised him with a steak knife to his thigh and this guy," Butch raised the pistol, "ended the argument."

"Anything on him?" Eli asked.

"Nothing."

"Where is he?"

Butch nodded toward the back of the house. "In a tarp out back. He'll be enjoying an Arkansas hog farm by dawn."

Hope stepped toward Jennifer. "You have a lovely home. You must have worked hard to get it so beautiful." With blood on the floor, the compliment seemed so out of place it caught everyone off guard.

"Uh… thank you," Jennifer said. She leaned the shotgun against the sofa. And eyed Eli.

"I need a little help, brother," Eli said.

"Let's go in—"

"We need to find Abena Williams and where she works," Hope said, interrupting Butch.

Butch gave Eli a *What gives?* look. Eli hid his disgust the best he could and gently nodded.

"Okay," Butch said. "A-B-E-N-A?"

"That's right," Eli said. He turned to Hope.

"Hope, I need you to stay here with Jennifer and make sure we don't get any more visitors. We'll be right back."

Hope looked at Jennifer, then at Eli. "Let the men do their work?"

Eli said, "No. We don't know who's after us. There may be more on their way. We need your help. I know more about the situation. You seem very capable. Please?"

Hope simply smiled and said, "Sure."

Eli followed Butch to his office at the back of the house.

"She's a piece of work," Butch said as he dropped into his chair behind the thick oak desk.

Eli wagged his head. "Tell me about it."

Butch pulled out his keyboard and input a few keystrokes. "Wow. What does this Abena do?"

"I think she may be a cleaning person or janitor."

"Where she works is hard to find. More security than I thought." Butch tapped a few more keys and waited. "Okay. I see."

"What? What is it?"

"Looks like she works at a place called JEG Research."

"What do they do?"

"Can't tell. But the building is leased by a John Gregory. He was a professor at TU. I'd say he's the owner."

Eli knew that some successful professors took their research outside of the university setting.

Butch hit a few more keys. "Okay. Here are some more recent papers. He develops specialized materials for oilfield applications. Looks like he holds several patents."

"Anything about batteries?"

Butch maneuvered the mouse and made a few clicks. "No. Nothing. How does she fit in this mess with Jim?"

"Don't know. She's been to my house and Jim's looking for us, I think. He may be protecting her for some reason. Thought it had something to do with lithium batteries based on what we just found in her apartment. Thought she was stealing technology."

"Nothing here on that, pardner. But she did work at TU for a while. Probably for that professor."

"I need to find her. Talk to her. Fast."

Butch kept working on the computer. "Let's see. Looks like

she's a first-generation Congolese immigrant if that matters. Arrived when she was 12. Gained citizenship with her mother seven years later."

Eli didn't know how that related to anything at this point.

"Full citizen for a long time. Fifty years old now. Single mother. Husband died quite a while ago. Has a son. You already know where she lives."

"We knew about her son. In Dallas. She wouldn't go there." Eli ran through his unanswered questions. Where was Jim? What was this discovery Hope was supposed to find? Was she telling the truth? And who is behind it? What's the reason this discovery was so important to them that they'd kidnap or kill for it? He remembered the meeting location Hope had given him north of Hominy and west of Wynona.

"Maybe if I came at this another way. They gave us a location for the meet at the deadline to give them whatever they are looking for. Can you access the oil and gas lease database? Maybe see who owns it."

"Yes. Give me the location."

Eli did.

"Holy shit, cowboy," Butch said, pointing at the screen.

"What?"

"Your old buddy owns it."

"What old buddy?"

"Lucian Blackwood. Blackwood Energy."

Eli's heart jumped into his throat. He could barely get out his next words. "Blackwood? You sure?"

"No doubt. The asshole that pushed you out of the business."

CHAPTER 15

ELI WAS BEING sucked into a black hole again. One he kept hidden from everyone, even himself most of the time. His soul fought back, desperately clawing for anything to keep him from going into that abyss. While he didn't understand why, he was certain something awful awaited him there. Something so terrible it would devour his soul and end him.

After Ravenel Energy had been purchased in a takeover by a large competitor eight years ago, Eli had decided to leave to stay close to his friends in Tulsa. A trusted headhunter had reached out and convinced him that Blackwood Energy would be a great fit. They'd been on a buying spree and had grown exponentially, Blackwood's son had suddenly left the company, and Eli's skills made him a great fit as the executive vice president over their operations. The good news had been they were based in Tulsa and they would agree to an employment contract that would protect Eli and his financial future. As it later turned out, the bad news was the company was led by Lucian Blackwood.

On the strength of his family's legacy, Lucian Blackwood had positioned himself as a critical cog in the city's machinery. The man behind the curtain, leading the city, its politics, and its citizenry to his own vision of prosperity. He'd initially welcomed Eli and given him a wide berth to pull the fragmented pieces of the acquired companies into a cohesive, focused, and growing enterprise. That is, until Blackwood slinked into Eli's office one day, five years later, and fired him for refusing to lie and inflate the oil reserves of the company to prop up the stock.

Eli had been devastated. It wasn't about money. Blackwood had been forced to honor Eli's employment contract, paying Eli millions. But the surprise termination, with no reason given, had been a very public shaming of Eli as a failure. Because it was a senior executive position in a public company, it had been announced on the mainstream business news and would bounce around the internet forever. And with the noncompete clause, it effectively ended his career.

It had triggered Eli's worst nightmare. The emotional destruction had pulled him into a deep depression and caused Eli to seek out Lizzy to help him manage to survive. His refusal to lie, to be just like his father, had destroyed his career, not saved it. Others had no idea, but Eli had hit rock bottom, alone. He and Lizzy hadn't yet found the key to fully resolve the issue, but anytime Blackwood came up, Eli quickly countered the spiral with a few affirmations. Now, he summoned his resilience and focused on saving his friend.

Butch seemed to sense Eli's reticence. "The guy's a snake."

The support helped. "All the more reason to think there is a link." Eli wondered if he had his answer as to why he'd been drawn into this. Was he the target? Did he unknowingly stumble on something three years ago before he was fired?

"I've gotta check both leads," Eli said. "And do it right now."

"You need me to help?"

"I won't ask you to do that. Not after what happened here. You stay with Jen."

"Then you'll have to take a chance on that woman out there to tell you the truth. Split up."

Eli wagged his head. "I can't do that. I can't trust her to handle figuring out where Abena Williams fits in. The woman has no filter, no fear, and I still can't tell when she's lying."

"Then the only solution is to keep her with you and do both together."

"That burns time. Takes twice as long."

"What about the Society?"

"That's what I'm thinking. We can run down the Abena leads and I'll have Hudson and Sonny start on Blackwood."

"I can help from here on Blackwood if they need me." Butch looked out the office window into the parklike backyard. "Can you tell Hope about Blackwood and see her reaction?"

"Won't work. I wouldn't trust any read I get from her. We'll just have to keep Blackwood our little secret for now."

Butch nodded, logged off, and stood. "It's late. You and Hope stay here for the night. My foreman will keep watch. You'll need your rest."

"Thanks, Butch." Eli stood and headed for the door. As he turned the corner into the hallway, he hoped a professional liar couldn't spot his lie. His mistrust would cost them time if she wasn't in on this. Jim didn't have much of that. But if Eli was the target, Lucian Blackwood would get another chance to ruin his life—this time permanently.

Eli entered the great room and spotted Hope and Jennifer sitting at the kitchen island. Jennifer was laughing as Hope finished a story about one of her old clients. Hope turned when she noticed Jennifer raise her head and stop laughing.

"You boys figure it out?" Hope asked.

Eli approached Hope, her eyes scouring him. With each step closer he became more conscious of his every movement and expression. His body tingled as if he were walking into a high-intensity force field. He carefully calmed himself and flushed the concerns from his mind. He stopped across the long rectangular island from them. Butch went to Jennifer and hugged her.

Eli nodded to Hope. "Yes. At least the next step in finding Abena Williams." He explained what they'd found and that they'd head out in the morning to find Professor Gregory.

"Anything else?" Hope asked.

"No," Eli said, fighting the urge to look at Butch.

Keeping her eyes on Eli, Hope stood and paused, then looked at Butch and smiled. "Thanks for your hospitality. Where would you like me to crash?"

Jennifer rose. "I'll show you."

As Hope and Jennifer passed Eli, Hope smiled. "Good night." They disappeared down the other hallway.

Eli looked at Butch, who shrugged.

Eli had a lot to learn about lying.

CHAPTER 16

LUCIAN BLACKWOOD WATCHED the dark pickup pull down the cobblestone driveway, wind around his home, and park in front of his detached office. A chill rattled though him. He turned away and walked to the side table that sat next to his favorite chair, picked up the remote, and pointed at the massive stone fireplace. It roared to life with a click, flames reaching high toward the open flue. He went to the crystal decanters and poured a glass of Jameson. It was a cool Saturday night, the first one in a while, and he blamed the chill on that. But deep down, he knew it was driven by his worry about the impending implosion of his empire and the news Bart Winchester carried with him.

As he walked to his leather desk chair perched behind his oversized custom desk, he took a sip and glanced at the pictures lining his paneled walls. Dignitaries, politicians, and sports legends had all lined up for those photo ops. Lucian and his family had commanded that respect for over one hundred years. He'd personally helped the city through its rebirth and had helped its citizens live in one of the best cities in America. Still, Jim Munro had given him the finger, through his investment banker, of course. That was the coward's way.

Winchester knocked on his office door. Blackwood sat, as he always did when receiving those who worked for him.

"Come," Blackwood said.

Winchester entered, his leathery face stretched taught by his scowl. The bill from his black ball cap shaded his eyes. Blackwood braced for the bad news.

"We missed," Winchester said taking a seat across the desk. "He was more capable than they thought."

"The less I know the better." Blackwood learned a long time ago the value of plausible deniability from his father. He didn't like having to employ Winchester or his tactics, but he had no choice. Not for a while.

Winchester nodded in a way that said he accepted Blackwood's position but didn't like it.

"Scott is a disease," Blackwood said. "He undercut me before I fired him, and his failure started us on this slide. We've lost another 15% in value. The quarterly reports will be out soon, and everyone will know. We need this. Without it, we're done."

Winchester shifted in his chair and removed his cap, setting it gently on the desk. "He won't find him. I've been assured of that. And we're already way ahead of him."

"Just be sure to get it before the weekend is over. That proxy battle is heating up. We can't hold her off much longer."

Winchester calmly folded his hands in his lap. "I can take care of her."

"No! You won't touch her. You hear me?"

Winchester smiled and placed the ball cap on his head. "That's what I thought. Just testing the waters."

"Leave her to me," Blackwood said.

"I'll move on. I have an angle to perhaps convince Munro to change his mind. If that doesn't work, we'll get it the old-fashioned way."

Blackwood didn't want any part of that. "Let me know when it's done."

Winchester stood. "Anything else?"

"No."

Winchester left.

Blackwood took another sip. He noticed the framed family photo from ten years ago. His son had left the company. His daughter was attacking everything he'd built. He wondered what the hell had happened. He glanced up and spotted the large portrait hanging over the fireplace. His father and grandfather stared back at him. His confidence melted and he felt like he was stuck in quicksand. He couldn't lose. No matter what. He chugged the rest of his drink and headed for the door.

CHAPTER 17

SATURDAY MORNING CAME early for Eli. Sleep had been elusive, and he'd tossed and turned in the luxurious queen bed in the guest wing at the back of the house. While he showered, a change of clothes magically appeared on the bed. He dressed and followed the smell of fresh coffee and bacon into the kitchen. Jennifer and Hope were there. Hope looked refreshed and showed no sign of suspicion.

"Good morning," Eli said.

Jennifer handed him an espresso mug. "Double, right?"

"Might be a triple this morning," Butch said, smiling as he entered the kitchen from the primary suite.

"Thanks, Jen. Can I do anything?" Eli said.

Jennifer turned and pulled a couple of plates from the stove. "Nope. It's all ready. Hope helped," Jennifer said, placing the plates in front of Eli and Butch. She gave Butch a hug and kiss and returned to her coffee.

Eli eyed the bacon, scrambled eggs, and warm biscuit on the plate. He noticed the two dirty dishes in the sink. "Thank you, ladies. Someone was up early."

"We don't have much time to waste," Hope said as she finished her coffee, planting the mug firmly in front of her.

Eli shared her impatience and downed his breakfast in minutes while the group ignored the events of last night as best they could by participating in light banter. They were interrupted by a knock at the door to the covered walkway that led to the garage. Butch rose and stepped outside, talking with a tall cowboy. The cowboy handed something to Butch. They both nodded, and the cowboy tipped his hat. They shook hands, and Butch came back inside.

"It's all clear. Somehow the sheriff called it an accident caused by a blowout. No mention of anything else. The problem here is taken care of."

Butch tossed Eli a key fob.

Eli stood and caught it.

"Take the truck. You all just need to be careful. We'll get your rig to the shop. Here's the address you asked for."

Butch handed the piece of paper to Hope. She entered it into her phone and tossed the paper on the island. They said goodbyes and headed out to the large, dual-wheeled crew cab pickup parked in the driveway.

Eli pulled the truck onto the section road. It was bulky but powerful. "Where to?" he asked.

Hope looked at her phone. "Looks like the professor lives right between you and me. Take the Broken Arrow Expressway. He lives just off Lewis, south of Twenty-First Street."

The traffic was light, and Eli watched the sunrise in the rearview mirror. After exiting onto Twenty-First, he headed south on Lewis. In minutes they pulled into the circular drive of the older, two-story, white, colonial brick home. The front porch had two towering white columns that supported the two-story-tall porch roof. Eli wondered if it was designed to intimidate anyone who entered the simple gray front door.

Eli turned off the engine. "We need to go easy here. We don't want to tip our hand."

Hope grinned. "That's all I do is easy." She opened her door and got out.

Eli did the same, and they met on the winding walk that led to the front door. The jagged leafless trees along the walk reached toward them and the frigid January gusts reminded him it was still winter. They reached the door, and he pressed the camera doorbell. It hadn't escaped him that an unannounced early morning visit to someone's house these days was like kicking in their door. He heard a man's voice say, "Wait there."

The door opened and the man, fit, around six feet tall, with salt-and-pepper hair and a close-cropped beard, appeared in a tartan plaid robe.

"Can I help you?"

"I'm so sorry to interrupt your morning, professor, but we need to speak. It's an emergency."

"You cops?"

"No sir. I'm Eli Scott and this is Hope Munro."

The man eyed Eli, then looked at Hope and opened his mouth. "Oh Christ. I know who you are."

"Hope Munro, sir." Hope offered her hand and smiled. "A fan of your work in the area of renewable frac sand coatings."

Eli looked at Hope, trying to hide his surprise.

Professor Gregory looked taken aback. Totally disarmed. Hope was good.

He slowly shook her hand. "I appreciate it. But I still don't appreciate you defending those assholes."

"I understand, sir. It's just a living. Not nearly as important as the work you do."

He turned back to Eli. "Look, if you want to talk business, call my office." He started to close the door.

"Wait," Eli said. "This is about Abena. We think she may be in trouble."

The professor stopped, reopened the door, and stepped onto the threshold. He scanned them both again. This one slower than his first. "How do you know Abena?"

"She came by our houses," Hope said. "We think she may have something for us."

It wasn't quite the truth, but Eli went with it.

"We weren't home," Eli said. He nodded toward the doorbell camera. "Our doorbell cameras recorded her."

The professor put one hand on his hip, keeping the other on the door. He looked off into the distance behind them. Then he stepped inside and held the door open. "Let's go inside."

The house was nicely decorated and clean. Like most older houses in the area, a parlor sat just off the entrance. The professor led them inside and stopped. He stared at Hope for a second. "You related to Jim Munro?"

"No—"

"Yes," Eli said, cutting her off. "She's his daughter."

"Hard to believe," the professor said, still focused on Hope. He seemed to take a relaxing breath. "He's been a great friend to the university and some of my work." The professor faced Eli. "The truth is, Abena hasn't shown up for work since Wednesday."

Alarm bells rattled Eli's nervous system. "Did you report that to anyone?"

"Yes. I had Nora call her son in Dallas and see if things were okay."

Eli felt like jumper cables had just shocked his heart. Hope didn't look concerned at all.

Eli turned back to the professor. "Who's Nora?"

"She's my lead researcher. She's known Abena since our days at TU."

"What did she find out?"

"Nothing. She wasn't in Dallas. Her son is headed up this morning. Said he called the Tulsa Police. He was connected to their Missing Persons Unit. They wanted to wait until he got here. Then he'd get them into her apartment."

Eli struggled to hide his crushing disappointment. "Did she work anywhere else?"

"No. Just for us. TU before that."

"What can you tell us about her?" Eli asked.

"You need to talk to her son."

"Between you and me, professor, she didn't look like she had much time to waste," Hope said.

"What do you mean?"

"Here, look at this." Hope pulled up the photos on her phone. The professor pulled a pair of tortoise shell glasses from his robe pocket and closely examined the two images.

"You may not like what I do, but I'm connected," Hope said. "I can find things out that even the police can't."

He pulled his glasses off and said, "She's very kind and helpful. Just a wonderful human being."

"What did she do in her time away from work?" Eli asked.

The professor looked out the window to his left and tapped his folded glasses against his other hand. Then he looked at Eli. "You need to talk to Nora. She knows her well."

"Where can we find her?" Eli asked.

The professor's face softened. He seemed to suddenly recognize Eli. "I have to tell you something. My son worked for you at Blackwood Energy before you left. An engineer. Said you were the best leader he ever saw. You cared about your people." He slipped his glasses back into his pocket. He locked eyes with Eli. "So I trust you. I'll tell you where she lives. The rest is up to you. Give me your number. That way I can text it to you, and I can give your number to her son when he gets here."

Eli didn't want to do that. Connecting him with the son meant connecting him to the police. But the cat was out of the bag. He didn't have a choice. The professor pulled his phone from his other pocket and Eli gave him the number. He glanced at Hope while the professor typed it into his phone. Her subtle smile made Eli feel like he was just where she wanted him. Between a rock, a liar, and a hard place.

CHAPTER 18

THE TRIP TO Nora Perry's home took ten minutes. Eli knew he shouldn't trust Hope, but driven by his commitment to find her father, he had no choice. The brick townhome sat behind an apartment complex along Riverside Avenue. With a view of the Arkansas River from her second-floor windows, Eli thought it would be a sought-after address. Nora Perry was doing well. He pulled to the curb in front of her unit and killed the rumbling engine of the oversized truck. The sun was now up, well into the morning sky, and Eli hoped Nora was at home.

"I'll take the lead with her. Again, we don't want to give away too much," Eli said.

Hope opened the door, stepped out of the truck, and slammed the door. Eli didn't know how much more of this he could tolerate. He left the truck and followed Hope up the steps to the wooden front door. Stepping around Hope, he knocked on the door. He didn't hear a thing from inside.

Suddenly, the door swung open. A young woman stood in the door, barefoot, dressed in the latest winter running gear.

"Miss Perry?" Eli asked.

"Come in. I've been expecting you." She swung the door open and headed into the narrow hallway. Eli and Hope followed. He assumed Professor Gregory had provided a heads-up about their visit.

Nora Perry walked like a scientist. Her steps were deliberate, almost measured. She was fit and carried herself well, shoulders back, head up. Her jet-black hair was pulled tightly into a ponytail that waved back and forth as she strode into the tiny living room. The furniture was functional in an IKEA kind of way. The unit looked sparse and hardly lived in. It was neat and clean, with no photographs displayed anywhere. Eli assumed she spent most of her time at work or on the Riverside Trail along the river.

She directed them to the sofa. "Have a seat. Please." She took the single chair facing them. Her expression darkened and lines of concern appeared in her ivory skin. "I understand you're trying to find Abena."

"Yes," Eli said. "My name is Eli Scott. This is Hope Munro."

"I know who you are," Nora said tersely as if he was wasting her time. Her eyes kept cutting to Hope like she was a threat.

"We have reason to believe she's been trying to contact us," Hope said. "We're not sure why, though."

Hope exhaled little too loudly. She looked as if she wanted to be somewhere else.

Nora eyed Hope, who was thumbing her phone, then turned back to Eli. "She's not shown up for work. That's not like her. I've known her a long time, and she's never done this before."

"Professor Gregory said you knew her at University of Tulsa?"

"Yes. There were a bunch of us that got to know her. She's a wonderful person. She works hard. Takes it very seriously. She was a bit like a house mother to us."

"What can you tell us about her?" Eli said.

"She's a single mother. Her son is older now. Lives in Dallas. She's worked cleaning our laboratories and offices at JEG and did the same in the chemistry and biochemistry labs and classrooms at TU."

"Any idea as to why she missed work?" Hope asked.

Nora stared at Hope. "Before I answer any other questions, let me ask you a few."

Hope glared back.

"Does your interest in Abena have anything to do with your line of work?"

Hope leaned forward. "What do you mean?"

"I know what you do to people. And I know the kind of people you work for. I want to know if your interest in Abena is related to any of that. I don't want her pulled into any of your bullshit."

"It's none of your business," Hope said.

"It's not related," Eli said, trying to defuse the situation. Hope was edging toward anger, and he knew that wasn't good.

Nora glared at Hope. "It *is* my business. But if you're telling me she's not representing one of her clients, Mr. Scott, I'll believe you. Professor Gregory told me about your reputation."

"Thanks for that. We're trying to find her. Now, what else can you tell us about her?"

"She's smart. Interesting. Single mother, like I said. She works hard. She even monitored some of our classes to learn more about what we did at TU."

Eli thought about the chemistry books at Abena's apartment.

Nora continued. "She even…" She stopped herself.

"What is it?"

Nora leaned back, seeming to weigh her options.

"What were you about to say?" Hope said.

Nora stayed silent.

"Look," Hope said. "She's in trouble. She'll probably be dead soon."

"Hope!" Eli yelled.

Hope jumped up. "She's involved in something way over her head. If you don't start telling us everything, her death is on you."

Eli stood. "That's enough, Hope."

Hope shoved him. Hard enough that he stepped backward toward the sofa.

"Well?" Hope said to Nora. Nora gave her the finger.

"You'll be sorry you did that." Hope pushed past Eli and headed to the front door.

"Sorry. I'll be right back," Eli said to Nora. He followed Hope out the door. "Wait."

She stopped and wagged a finger in Eli's face. She started crying. "This is going nowhere." She turned and walked away.

"Where are you going? You don't have a—"

A black limo pulled up. Hope jumped into the back seat and slammed the door, and it sped off.

Eli pulled out his phone and snapped a photo of the departing car. He checked the image and shoved the phone back into his pocket. He wondered what had just happened. He also wondered about the limo. Had Hope called it using her phone, or was it scheduled?

He looked behind him and saw Nora standing in the doorway. He dropped his head and walked up to her. "I'm so sorry about that."

She folded her arms. "Didn't surprise me."

"Look. I have a friend. A mentor. He's been taken. I can't go to the police. Abena may somehow be linked to him. She might be able to help me."

"Is she in danger?"

Eli spread his arms, palms up. "Honestly, I don't know. But I can promise you if she is I'll do everything I can to get her out of it. Including getting the police involved if I have to."

"Based on my conversation with her son this morning, they already are involved."

Eli knew that wasn't a good thing. "What were you about to say in there?"

Nora looked down at the ground, then up at Eli. "We give some of our old equipment to Abena. Stuff that's being replaced. I think she was selling it to make extra money to send to family members back home in the Congo. I just don't want her to get in trouble for doing that."

"Trouble?" Eli stepped closer.

"Yes. Professor Gregory and I have been doing that for a while. I'm not sure it would be okay for her to resell it."

"Let me ask you this. Was any of the work you were doing associated with batteries?"

"Batteries? You mean lithium-ion batteries?"

Eli nodded.

"No. Our work and equipment were used in the generation of renewable organic compounds for the oilfield. No batteries."

"Any idea as to where she would be?"

"No. Believe me, if I knew I'd be there already."

"Thanks, Miss Perry."

She softly smiled. "Nora."

"Thank you, Nora."

Eli spun and headed down the front walk.

"Eli," Nora called out.

He stopped and turned to face her, his interest suddenly acute. She waited and he walked back to her.

When he stopped, she said, "Abena is smart. Not smart, but brilliant. She was ten times brighter than any of my students. If she had kept that equipment, she could have used it to test any hypothesis, including anything to do with lithium-ion batteries."

Eli examined her eyes. She looked truthful but sad. He nodded. "Thanks for that."

"Just find her. Please." She turned and walked away.

Eli now knew one thing for sure: He needed to find Abena Williams.

As Eli walked to the truck, he wondered what Hope was doing. Maybe Nora's challenge to her manipulation set her off. But the car had come too quickly. Maybe it was one of her clients needing help, or maybe it was something else. With Hope, he couldn't tell. She had him doubting everything she'd told him and doubting himself. He knew he needed help.

He texted Lizzy to see if she would meet at the coffee shop on Utica. Her reply was an instantaneous yes. He entered the truck and called Hudson. It was time to find out about Blackwood.

CHAPTER 19

AFTER TEXTING HUDSON and asking him to dig deeper into the Blackwood connection, Eli drove away from Nora Perry's home. He battled the memories pulling him down to a place so dark and deep that he needed Lizzy's help to get his head straight. Hope's behavior was a mystery, too.

Eli pulled into the coffee shop in Utica Square, the posh shopping venue just down the street from Lizzy's practice. Leaving the truck, he saw Lizzy in the back corner booth. He took a deep breath and immediately felt her presence. Their connection was strong, and it had helped them both. He stopped at the counter, bought two double espressos, and headed to Lizzy in the booth.

Lizzy greeted him with a smile. "You look like you've been rode hard and put up wet."

Eli dropped into the seat across from her. "A long two days."

"Let me guess. She's driving you crazy?"

"How'd you know?"

"Your history of dealing with the personal costs of lies and deceptions with your father."

As usual, Lizzy had hit the nail on the head.

"I'm confused by her behavior." Eli paused, weighing whether to get Lizzy involved in the Blackwood issue.

She read his consternation. "What is it, Eli?'

"It's the Blackwood thing again. I'd hate to get you involved any deeper in this."

"Don't worry about that. This is a session. Confidential." She reached across the table and squeezed his arm. "Let's take it like a box of chocolate truffles—one piece at a time." Lizzy grinned and pulled out her small notebook from her folio. "What do you mean 'confused'?"

"She clearly is concerned about her father. I think that's true. But I still can't tell when she's telling the truth or lying."

"Did you confirm that Jim is missing?"

"Yes. He's been missing and silent since Wednesday night."

"So you know that's true?"

"Correct."

"And what makes you think she cares?"

"What?" Lizzy's question made him think. "Her sincerity. Her tears. Her determination." Lizzy made another note. "And what made you come here? To see me?"

He explained Hope's tantrum and disappearance. "I guess I felt stunned by that. Like I said, she says she loves her father, but I didn't understand why she fled."

Lizzy wrote something down again. "Where'd she go?"

"Don't know. But she was angry and crying."

"Angry and crying," Lizzy repeated, making a note.

She looked up and gave Eli a look he'd come to know well. It was a gentle, warm expression. He immediately relaxed, knowing help was forthcoming. "Look Eli, just like I said before, the behaviors you are describing are still consistent with those of a full-blown sociopath."

"I know we talked about that before, but I just can't believe she doesn't care about her father. I can see it."

Lizzy looked away and exhaled. Then she locked eyes with Eli, leaned across the table, and whispered, "You're fighting this a bit. I can see there is a connection to her. What is it?"

Eli thought for a second. "It's Jim."

She covered Eli's hand. "No. Go deeper."

Eli closed his eyes and focused on his breath as she'd taught him. His thoughts drifted by, like a news crawler in the fog. Then, it struck him. "It's the *connection* to her father. I feel that."

"And where does that feel like it comes from?" she whispered.

Eli allowed the feeling to rise from the darkness. He suddenly felt punched in the stomach. "From what I didn't get from my father but got from Jim."

She nodded. "Good work." She let go of his hand and leaned back.

"It's not her feelings, it's yours—from a long time ago. Fight projecting them onto her. She'll only do something to win—feel superior. To do that she'll lie, manipulate, and steal whatever she thinks is valuable to others.

Eli felt a bit like a fool. He hated liars but loved Jim. He'd unknowingly assumed Hope, despite her sociopathy, felt the same way he would about her father. Eli took in what Lizzy was saying. It was difficult to accept. He'd seen it with his own eyes: Hope acted like she cared about her father. But he trusted Lizzy. And Hope had lied repeatedly. Publicly for her job.

Again, Lizzy seemed to read him like a book. "You're a good man, Eli. Let me cut through the BS and be a short looper for a minute." She looked to the side, as if plucking a thought that was floating past. "Always remember she's a predator. She has no conscience. None whatsoever. She's a master manipulator who can spot a weakness or strength in you or another person quickly, then exploit either. She can act better than most professional actors to mimic our emotions. Not *feel* them. Ever. But it makes her invisible to those of us with a conscience. Professionals like me, and good people like you. We just can't imagine the depth of her condition."

"Our conscience makes us weaker?" he asked.

"No. It makes us susceptible to manipulation if we aren't equipped to deal with a sociopath. We have difficulty comprehending their motivations."

"Sounds like a liability to me."

Lizzy looked around the room, then focused back on Eli. "I believe our conscience is the most powerful force in nature. It's what sets us apart from every other living thing. It connects us all—that ability to care about another human, sometimes all of humanity."

"Okay. I think I can see that now. But how can I use that against her and save Jim?"

"Remember that her only motivation in life is to win. To dominate. To be seen as superior. She doesn't care about anyone or anything else. Remember she knows you far better than you can ever know her. She's already studied you and seen how she can manipulate you. She just showed you an example."

"How?" he asked.

"When she stormed out crying and left in the limo. That's her pity play. She wants you to feel sorry for her. To feel guilty. It's a hallmark of her condition."

He understood. Hope had done it earlier when she'd teared up. But Eli needed a weapon. "What can I do? Can I use this against her?"

"Yes. Verify what you can. Independently. Don't base your decisions on anything else she does or doesn't do or say. And keep your emotions in check. And remember, she can't feel any emotions. So those she shows you aren't real. They're manipulative."

"That's a tall order. I have to think like her."

"No. You have to think like *you*. Evaluate everything using your intellect, not your emotion."

"I think I've got it. Back to my original question. How do I deal with her lies?"

Lizzy chuckled. "You'll love this." She closed her notebook.

"Treat everything she says as a lie. Unless you can verify it, it's a lie she's using to manipulate you."

Lizzy was right. He didn't like that answer. It didn't square with what he was *feeling*. There was one thing he knew was true. His mentor and friend was missing. Probably in trouble due to some mysterious invention involving Abena Williams. Now Hope was missing too, and he was about to find out where she went.

"What about the Blackwood issue?" Lizzy asked.

"It's back. And I can't shake it."

"Why is it back?"

Eli looked away. "I don't think I should tell you. I don't want to put you in that position."

Lizzy paused and side-eyed Eli. After a few seconds of staring at Eli, she nodded. "Okay. Tell me about the *feeling*."

Eli described it. "I need to keep a clear head here. I need to act accordingly."

"Okay. Let's try this." She pushed her pad aside. "Close your eyes and try to feel those feelings again."

Eli did. The soul crushing shame and fear surfaced quickly.

"Hold on to that and think about the EMDR. Are the feelings close to the same?"

"Yes. Yes!" Eli made the connection. "Does that mean it's connected to Mom's problem?"

"Tell me about that night. The one that came up in EMDR."

Eli looked down at his hands and recalled that night. "It was late one night, and I awoke with that 'uh oh' feeling ripping through me." He looked up at Lizzy. "You know, the one you had as a child when the bottom of your stomach dropped out because you'd been exposed for doing something wrong. I heard a commotion in the house and listened to my father's voice talking with strangers. My bedroom faced the front of the house and was right next to my parents' room. Something was wrong, but I was afraid to go find out. I was supposed to be asleep. Then, I noticed the flashing lights through the curtains and rushed to the window, opened the curtains, and peeked over the thick white sill."

"Okay. Go on," she said.

"An ambulance sat in the driveway, its gumball machine flashing and bright light streaming out from the back. My body knew the terror before my mind did. I felt the acidic sickness and the tears rolling down my cheeks. I must have stood at that window for ten minutes or so. Then I saw them: two men from the ambulance had my mom on a stretcher. She was under a sheet but strapped in. They gingerly lifted it off its wheels when they reached the steps down to the driveway. Each time the lights flashed, I could see my mom. She wasn't good. She wasn't happy. She wasn't moving. The tears were cascading down my cheeks, and I was bawling in an effort to get this dark feeling out of me. But it didn't work. No matter how hard or how long I cried, the feeling remained.

"I don't remember if my neighbor told me, or if I overheard him telling someone on the phone, but I quickly knew my mom had tried to kill herself. That revelation consumed me, and the feeling of wrongness, not being enough for her, seeped into my bones. There was never any explanation, and just like mom's other problems, I knew the rule was never to speak of it. That night my mom made it… but I didn't."

"What happened after that? Did your father explain it to you when he returned?" she asked.

He felt his anger swell. "No! He only came back to see if she'd died. For the insurance. Three days later he got caught and sent to prison. I never saw that bastard again." Eli took a breath, then continued. "After she returned, I was happy she did. But from that day forward when my mom was happy, I was happy. When she was 'sad', the demons came from the darkness and smothered my innocent childhood joy."

Eli could see Lizzy was struggling. A tear escaped her eye and ran down her cheek. She sniffled, wiped the tear away, then asked, "How old were you?"

Eli could feel something coming up quickly from the darkness. "Six or seven."

"Just a little boy worried about his mom."

Eli felt the lump in his throat. "Yes."

"And what emotion was that you were feeling?"

"I was afraid for her." Eli had trouble getting the words out. "No, that's not it. I was afraid for me. I thought she was leaving. Leaving me. No one told me, but I felt like I wasn't good enough."

Lizzy reached out for him again and squeezed his arm. "You were just seven years old. No one explained it to you then, but it wasn't you. It wasn't your fault. It's not your fault. Can you see that?"

Eli thought about that moment. Then and now. He realized where that "voice" that kept telling him he wasn't enough came from. He nodded.

"What emotions were you feeling?"

"I was afraid. I felt ashamed."

"And what did you feel earlier?"

"The same thing."

Lizzy nodded slowly at him and sat back. "It doesn't mean you didn't feel those things when Blackwell fired you. But they triggered that childhood fear and made it that much more intense."

Eli let out a deep breath.

"Better?" Lizzy asked.

"Yes. Yes. I think I'm good. Thanks, Lizzy. You're the best."

She flashed another smile. "I know."

Eli checked the time. "I gotta go." Eli stood.

Lizzy joined him in the aisle. She leaned in and hugged him. Then she whispered, "You don't need to save her. Save Jim. Be careful, my friend."

"I will."

CHAPTER 20

ELI SAT OUTSIDE the coffee shop in the oversized pickup and watched the shoppers in Utica Square. He wished he could be one of them. It was late Saturday morning, and the posh outdoor shopping venue had come to life. Late-model European and American luxury cars and faux SUVs occupied the parking spaces surrounding him. Women dressed in their designer winter coats, a few accompanied by their male companions, scurried in the chilling breeze between the shops and cafés. Instead of enjoying a leisurely Saturday, his mind raced through his options to find his friend. According to Hope, Jim only had thirty-six hours to live.

Lizzy had said to treat everything Hope said as a lie, but Eli couldn't do that. He couldn't risk Jim's life that way. Lizzy had helped him see that his conscience wouldn't let him believe that she didn't care about him. He needed to find her to sort through her lies. The only ties to Jim were through Hope, Abena Williams, and maybe Blackwood. He pulled his phone from his pocket and examined the photo of the fleeing limo. It was a black Town Car. He enlarged the photo and examined the Oklahoma license plate, memorized it, and called Butch.

Butch answered on the first ring. "Hey, cowboy."

"Hey, Butch. I need a plate run." He heard Butch's footsteps then a door close.

"No problem. Give me the plate."

Eli did.

"Hang on." He heard Butch give the plate to someone on his office phone. After a brief pause, Butch said to Eli, "Shit, man. Are you following Blackwood?"

Stunned, Eli wasn't sure he'd heard Butch correctly. "What?"

"The plate. It's a Lincoln Town Car registered to Blackwood Energy."

Eli didn't want to believe what he was hearing. Lizzy had been proven right. Hope had been lying the whole time. A white-hot flare fired off in his gut.

"She was working for Blackwood," Eli said.

"Who?"

"Hope Munro suddenly took off in that limo."

"If she's working for Blackwood, that—"

Eli cut Butch off. "That means they've been working together. She may be behind the whole thing."

"Careful, pardner. If that's the case, doesn't that make you the target, not her father?"

The revelation twisted inside him. He'd been used. How did he miss it? She'd been manipulating him the entire time. Now he needed to find her for another reason.

"Thanks, man."

"Be careful!" Butch said.

"Later." Eli ended the call. He'd deal with Hope once he found her. But Blackwood was a snake, and he was in this with her. He knew of several reasons Blackwood would need an image consultant, but Jim was missing, and as far as Eli was concerned, Blackwood and Hope were prime suspects. His hate grew even more toward Blackwood. It was something he'd never thought possible. He dialed Hudson's number.

"Hey, mongrel. I was just about to call you," Hudson said.

"What you got, Hudson?"

"You sound like you have a burr in your saddle."

"Several."

"Well then, this won't help."

"Okay. Let's hear it."

"I went up to the lease north of Hominy. It was Blackwood's all right. The cattle guard was locked, and a freshly painted trespassing sign was up."

"You didn't get in to see it?"

"Ain't no hill for a stepper. Obviously, you don't know who I think I am!"

Despite his simmering anger, Eli chuckled. "My bad."

"It's an old lease. Had a shut-in well. Think it was drilled to the Mississippi Chat. That play had been resurrected by horizontal drilling and fracking but there was no new well staked anywhere on the lease. There's an old doghouse that looks like it's been recently moved in. Locked up tight. There was a camera on the power pole, so they probably saw me. I don't give a shit, though. Those hombres are up to something."

Eli thought about Jim trapped inside the steel-sided trailer. "Could somebody be inside the doghouse?"

"It's possible."

Eli's spirits lifted a bit. "Okay. This may be easier than I thought. Thanks, Hudson."

"Whoa there. There's more."

"More?"

"Yeah. Went to the café on Main Street to have a cup. Heard that someone has been using the old former Ravenel Energy area office for the past few months."

"Our old office?"

"Yup. Been shut down since you left years ago. But Sherry's

sister, who still works the morning shift at the café, said she'd heard some guy from Tulsa had rented it."

"You think it's Blackwood?"

"Nah. Might be Jim. That would tie to his request for some security up here."

Eli's mind raced. The old office was isolated in an abandoned area of Hominy. If Jim was renting it, he could be hiding something.

"One more thing. She said she'd seen an old blue Toyota heading in that direction down Main several mornings."

Eli stiffened in his seat, every muscle in his body rigid. "A blue Toyota?"

"Yup."

"I'm coming up this afternoon."

"Thought you'd say that. I already gave Sonny a heads-up."

Eli started the truck. "See you soon. I'll call when I get closer. It might be a minute. I have to stop by the house."

"Let me know." Hudson hung up.

Eli backed out of the parking space just as his phone rang again. He didn't recognize the number, but it had a Tulsa area code. He pulled back into the space.

"Hello?"

"Mr. Scott?" A young man's voice.

"Yes. Who am I speaking with?"

"This is Darnell Williams. Abena Williams's son."

Eli's breath caught in his throat. He cleared it. "Yes?"

"I got your information from Professor Gregory. From her work." His tone was measured. Careful.

"Yes. I spoke to him earlier."

"Well, he said you were worth talking to. Can you meet me?"

Eli wondered if he'd already met with the police at Abena's apartment and if this might be a setup. Eli could have been spotted at his mother's apartment. Dodging Darnell didn't seem fair, though. "Yes. Where and when?"

"I'm at Mom's now."

The setup scheme now took root in Eli's mind. Were the cops setting a trap? And Darnell just acted as if Eli should know where his mother lived. He needed to play clueless.

"And where is that?" Eli said.

"Quail Ranch Apartments. Number 217. Can you come now?"

Darnell seemed eager. Eli didn't know if it was because his mother was missing or if it might be Darnell was nervous about a ruse. Eli didn't have a choice. Darnell already knew Eli had been looking for his mother. If the cops weren't in on this, this might be a way to keep it that way. With Blackwood involved somehow, cooperating with Darnell to find his mother first was a smart move. Blackwood had a hand in most elected officials' campaigns, and no telling what they might do if they found her first.

"Yes. I'll be there in fifteen minutes."

CHAPTER 21

LUCIAN BLACKWOOD WATCHED the flags in the park fifty-one floors below him. They appeared to vibrate in the stiff north wind. He heard it whistle against the thick plate glass and eyed the dark stormfront building to the northwest. He felt the warm air from the sleek metal floor register against his skin but still battled a chill from within. From a deep well he had always ignored, the image of his father calling him an idiot rose up and squeezed his chest. It would soon be noon, and he'd have exactly forty-eight hours before all his father had built came crashing down. The worst part wasn't the memory. It wasn't even his own doing. The worst part was that his demise would be at the hands of his daughter.

He heard a knock and turned away from the window. Bart Winchester stood in the doorway, and he nodded him in. Winchester's stare unsettled him as he strode to the desk, never removing his attention from Lucian. His dark cap, long face, and thick rigid frame had been chiseled from the grizzly work he'd done as a special forces operator and later as a CIA contractor.

"She here yet?" Blackwood said, doing his best to hide his anxiousness.

"Soon. The car picked her up fifteen minutes ago." Winchester approached Blackwood's desk.

Blackwood grabbed the high back of the black leather chair, turned it, and sat. Winchester continued standing.

Blackwood looked up. "What is it?"

"You know I don't trust her."

Blackwood took a breath and leaned back, his eyes locked on Winchester's. "You know, it's not about trust. It's about results."

Winchester's face turned sour. He leaned down, supporting himself with his hands on the desktop. "I hear you, but you know what she is."

"I know exactly what she is. She's the person that got a U.S. Senator re-elected after he got caught red-handed with that intern. She's the woman who helped that weird google boy build his company into a billion-dollar business by delivering government support, and contracts, that he'd never get on his own after he got caught up in that bitcoin scandal. It's the eleventh hour and unless you have a better idea, we need her to get her father to change his mind."

Winchester sat down and swallowed his challenge.

"Nice to be wanted, boys," Hope said as she flittered into the office.

Blackwood raised his head. "Where are we?"

Winchester didn't turn or acknowledge her. She took the seat next to him. Still, he didn't look at her.

Hope glanced at him, then back at Blackwood. She shrugged.

Blackwood narrowed his eyes on her. "Did your father change his mind yet?"

Hope smiled. "Did you live up to your part of the plan?" She turned and eyed Winchester.

"It's all in play now," he said to Blackwood, still refusing to look at Hope.

"And you're sure this will work?" Blackwood asked Hope.

"No." Winchester said before Hope could answer.

She wagged her head and laughed. "Yes. The Williams woman is the key. This will flush her out."

Finally, Winchester turned to Hope. "You mean the janitor?" he said, sarcastically.

Ignoring him, she said, "It will work. Perfectly. Once she's found, dad said he'll sign the agreement."

"On the spot?" Blackwood asked.

"Yes."

Blackwood grabbed onto her answer like a man grabbing a life preserver on a burning boat. He hated having to rely on her, but he had no choice. "He'd better," Blackwood said as he nodded toward Winchester, who smiled. "It has to happen tomorrow. The board officially meets at noon on Monday. They'll have no choice but to authorize a special shareholder vote. The one my daughter has been pushing for. The earnings release will tank the stock and she'll win. It has to happen tomorrow." Blackwood left out the part about the collapse of his shares due to a margin call.

"He said he'll sign," Hope said.

"Where is he. I'd like to hear it myself," Winchester said.

Hope focused on Blackwell, not Winchester. "That can't happen. If you do anything to try, the deal's off,"

Winchester looked at Blackwood. "Bullshit."

Blackwood glared at Winchester and wanted to choke him. He slammed his hand on the desk. "That's enough!"

Hope grinned.

"Now," Blackwood said, "What about Scott?"

"I need him to get to Williams," Hope said.

Winchester folded his arms and huffed. "He's a problem. One that needs to be dealt with."

Blackwood leaned back and considered that option. Scott had been a pain in the ass when he worked for him. Mr. goody two shoes. Mr. shareholder value. He'd gone against Blackwood and his efforts to keep control over the people in the organization from the start. But he needed to be careful. He needed plausible deniability.

"You do what you need," Blackwood said to Hope.

She stood. "I'll keep you apprised of my progress."

As she walked out the door, Winchester said, "You do that."

CHAPTER 22

ELI WASN'T USED to lying. As he made his way to south Tulsa, he thought about the ones he may have to tell. He wanted to puke and rid himself of this feeling. But the problem wasn't in his stomach. It was wherever his conscience resided. He hated liars and hated lying. His poor judgment about Hope had ripped any confidence he'd gained to pieces. And he felt stupid for ignoring Lizzy's good advice. As a result, he was swimming in a sea of self-doubt.

He knew this could be the end. If the cops were there and had his prints, or someone had identified him on a doorbell camera at the apartments, he'd immediately be a suspect. Probably locked up. Even if the cops weren't there, he'd be forced to act as if he'd never been there to earn Darnell's trust. It was his chance to get information about Abena that might lead him to her and ultimately to Jim. He needed to get north to Hominy. But first he had to face Darnell.

Eli turned into the familiar parking lot of Quail Ranch Apartments but parked near the office, as if he'd never been there before. Walking from his truck, he acted like he was searching for the apartment number. When he got close, he spotted a young Black man waving from Abena's balcony.

He found the stairs and climbed them, and with each step, he battled the urge to flee. He reminded himself of his courage to face adversity. Darnell stood in the doorway of the apartment. He was a muscular, angular young man with a high and tight haircut and round wire-rimmed eyeglasses. His eyes were wide and bright, but the sags beneath them reflected his concern and lack of sleep.

"Mr. Scott?" Darnell extended his hand.

Eli shook it, noting his firm grip. "Call me Eli. Please."

"Come in."

The place looked the same. Still ransacked. But no one was there with handcuffs and Eli relaxed a bit.

"Wow. Who did this?"

"We don't know yet. The police were here and did their work. Said they'd process the prints they found. The only thing missing is my mom. They put out a bulletin this morning."

"Sorry that she's missing."

"I appreciate you."

"What can I do for you?"

A look somewhere between concern and suspicion drifted across Darnell's face. "Professor Gregory said that you were looking for her, too?"

"Yes. I am. She came to my house, and I wasn't there. She looked worried and rang the bell several times. The security camera caught a clip of her. I was trying to find out why she was there. She looked like she needed help." Eli felt good about telling the truth.

"Can I see the clip?"

"Sure." Eli showed it to him.

"That's my mom all right. She does look worried. Why your house?"

Eli forced himself to relax before he lied. "I don't know."

"Then why are you trying to find her? Most would just let it go."

Eli refused to let Darnell's challenge unnerve him. "For some reason I feel like she needed my help."

Darnell paused, looked away, then returned his focus to Eli. "Look, I know about you. You were a good leader. I work with some folks that worked for you. Got a good rep. But why would she need your help?"

"Look, Darnell. I don't know. I just feel like I want to help. That's all."

"That's nice of you."

"What did the police tell you?"

"The first step was the bulletin and processing the prints from here. Told me to sit tight."

Eli imagined the discovery of his prints followed by his immediate arrest, and it made him sweat. "Would you mind telling me about your mom? Maybe something will strike a chord with me."

Darnell eyed Eli, appearing to weigh his options. "Okay. My mom is from the DRC."

"The Congo?"

"Yeah. Came here when she was young with her mom and dad. They'd all worked in the artisanal mines there and wanted to get away."

"Artisanal mines?"

Darnell's jaw tightened and he narrowed his focus on Eli. "Nice words made up by some fat cats to describe the hand mining of minerals. They were handling cobalt. It's slave labor. They get next to nothing for their work. Kids, their parents, they all get hurt or sick."

"That sounds terrible."

"It is. Mom's dad was sick when he got here, then her mom got cancer too. They both died and she dropped out of her first year of college and went to work. Then she had me. She's a great mom and did everything she could to see that I got my degree. Worked two jobs."

"Is that when she worked at TU?"

Darnell hesitated, then slowly nodded, perhaps buying time to evaluate his reply. "Yeah. She worked as a customer service person during the day from home to take care of me. See, my dad died when I was in third grade."

Eli wagged his head. "Sorry to hear that."

Darnell seemed to respond to the empathetic gesture. "Thanks, man. Anyway, she did the single mom thing, then when I graduated from TU she started monitoring classes."

"What kind of classes?"

"Chemistry. Biochem. See, she'd wanted to be a chemist before her parents died and she was forced to drop out. She's smart. Real smart. Never really got a chance to prove it. Because of her lack of formal education, her gender, and the color of her skin. You know how it used to be around here. I'd heard you did your best to change that at Blackwood."

Eli softly smiled, thankful for the recognition. "I did. What about her work now?"

"She loves working with Professor Gregory and Nora. They're like family to both of us."

"Did she say anything about doing anything outside of work?"

Darnell pulled back, crossed his thick arms, and furrowed his brow. Suspicion filled his dark eyes. "Why would you ask that?"

Eli knew he'd hit a nerve. "Just trying to figure out what might be the reason she was at my house."

Darnell stood firm, waiting with his arms still crossed. He clearly didn't want to go there. He was hiding something.

"Is there something you're not telling me?"

Darnell uncrossed his arms, went to the door of the apartment, and opened it. "I think we're done."

"I'd like to help."

"Goodbye, Mr. Scott. Thanks for coming by."

Eli left the apartment not wanting to anger Darnell any further. If he was hiding something, he was probably hiding it from the police too. As Eli walked to the truck, he wondered what Williams family secret had to do with Jim. One name kept searing itself into his mind. *Lucian Blackwood.*

CHAPTER 23

ELI WAS HEADED into the mouth of the beast that had destroyed him three years ago. As he drove to the offices of Blackwood Energy, he felt the struggle begin. It was as if he were back there already, being escorted from the building like a criminal. The shame gremlins were back, hacking away his self-confidence, telling him his flaw was deep inside him, fatal, and of his own doing. He should have managed his tenure with Blackwood more effectively. Instead, he'd let everyone down: his employees, his family, his friends, the needy, and everyone who had relied on him. He was on an elevator to hell. A hell of his own making.

Eli knew he had to "feel the feel" as Lizzy had taught him. But then he needed to take control of his emotions. He remembered the session this morning. That was then and this was now. As far as he was concerned, his so-called failures were the ingredients of wisdom he'd already paid for, and life was about having the courage to act on that wisdom. He leaned into the empty worthlessness coating his being and inhaled it. Then he focused on his purpose in life: to make the world a better place by using his talents to help others. And at this moment, Jim Munro needed *his* help. He exhaled and envisioned tossing the sticky gremlins where they belonged—in the past. He wasn't helpless anymore. He was a Marine veteran who was physically and mentally able to meet any challenge.

A block away, he pulled the truck to the curb and stared at the glimmering fifty-two-story building. Focused on the top floor, he knew the answers he needed hid inside. The afternoon sun was overhead, and it warmed him as he left the truck and walked to the entrance of Blackwood Center.

Based on what he knew, Lucian Blackwood would be there. According to Eli's sources, Blackwood was experiencing a seismic shift in his world, an earthquake that could crumble what was left of the Blackwood dynasty that had been built by his father. His wealth was vaporizing, along with his influence, as his oil company had been crippled by a long string of failed investments. Accelerating his own fall was the fact that he'd pledged his stock to secure loans to invest in a plethora of nonenergy investments, all of which were failing and heading to a margin call that would be the death knell to his stock holdings in Blackwood Energy which would also finish off his reputation and power.

As a result, Blackwood was under attack by his own daughter. Sarah Blackwood had refused to take any part in her family's enterprise. Instead, she'd joined Baker Capital, an ESG-oriented hedge fund that had become one of the most feared environmental, social, and governance activists on Wall Street. As a young partner, she'd targeted her father's firm for his refusal to recognize the effects of global warming and his lack of good governance, which was reflected in the makeup of his crony-filled, all-white-male board. All issues Eli suggested should be addressed before he was fired. In addition, Blackwood's affairs with several women, both inside and outside the company, were a liability and a distraction. Eli assumed they also provided more emotional fire to Sarah Blackwood's efforts. She'd watched her mother experience the humiliation and refuse to leave him—something Eli knew all too well. Eli suspected that Hope was involved in burnishing Blackwood's image through this proxy battle, and it would provide cover for their hand in Jim's disappearance.

He reached the glass wall and double doors that guarded the entrance to the building. Walking to the far-right door, he pushed the button for after-hours entry. The security guard at the desk answered, and Eli looked into the camera hovering above him.

"Eli. I'll be damned," the guard said through the speaker.

"Hi, Gerard. Been a minute. Hasn't it?" Eli said.

"Yes, sir. I'm sorry. Not sure I can let you in."

"I'm sure you can let me into the lobby so I can talk to you."

After a short pause, Gerard said, "I think that would be okay."

The magnetic lock buzzed and Eli opened the door and headed across the massive lobby to the security desk that sat in front of the bank of glimmering silver elevators. Gerard stood to offer his hand across the long counter.

Eli shook it. "How've you been?"

"Busy. Lots of visitors lately."

"I'll bet."

"Ginny and the kids doing all right?"

"Yes. They're great. You wouldn't believe how big the kids are now."

"That's great to hear." Eli leaned on the counter and lowered his voice. "Is the old man in today?"

Gerard sat back down and glanced at the bank of monitors and the computer screen in front of him. "I don't think I can tell you that."

"Look. I need to speak with him. I know he's probably up there. He probably dragged Virginia in there today, too. Just call her and ask if he will see me. It about something I know he'll want to hear." Just the thought of being face-to-face with Lucian Blackwood wracked his nerves.

"I can do that. But I didn't say he was here."

"I've got your back, Gerard."

Gerard picked up the phone and had a short, muddled conversation with the person on the other end. He hung up the phone.

"She said for you to wait here."

"Is he coming down?"

"Just said to wait here."

"Okay. Thanks."

The reply made Eli uneasy. He tried to hide the fact that he was about to jump out of his skin. Was Blackwood coming down? Or was he sending his goons to throw him out? Eli was sure he wasn't violating anything in the agreements he had signed, but that wouldn't matter to Blackwood.

Eli suddenly wasn't sure what to do with his hands. Then he caught himself and focused. No matter what happened, he would still be the man he was, and Blackwood would still be an asshole. Crude, but it helped. Finally, the executive elevator behind the security desk dinged. The doors parted and Hope strutted toward Eli and Gerard.

She looked refreshed. She smiled at Gerard, gently placed a hand on his shoulder, and said, "Could you please give us a minute, kind sir."

Gerard rose, grabbed his phone, and walked away.

"Hello, Eli," Hope said as if the last twenty-four hours had been erased.

Eli knew it was best to hold his temper but knowing and doing were sometimes two different things. "What the hell are you doing here?"

"Why the hostilities?"

"You forget you ran off. To this place of all places."

"I don't know what you mean. I did leave to get to a meeting I had previously scheduled. I had to. I have a business to run. But I also need to find my father." A tear formed in the corner of her eye.

Eli remembered what Lizzy said. Treat everything as a lie. He did.

"I don't think that's true. Otherwise, you would have stayed at Professor Perry's."

"She had nothing to offer. Nothing. She was wasting my time, and I had a meeting to get to."

"Are you working for Lucian Blackwood?"

She took a breath and slowly let it out. "I think I can tell you that I am. It's probably out there somewhere. I'm helping him with his proxy battle."

"I assumed as much. Anything else?"

Her demeanor didn't change. "I don't think I care to share the details of my engagement. That's private and confidential. I don't share what I'm doing with my clients. It's privileged."

Eli ignored her answer. "I need to see Blackwood."

"Sorry, Eli. He won't meet with you."

Eli couldn't tell her what he suspected, especially since she might be involved. How, he didn't know.

She smiled and looked into his eyes. She reached out and touched his forearm. "You're a good man. I know that. And you're helping me find my father. That's what's most important. You've been very good at it so far. You're a great friend to my father. As capable as he told me." She let go of his arm. "We only have until tomorrow evening. Anything I can do to help?"

Eli shook his head. "I'll call you if I need you."

"I'll be done here soon. I'll call you." She began to turn away.

"Wait. I have a message for Blackwood."

She turned back, her expression still soft and welcoming. "Yes. What is it?"

"I know more than he thinks I know."

She cocked her head to the side and snarled. "That's it?"

Eli stared at her. She stared back like the predator she was. She waved to Gerard, then disappeared behind the elevator doors.

Gerard glanced at the elevator door and dropped down into his seat. "Sorry about that, Eli."

"Not your circus, Gerard. Thanks for the help."

Eli turned and walked toward the doors.

"Hey. You dropped this," Gerard said.

Eli turned and saw Gerard trotting toward him with a piece of paper in his hand. He placed it firmly in Eli's palm and looked him in the eye for a long moment. "Nice to see you."

Eli slipped the paper into his pocket until he'd left the building and was back inside the truck. He retrieved it and unraveled the crumpled note.

Sarah 457 Mayo Hotel

CHAPTER 24

SARAH BLACKWOOD EYED her long checklist as her team leader, Brian, waited on the call. At 2:30 on a Saturday she'd rather be in Santa Monica enjoying espresso standing on the promenade in front of the Miramar Hotel, gazing down at the shimmering Pacific Ocean. Instead, she was holed up in a dark hotel room that smelled like stale coffee and cardboard. She finished scanning her list and looked up at the wall of disheveled bankers boxes that held what she hoped was vindication for what she'd done.

She reached for the phone sitting with her on the luxurious bed and tapped it off of mute. "Hey, Brian?"

"Yeah, boss?"

"I think that's everything I had. What are we looking like on your end?"

Brian Costa was a workhorse. An MBA from SMU and her most trusted senior analyst. He led the team of junior analysts, analysts, and research associates she'd handpicked for this job.

"I think the results they'll announce will tank the stock. Our estimate is that it will hit thirty dollars a share and put Blackwood's value at twenty billion. That's down over sixty percent in the last three years. A negative fifty-eight percent return including the dividends." As usual, he had a tight grip on the numbers, but there was doubt in his voice.

"That's good. Why am I hearing that tone in your voice?"

She heard shuffling papers on the other end of the call.

"Looks like we have twenty-nine percent of the institutional shares lined up. We need around forty percent to get the rest to fall in line. That excludes our holdings.

"And what did their benchmark competitor do during the same period?"

"The opposite. Nearly a two hundred percent shareholder return." She'd worked closely with Brian for years. Normally he'd be energetic and ready to drive a stake in Blackwood Energy's heart. "So what's with the somber mood. They announce. We win."

Brian sighed. "I picked up a rumor. They have something else coming. Another announcement. That rumor has the other shareholders scared. It's supposedly an announcement that would turn it all around. Quickly."

Sarah leaned away from the phone. She wondered what it could possibly be. A white knight with loads of cash? That wouldn't have that kind of effect. It would have to be something that would create a ton of value immediately. She felt as if a hand was reaching from her past and pulling her under. If true, she'd fail and wouldn't prove to anyone that her father was the person she knew he was. The one who left such a chasm in her heart. The one who'd destroyed so much. It would be swept under by a blizzard of buying then crash once the truth got out. But her father and his board would survive the vote, and her mother would still be stuck with him.

"You still there?" Brian asked.

"What do you think?"

"I think it's that image consultant. I think she is spinning a web of misdirection and confusion on the numbers, and I wouldn't put it past her to put her lies into the market."

"So you don't think it's true?"

"Didn't say that. But if I were to handicap it, my money would be on her putting lies into the market."

Sarah already hated Hope Munro, even before she was involved with her father. She'd rescued some of the most misogynistic creeps Sarah had ever seen. Only because they had billions. Now her father would be added to that list.

She leaned back into the phone. "What do we need to counter this?" she asked firmly.

There was an uncomfortable delay on the other end of the call.

Sarah leaned closer. "It's okay. You can say it."

"We need dirt on your father. We need to be able to make it stick. We need to disprove the rumor."

She climbed out of the hole she'd just fallen into. She mustered all of her strength to hide her devastation. "By Monday?"

"Afraid so. No sure how we do that."

"I'll get back to you." She ended the call.

Her father had wrecked her childhood. He'd ruined her ability to trust. She'd tried to, but the men she'd dated always wanted more than she could give. Now her work was her fortress of safety and solitude. She hated to make the next call, but she promised herself she'd always have as much courage as anyone.

She dialed the founder and managing partner.

"Sarah! Good news, I hope." Clifton Brill was an eternal optimist. He also expected partners to deliver on their promises.

"Hi, Cliff. Look, I won't sugar coat it. It's going to be close."

"Close! I thought you said there was no way you'd lose. You said I should put you on this and take a meaningful position in Blackwood Energy stock."

She was quickly on the defensive. "We still can make a great return."

"Then what's the problem?"

"There's a rumor. We think it's being spread by Hope Munro. It's got shareholders jittery. We may not win the proxy vote. The shares may rise on the rumor."

"We're betting on a rumor?"

She felt on the run now. "Not entirely. If I can disprove it, we can still win. Just as we planned."

"But we have to time the sale to make any profit before the rumor is proven untrue and the shares collapse." He yelled something away from the phone. "Don't put us in that position. You hear me, Sarah. I like you, but this is not good. If you miss on this one after you got us into it, I'll have no choice but to let you go." The phone went dead.

CHAPTER 25

ELI SAT IN the truck and stared at the message in his hand. He didn't know Sarah Blackwood, other than a brief introduction by her mother at a charity event seven years ago. She lived in Santa Monica where her company was based. He needed to get to Hominy, an hour's drive to the north, and he was running out of time. It was already 1:30 p.m. Every minute felt like another nail in Jim's coffin. But the Mayo was only a few minutes away, and Gerard had given him the note for a reason. After all, he'd risked his job by giving it to him.

Eli jammed the note into his pocket, shifted into drive, and headed to the Mayo. When he arrived, he found a parking spot a block away on the street and trotted to the entrance of the art deco hotel. Two valets stood on either side of the door flanked by the towering Dorian columns carved from stone that felt like sentries guarding the hotel's secrets. Built in the twenties with the momentum of Tulsa's early oil boom, Eli bet it held many. He hoped it would hold a few new ones, too. He nodded to the valets and headed inside.

The lobby was just as impressive, the white marble floor checkered with black inlaid squares giving a nod to the roaring twenties. Four glowing chandeliers dangled from the two-story ceiling, bathing it in an aged yellow hue. Ignoring the front desk, he headed up the grand stairway to the elevators. In seconds he was on the fourth floor. The doors opened, and he found his way down the hallway to Room 457.

He was about to deal with an environmentalist—one that had no time for an oilman, let alone one that worked for her father. He settled himself and tapped on the dark-brown door. His knock sounded deep against the thick wood. He stepped back and smiled at the peephole.

"Can I help you?" The woman's voice from inside was melodic.

He stepped back so she could see him through the peephole. "Yes. Miss Blackwood. I'm Eli Scott. I don't know if you remember me, but I worked at Blackwood Energy a few years ago."

"Did my father send you?" Sarah's voice was now firm and cold.

He didn't like talking through a closed door. "No. If you knew how my tenure ended there, you would know that's not plausible."

The deadbolt clicked and the door opened. Her dark eyes were wide, and her red lips glistened. She'd cut her blonde hair short. She was taller than he'd remembered, and her eyes met his, then shifted left and right as she checked the hallway.

"I remember now. You're the one." She let the door drift open but held on to the knob.

"The one?"

"The one person at that company who wasn't just about the money."

"Thanks, I think. I need to speak with you about something important."

"And what would that be?"

Eli looked right and left, then whispered, "I can't talk out here."

She leaned forward and whispered, "You can't talk in here, either." She leaned back and grabbed the door handle.

"Wait. Can we talk downstairs?" Eli asked.

She pushed the door toward him, narrowing the gap. "Not till I know what this is about."

Eli raised both hands. "Okay. Okay. Look. A good friend of mine is missing, and I think your father is involved."

"What?"

He dropped his hands and stepped closer to the door. "I think there's a connection, but I don't know what yet."

"Go to the cops." She started to close the door, but Eli stopped it with his hand.

"Wait. Please."

Her eyes flared and she looked at his hand on the door, then at Eli. "Do you want to keep that hand?"

Eli pulled his hand from the door. "I'm his friend. I can't go to the cops. If I do, whoever has him said they'd kill him." Eli didn't know if that was a lie or the truth, but he needed to use it.

"And who is this friend?"

"Jim Munro. He used to be my boss at Ravenel Energy."

Her face relaxed, then a wave of concern spread across it. "Jim is missing?"

Her answer sent a jolt though him and he pulled back. "You know him?"

"We've invested in one of his companies. Good guy, great investment. He cared about the damage your business had done to the environment, unlike most of you." She looked over her shoulder. Turning back, she said, "Let me clean up a few things." She closed the door in his face.

Eli could hear papers shuffling and what sounded like lids being placed on cardboard boxes. Less than a minute later, she opened the door.

"Come in," she said.

Eli stepped into the room. As he passed her, the scent of lavender floated into his nose. The room was a single king. Not the usual for the spendy Wall Street hedge funders he'd known. White bankers boxes were stacked against one wall, some with files jutting from their tops. He wanted to point out how many trees she'd destroyed. A square black flight case was underneath the side table, and a brief case hung over its chair.

Apparently noticing his focus on the boxes, she said, "I've been working." She closed the door. "Now tell me about Jim Munro."

Eli wasn't sure how much he could trust her, but it was certainly more than he could trust Hope. Everything he'd heard about her said she was a person of character. Her track record of not supporting her father had been clear. But blood ran deep, so he told her the headlines, leaving out anything about Abena Willams.

She moved past him toward the table. "Jim Munro's daughter is working for my father, against me."

"I know that," he said, following her.

She stopped at the table and turned. "That puts me in a precarious position."

He stopped, not wanting to crowd her. "I understand."

"So what do you want from me?"

"I need to understand if you think your father could do something like this, and if so, how he would get it done. Obviously, he can't do it himself."

"To answer the first question… yes." Her eyes narrowed on him. "If it gets him money or power or gets his rocks off, he'd do it." She looked around the room. "As far as the second question, we know he's used third-party contractors before, mainly to cover up his misdeeds. That's what Hope Munro is doing for him." She raised one eyebrow, inviting him to respond.

"Who else has he used?" he said, hoping she continue providing information.

"Everything goes through his current head of security. The guy's a pit viper. Former CIA contractor who worked in Iraq doing God knows what. He came on six months after you left. Anyone else is hired by him."

He hoped to keep her talking. "What's his name?

She looked ill having to say the name. "Bartholomew Winchester. Goes by Bart."

He nodded and gave her a gentle smile. "Okay. Thanks for that information."

She grabbed the back of the chair and leaned over the table, her eyes flashing a warning. "If you meet him, you won't be thanking me." She took a beat with a slow cleansing breath and released the chairback. "How come you left?" she asked, as if she were interviewing him.

Eli thought for a second. His severance clause wouldn't let him tell her the truth. "I have no idea why, other than I lost respect for your father."

"Join the club," she said. The conversation had felt all business until this point. Her stern demeanor softened a bit. "I heard you were good to your people. That probably pissed him off."

Eli shrugged.

Her expression hardened again, into a frown. "Well, he's run the company into the ground. Since you left, the value of the company has dropped by half. We think there is lots of value to unlock with him and his cronies gone. The environmental damage caused by his denial of global warming is mounting by the second." Eli felt the hair stand up on the back of his neck and wanted to argue the point. He smiled silently instead.

She appeared as if an idea suddenly showed up. One she hadn't thought of before. "You know what? Take a seat."

Eli went to the table, moved the briefcase to the side, and sat.

She sat facing him, folding her hands on the table. "I don't like your industry. Not at all. But you seem like a decent guy in a shitty industry. She paused, then said, "How would you like to help me? I help you, you help me. Seems fair."

Eli was suddenly cautious. On one hand, he was getting what

he wanted. On the other hand, battling Blackwood out in the open could be a problem. "What do you mean?"

"I mean you know the company as well as anyone on the outside. You also know my father better than most after working for him for nearly five years. I need to show that he's not the best leader for the business going forward."

She'd turned the tables on him. Eli chose his words cautiously. "I'm not sure my contract allows me to do that."

She waved off his concern. "I'll have my legal team look at it. We'll set up whatever ethical walls we need to protect you. You point and I'll dig."

Eli decided to test her commitment. "I only have until tomorrow at 7 p.m. to find Jim."

She took that in, covering her lips with her index finger.

She slapped her palm on the table. "Let's do this. I'll help you get Jim back and then you help me."

Eli didn't have to think long. Sarah had access, even if it was through her mother. He had nothing right now that would get him in to see Blackwood. She seemed to have no problem taking her father down. Perhaps they were aligned on that. She'd have access to the building, too. Probably after hours. Or at least her mother would.

"You know what? It's a deal." He reached across the table to shake her hand.

She smiled and shook it. Her hand was firm but smooth and warm. They held the shake a little longer than Eli had planned, then quickly let go as if the sensation shocked them.

She settled back in her chair, smiled at Eli, and nodded. "I think I'm gonna like doing this."

CHAPTER 26

ELI PONDERED HIS next move as he sat across from Sarah. As his attention left the room, he felt as if he had all the pieces on the table now. With Sarah's cooperation and commitment, he could get to Blackwood. He had a lead on Jim in Hominy and a lead on Abena but no location. There were two paths to his success—and his survival. His first choice was finding Jim before the deadline. He was sure that path went through Blackwood. His second choice was to find Abena Williams, find out what this invention was, and deliver it to the kidnappers. Neither had the certainty of success he wanted, so he needed to pursue both.

His eyes found Sarah again, and a long dormant sensation rose from a place deep inside him. There was something about her—something that shook him to the core and said to pay attention to her. It wasn't a warning. It was a force that pushed him toward her. The last time he'd felt like this, he'd trapped himself in a relationship so toxic, it nearly cost him everything. He breathed and pulled back on the throttle.

"What? What are you thinking?" Sarah said, snapping him out of his head.

Eli gathered his wits again. "I need to go somewhere before we get to your father."

"Where would that be?"

"Hominy."

Sarah leaned toward him, put her elbow on the table, and thrusted her hand out to one side. "Hominy? In the Osage? What's up there?"

"A clue. I think it may be critical."

"Can you tell me what it is?

Eli knew his answer would start down the road that led to her father. "Yes. Someone leased the old area office Jim and I started in years ago. The scuttlebutt is that it might be Jim."

She glanced at the boxes, then nodded at Eli. "Let's go. The sooner we find him, the sooner we can deal with my father."

Eli was a bit surprised. "It could be dangerous."

"Two may be safer than one," she said, standing. "Let me get a few things together, and I'll meet you downstairs."

The support warmed Eli but environmentalist or not, he didn't like putting her in harm's way.

"You sure?"

"If you knew me, you'd know I don't do anything I don't want to."

"I appreciate you." Eli stood and headed out. On the way downstairs, he texted Hudson and they agreed to meet at Sonny's trailer in Hominy.

After waiting in the lobby, he spotted Sarah walking down the grand staircase. She'd changed into her jeans, a thick sweater covered with an insulated vest, and boots. She carried a small black duffel and jacket in her right hand. She moved like a woman who could handle herself. Confident, fit, and with purpose. She joined Eli in the ornate lobby.

"Ready?"

"I am. I'm parked down the street."

They left the hotel, and Eli noticed the winter sun was sitting low in the sky. It was nearing 4 p.m. Fighting a stiff, chilly north wind, they made it to the truck. She eyed the dual-wheeled pickup and its deer catcher, muddy running boards, and a scratched-up toolbox that sat beneath a louvered headache rack against the back of the cab. She headed to the passenger's side. "I didn't figure you for a rancher."

"It's a loaner," Eli yelled over the wind. They both got in. "My normal ride had too many bullet holes." He looked at her for effect.

Appearing unfazed, Sarah set the duffel on the seat between them and patted it. "That's why I brought this."

Eli glanced down at it. He assumed it was a weapon. He wasn't surprised. A tough woman raised in Oklahoma who knew how to defend herself wasn't unusual.

"Let's go, cowboy," she said.

He shifted the truck into gear and chuckled to himself.

"What is it?" she said.

"That's what the guy who owns this truck calls me."

He did a U-turn and headed for Hominy.

CHAPTER 27

THE TRIP TO Hominy took an hour, and Eli knew the highway was patrolled regularly by state troopers. The winter sun was setting and storm clouds thickened on the horizon to the northwest. He gave the truck a little more gas. Hugging the speed limit was like pulling teeth for Eli. But the company was good and each of them shared a little about themselves. He also filled Sarah in about what had transpired over the last few days regarding Jim. He'd decided to share Abena's story, too. Sarah had listened with interest and understood the links with her father. She rode in silence for a few minutes digesting what he'd told her and scrolling through her phone. Then she put her phone away and looked at him.

"You were quite a basketball player back in the day," she said.

Eli guessed she'd been checking up on him online. "I could play, but that was a long time ago."

"I saw where you turned down a half dozen offers from Division One schools."

"That I did. I was starting my senior year when 9/11 happened. I couldn't get rid of the image of all those innocent people in the towers and on the planes who never had a chance. We had lived in Maryland, not too far from the Naval Academy, when I was a kid. I'd badger my mom every Saturday to take me there. Some days she'd acquiesce and take me. I respected those young midshipmen and their commitment to serve. To defend those who couldn't defend themselves. We moved to Pittsburgh when I was entering middle school. In my senior year, I enlisted. My mother was shocked. She hated the idea, but in the end, she supported me. And I knew I needed time away."

"Away from your mom? Sounds like me."

Eli remembered Lizzy's coaching on being vulnerable and open, but he also knew about oversharing. "Let's just say it was tough growing up in that house."

"I sure get that. How long were you on active duty?"

"Six years. Then on to Penn State and a degree in chemical engineering. My first job was with Ravenel Energy. After they were bought and moved to Houston, I took a package and went to work for your father."

"Why would you do that?"

Eli laughed at himself. "First, I got to stay in Tulsa. Then, based on what the headhunter told me, I thought he was open to change. I thought it was a place where I could make a difference. For the people who worked for me and for the public we served."

"And now?"

"I lost respect for him and some of the leadership team. I was working twice as hard and getting nowhere. It wore me out. Then, he fired me." Eli shifted in his seat. "My turn."

Sarah tried to quell her smile. "Okay."

"Where did you go to high school?"

"Jenks."

"Nice neighborhood. Big rival for Union."

"It was. A good school, too."

"And college?"

"Harvard. Undergrad and MBA. Daddy wouldn't have it any other way," she said, her voice dripping with sarcasm.

"Why didn't you work for Blackwood?"

Sarah's bright face turned dark. "He wanted me to. But I told him to shove it. I think it was the third affair Mom told me about. I saw what it was doing to her and didn't understand why she put up with it. I didn't like the way he treated his people, especially those who didn't look like him. He denied global warming and the fossil fuel connection. Didn't want to be a part of that. I took the job with Baker Capital in Santa Monica. As far away from here as I could get. But now here I am exposing his bullshit."

"I think global warming is real and we need new forms of energy. Like Jim is working on. But what is everyone supposed to do until we have an economical alternative?"

She turned to him, her eyes flashing. "Spoken like a true oilman. The sooner your kind stops pumping more of it, the price will go up, and those alternatives will be economic."

That pissed him off. "That won't get the children to school and their parents to work. That won't provide all the products that touch our lives every day. The shampoo you use, the hot water in your bath, the clothes you're wearing. It's just not that simple." Eli realized he was almost shouting. He settled back in his seat and looked ahead. "Sorry."

She looked forward through the windshield and sighed. "Enough of that."

After a couple of miles of silence, Eli nodded to the small black gun case at her feet. "Where'd you learn to shoot?"

"My father. We had actually been close when I was a kid. I'd called him 'Super Daddy' when I was four and had proudly shared every soccer trophy with him. Took me hunting when I was seven. I loved it. Then I kept going. Joined a gun club. Skeet. Got proficient at handguns as a teen." She smiled again at Eli. "Kept some of those pesky boys in line."

"Any of those pests ever stick around?"

She raised one eyebrow, still smiling. "Eli Scott. if I didn't know better, I'd say you were flirting with me."

His face warmed and he tried to fight his embarrassment. "No. I'm sorry. I…"

She punched him in the shoulder. "Just teasing. There were a couple but nothing permanent. How about you?"

It was the question he dreaded. It took a second to assemble his answer. Those damn gremlins were rumbling again.

Apparently, the pause became awkward, and Sarah said, "You don't have to answer that."

"You know, I don't mind. I had a couple who came close, but like you, nothing permanent."

Sarah looked forward again, grinning, and silently nodding.

They were quiet for a couple more miles.

As they rolled into Hominy on Highway 99, Eli glanced out his window. The sun was setting to the west, giving the approaching storm clouds a golden outline. Eli knew it would be dark soon, and that cut two ways. The cover of darkness would aid them in their clandestine search of the old area office, but it would also provide cover for anyone wanting to end their search—and them. He pulled to the stop sign at the intersection of Highway 20 and Highway 99.

"Is this it?" Sarah asked, looking around.

"No. To go into town, we turn left up here."

"I've been through here on the way to Pawhuska but never saw the town."

"Funny story. When I first came into town for my first job it was foggy, and I drove right past Hominy. Ended up at a gas station in Pawhuska and asked directions to Hominy. The two guys working saw my Pennsylvania plates and couldn't stop laughing before they told me I'd driven right past it."

"Poor Yankee," she said.

"That was me," he said as he passed Main Street and turned right instead. A two-story brick house with a wraparound porch, two double-wide trailers parked on the other side of its driveway, appeared atop a small hill.

"Is this the trailer you told me about?"

"Yes. Sonny and I were neighbors for a while here."

"You *chose* to live in a trailer in Tornado Alley?"

"Best I could find at the time. Besides, they were tied down," he said.

"That wouldn't matter."

"Just kidding. The landlord, Willie, there in the house, had a storm cellar. He'd let us use it."

Sarah shook her head. Eli pulled up the driveway and parked next to the second trailer beside two pickups.

He shoved the truck into park and watched her as she pulled a pistol from the bag, checked it, and clipped it on her belt. She shrugged on her vest, covering the gun, and reached for the door.

"You do know what you're doing."

She shrugged and got out.

Eli left the truck, and together, they walked up the steps to the trailer door. Eli knocked.

Sonny's hulking figure filled the doorway. His round face lit up when he saw Eli. His high cheekbones and dark almond-shaped eyes accentuated his infectious smile. He stepped out, gave him a bear hug, and lifted him off the porch. Sarah stepped back, appearing uncertain about what was going on.

"Don't worry. He always does this," Eli said, grunting, as Sonny set him down.

"Don't you look like a piece of crap," Sonny said, still grinning.

"Great to see you too, my friend," Eli said, patting Sonny on the shoulder and smiling.

Sonny settled himself and turned to Sarah to offer his hand. "This guy has no manners. Sonny Johnson at your service, ma'am."

Sarah shook it. "Sarah. Nice to meet you."

"Come on in. Hudson's inside." Sonny turned and ducked inside the door.

Eli waited for Sarah, who raised her eyebrows on the way by. He followed her inside and closed the door.

"Hey, hombre," Hudson said. He sat at the small kitchen table with a pad of paper in front of him. His wiry figure sat backward in the wooden chair with his arms wrapped around its back. His trademark oil-smeared University of Oklahoma trucker cap sat tipped back from his forehead. A well-worn brown leather jacket hung from his shoulders. His huge hand held a Coors. When he spotted Sarah, he stood and removed his cap. "Sorry," he said. He offered his hand.

She shook it. "I'm Sarah. You didn't need to get up."

"You don't know my Sherry. She'd string me up if I didn't." He laughed. "What's your last name? You look familiar."

"Blackwood."

"Shit," he said. "Oh. Sorry again." Both he and Sonny looked stunned.

"She's good, guys. She's on our side."

"Okay. Good to know," Sonny said. "Would you like a seat?" He pointed to the couch.

"I'm good," Sarah said. "We've been in the car for a while."

Hudson killed his beer, tossing it in the kitchen wastebasket, and walked past the table, picking up the pad on the way by. He stopped next to Sonny, forming a circle with Eli and Sarah.

"What's the plan, guys?" Eli asked.

Hudson turned the pad so Eli and Sarah could read it. He pointed to the large rectangle on the hand-drawn map. "Here's the old office and oilfield maintenance shop. I'd guess if there is something set up inside, it would be in the shop. The park is behind it, and we'll go in there."

"Yeah," Sonny said. "But one complication. Looks like it might snow any minute. We may leave tracks."

"Right. So be aware of that." Hudson pointed to the front corner of the shop. "We'll need a lookout here."

"I got that," Sarah said.

"Damn. You sure?" Hudson asked.

Sarah pulled her vest back, exposing the gun.

"By gum, I guess so," Hudson said. "Anyway. The rest of us will enter here. I'll get us in, and we'll sweep the shop first."

"Do you have a key?" Sarah asked.

Hudson did his best to mimic Sarah's move and pulled a lockpick set from the inside pocket of his jacket. They all shared a chuckle.

"Anyway, it will only take a minute or two, depending on what we find. Then Sarah will reposition here." He pointed to the side of the front porch of the adjacent rectangular office structure. "We'll run that in less than a minute. Then we're out. All in, we're exposed for five minutes, six max. Then back through the tree line and to the truck."

"What about cameras or alarms?" Eli asked.

"Didn't see any. If Jim leased it, it might not matter," Hudson said.

"If he still controls it," Eli said.

"Questions?" Hudson asked.

"What are we looking for?" Sarah asked.

Eli leaned into the circle. "Any indication that Jim rented this and any indication as to why. Obviously, we're looking for Jim and Abena Williams. I sent you all the photo from my security camera of her."

They all nodded.

"If we encounter unfriendlies?" Sarah asked.

"Make 'em friendly with that thing on your hip," Hudson said. "They already tried to kill Eli and Butch and Jim's daughter."

Eli thought about Hope. She'd said it was his fault she'd left. On some level, maybe she was right. But he flushed the thought from his mind. He couldn't afford it. She was working with Blackwood, and he suspected he was behind this. They were about to find out for sure.

CHAPTER 28

ELI KNEW TO trust his instincts, and as he drifted the truck into the gravel parking space facing the park playground with his headlights off, his body tingled as it had before every combat engagement. Instinctively, he touched the Glock tucked under his jacket. Sonny's prediction had come true. A light snow danced down the windshield. The leafless tree line provided some cover for the large crew cab in the darkness. To the casual observer, the difference between a ranch truck and an oilfield truck wasn't discernable. With an oilfield boneyard just around the corner, containing a few pumping units, tanks, and tubing, there was a plausible reason for the truck to be there in the first place.

He reached to disable the dome light. "Everyone ready?" He got a nervous nod from Sarah in the front seat, looked behind him, and Sonny and Hudson nodded confidently. He zipped up his jacket only a quarter of the way to maintain quick access to his gun. Quietly, they all exited the truck. The snow tickled his face as they headed into the tree line. The familiar aromatic smell of the oilfield lingered in the air. Side by side, they worked their way through the trees and settled at the edge, squatting to observe the office and shop before going further.

A single halogen light hung from a utility pole between the two buildings. It cast long shadows on the outside of the structures. Eli felt the cold snow on the back of his neck but ignored it. They'd be exposed for the first thirty yards until they reached the shadows at the far side of the shop. The two windows on the wall of the shop facing them were blocked with white plywood. He noticed the snowfall was heavier and now coated the ground. They'd leave a trail.

He looked at the group. "Let's go. I'll go first. Hudson and Sonny follow. Sarah will bring up the rear." They all nodded. He moved quickly across the flat ground. Not a run, but not a walk either. Halfway there, he heard a dog bark behind them. He hadn't considered a guard dog, but he quickly realized it was coming from a house beyond the park. He curled around the dark side of the shop and settled at the front corner. Everyone joined him. He looked around the corner and spotted the front door of the shop. It was still in the shadows, covered by a flat corrugated-aluminum awning, two garage doors just beyond it.

He waved Hudson around. Hudson tapped him on the shoulder on the way by and knelt at the front door. Removing the lockpicks, he worked the deadbolt then opened the door and looked inside. He gave Eli a thumbs-up. Eli waved Sonny around and Sarah stopped next to him. She pulled out her pistol, silently patting Eli on the back. Eli turned the corner, pulled out his Glock in his right hand and a flashlight with his left, and followed Sonny inside, closing the door behind him.

The shop hadn't changed much in fourteen years. The small office just inside the door still had the same filing cabinet, metal desk, and chipped wooden chair. Hudson, Sonny, and Eli gathered at the door to the bays for the shop. It was already ajar. Darkness waited inside. Using his fingers, Hudson counted down from three. He opened the door, and Eli pushed in and swept the area with his flashlight. Stunned by what he saw, he stopped, and Sonny ran into his back. It looked like someone had converted the vehicle bay into a makeshift laboratory. Someone else had tossed the place looking for something. Broken glass covered the floor and glimmered in his flashlight beam as it swept the first bay. Paper was scattered everywhere. A couple of lab refrigerators hung open, their contents broken and piled in front of them. Metal stands stood atop three long metal lab benches in front of him. They were covered with scattered laboratory glassware, chemical bottles, centrifuges, an older chromatograph, heating elements, and makeshift vent hoods. Just beyond the tables, his beam hit a dark-blue vehicle. Running the beam over the profile of the small car, his heart jumped in his chest when he recognized the old Toyota Corolla. Abena's Corolla.

Realizing it was clear and no one was inside the shop, Eli said, "Holy shit!"

"It's hers, isn't it?" Sonny said, moving next to Eli.

Eli kept the beam focused on the car.

"Don't stand there looking like a tree full of young owls," Hudson said as he walked past them with his own light. "Let's finish and get out of here."

They completed their sweep of the shop. Eli knew Jim had apparently rented the place. He didn't know if it was for Abena, or if they were working with someone else.

When they walked back through the first bay and headed for the office, a gunshot rang out. Then two more, and those slugs hit the metal exterior of the building.

"Sarah!" Eli yelled as he headed for the front door. He took cover to the left of the door, Hudson and Sonny behind him. He swung it open with his right hand. Two more shots hit the doorframe. There was no return fire.

"Sarah!" Eli glanced over his shoulder. "Cover me, guys."

"Right behind you," Sonny said.

Sonny and Hudson let loose, sending fire toward the front of the office next door. Eli scrambled into the shadows to the left around the corner. He retraced their steps and headed to the back corner of the building. She wasn't there. Eli heard Sonny and Hudson exchange fire with the attackers. In the darkness, he wondered where she'd gone. Had they taken her? He looked for blood in the snow and saw none. Then he spotted her tracks leading around the back of the shop. She wouldn't have run. Didn't seem like the type. Then it hit him. Following her tracks, he sprinted around to the back of the shop and saw her disappear around the back of the office building. Stopping at the back corner of the shop, he realized what was happening. *Smart woman.*

With driving snow pelting him in the eyes, he began firing at the front of the office. Hudson and Sonny did too. The constant hail of bullets made the bad guys pull back. A single shot rang out from the far side of the building, and Eli stopped firing and listened. *Silence.* One shot could mean two things, one bad and one worse. He couldn't live with himself if he'd gotten Sarah killed.

"I'm going after them," Eli yelled. He ran through the snow all the way to the front corner of the office. It was still quiet. Eli planned for the worst.

Leading with his Glock, he pivoted around the corner just as Sarah shouted, "It's clear!"

Her voice came from around the next corner. From the far side of the office building, outside. He ran across the front porch and turned the second corner. Sarah stood between two men. She was shaking. Eli doubted it was the cold. One thug was sitting up, writhing in pain, and holding his bloody shoulder. The other man was face down in the snow. Eli could see the thug's back rising and falling rapidly. His hands were tied behind him with his belt.

"This one might talk," she said, pointing her shaking hand to the man who was face down as she rolled him over with her foot. She pointed her gun at the other man. "This one thought a girl wouldn't shoot."

Both men were rough, unshaven white guys with shaved heads. Eli noticed the tattoos on their necks. He walked up to Sarah and put his hand on her shoulder. "Great to see you."

"You too," she said, smiling. "You too."

Sonny and Hudson raced up behind Eli. "You okay?"

"We're good. She got them both."

"Damn," Hudson said, pushing his cap up on his forehead. "Good job, cowgirl."

Eli turned to the man who was bleeding. He pointed his gun at him. "Who are you working for?"

The man looked at him with his dark, deep-set eyes, then glanced at his accomplice lying on the ground. He turned and spit on Eli's boot.

"We got this," Hudson said. "You get that ink in Big Mac?" he said, referring to the prison in McAlester.

The man didn't answer.

Sonny moved around Eli. "Pardon me," he said to Eli, grinning. He stopped in front of the wounded thug, a little to the right of him. "I think you need pressure on that to stop the bleeding." Lifting his huge left boot, he rammed it into the man's shoulder, knocking him on his back. He pinned him to the ground. The man screamed in pain. Snow stuck to his stubble.

"I don't think I heard what you said?" Sonny said.

The man stayed silent until Sonny put most of his weight on the man's wound. "Who hired you?"

"Some guy we didn't know. No names, just cash," the thug said, grunting.

"What did they pay you to do?" Hudson asked.

He stayed quiet.

Sonny stomped harder on the wound.

Once the man stopped screaming, he said, "Kill anyone that goes in there. Bonus if we did."

"Where do you go to get bonus payment?" Eli asked.

"Nowhere. The guy said he'd find us."

"What's he look like?"

"Mousy-faced guy. Looks like a killer, though."

Eli looked at Sarah. "Winchester?"

She nodded.

"What was going on inside that shop?" Eli asked.

"No idea. We just got out. The guy hired us right away. In McAlester." The thug looked at the other man, now sitting up on the ground. The man just shook his head.

Eli patted Sonny on the back.

Sonny pulled his boot from the man's shoulder.

Eli turned to Hudson. "We need to get going."

Hudson pulled out his phone, turned his back to the blowing snow, and typed. He waited seconds for a reply. "We'll take care of this. You guys get out of here. We got a few minutes before the police respond."

"How do you know that?" Sarah asked.

Hudson held up his phone and smiled. "Son-in-law." He texted again. "You guys get out of here. We'll clean this up. A couple of NLBs are on their way."

"NLBs?" Sarah asked.

Eli and Sonny answered in unison. "Nine Line Bind Society."

CHAPTER 29

ELI WAS WORRIED about Sarah. She shivered in the front seat of the pickup truck as they made their way north on Highway 99. She stared straight ahead and bit her lower lip. Eli remembered what it was like the first time he shot another human being. At least he had been trained to do so.

"Are you doing okay?"

She glanced at him and nodded. She turned back to the snowy road ahead.

"They would have killed us all," he said.

She nodded without looking at him this time.

"You saved us. And you've helped us maybe save Jim and Abena."

She turned to him. "I know. I just never..."

"I know."

She seemed to realize something. "I guess you would. Marines and all."

"It will serve a greater purpose. It wasn't just you, it was all of us. Working together to save my friend."

The corners of her mouth turned up. Not quite a smile, but an acknowledgement.

"You still good doing this?" Eli asked.

She sighed, seemingly shedding her burden. "Yes. If they are there, it will be worth it. How long till we get there?"

"Just a few minutes. The snow is letting up. When we get there, we'll have to go in on foot."

The truck's heater warmed the cab. They turned west just before Wynona and headed down the section line road.

"Do you think they're there?" she asked.

Eli knew they had to check out the doghouse. Based on what they'd found at the shop, Jim and Abena could be together and held at the Blackwood lease.

"We know they may be together. If we didn't check it out, I'd be crushed if they were and something happened to them. I know Hope Munro was probably lying, but I have to check it out anyway."

He suspected Blackwood was behind this, but the reason why he'd resort to kidnapping eluded him. It didn't make sense. Why risk everything by taking Jim and Abena?

"What do you think they were looking for at the shop?" Sarah asked.

"I think it was some type of scientific breakthrough, probably involving organic compounds. It was a makeshift lab, but it was ransacked. Whatever it is, it must be worth a fortune to cause all of this. I just wonder, if it's that valuable, who was the inventor? Why was Jim involved? Did he invent it with someone's help? How did Abena fit in? Her car was there. Her apartment was ransacked too. Was she a courier of some type? Then again, her son said she was brilliant. Perhaps she was the inventor working with Jim."

"Abena? A cleaning lady?"

"It could fit."

They crossed the next section line a mile in. He slowed the truck, pulled to the side of the gravel road, and killed the lights.

"It's up ahead. We walk from here."

They left the car and walked down the dark road. With each step closer to Blackwood's lease, Eli's body amped up a little more.

It was a strange mix of surging energy and outright fear. Finding Jim alive or finding something else. The snow had stopped, but it had gotten much colder. Eli kept his hands in his pockets to keep them warm and working, especially his right hand. Sarah seemed fine, but he'd insisted she stay behind him. The snow that had fallen was deep enough to muffle the crunch of each step on the gravel road. Before reaching the lease road, Eli cut into the blackjack oak forest. The leaves had turned brown but remained on the trees, providing adequate cover. With no moon, he couldn't see more than four feet in front of them.

After carefully picking their way through the trees, he spotted the square clearing that would become the drilling pad. All vegetation had been removed, dirt grated flat, and surface graveled. But there was no stake marking the well location. They wouldn't drill for a while. On the opposite side of the clearing, he spotted the doghouse. His optimism rose when he saw the power line running from the utility pole to the trailer. A camera sat atop the pole, but he could see the wire providing power was disconnected.

They waited and watched from the tree line. There was no movement. The trees rustled in the wind enough to cover the sound of anyone trailing them. Eli decided they needed to move quickly.

They worked their way around the perimeter of the pad, staying in the tree line until they reached the doghouse. The blue metal trailer looked like an elongated caboose with a metal-covered porch welded on the front. There was a single door on the porch with what looked like a train window beside it. There were no windows or doors on the back side of the structure. It sat flat on the ground on its skids. The gravel surface around it had been recently disturbed.

Eli moved up next to the back wall and listened. He couldn't tell if there was anyone inside or not. He'd have to take the chance there was. If Jim and Abena were in there, they'd be heavily guarded.

"Stay here until I get the door open," he said. "If something happens, go back the way we came."

Sarah rubbed her hands together and blew on them. She didn't look like she was going anywhere.

Working his way around to the front entrance, Eli saw the padlock on the door. He spotted a four-foot section of pipe leaning against the doghouse. Picking it up, his pulse pounded. He smashed it into the padlock, dropped the pipe, and grabbed his Glock and his flashlight. Using the wall for cover, he threw the door open. There was no response. Nothing. He stepped into the doorway and scanned the long trailer with the light. It was pristine. No sign of Jim or Abena. No one had used the trailer. He sighed, letting his optimism drain into the empty trailer. Hope had probably lied. Sarah appeared in the doorway, and Eli turned on the overhead light.

He turned to face Sarah and shook his head. "Come in. Close the door. We'll warm up in here before we head back."

She closed the door and stepped inside. She sat on one of the long benches welded to the floor in front of the row of lockers. Eli reached down and clicked on the electric heater at his feet. The trailer quickly warmed.

"What now?" Sarah asked.

Eli went over and sat next to her.

Sarah tousled her hair, and it fell gently into place. She patted the small space between them. "Scoot over here. I'm still cold."

Eli did. He hadn't been this close to a woman in a long time. Despite his painful disappointment, he swore he felt an invisible force pulling him to her. It was a wonderful but unnerving feeling for him. She was still Blackwood's daughter. "They're not here, obviously, but this could still be the meeting point. We have no idea where they are, and we don't have whatever they are looking for to trade for Jim. I doubt they'd make the trade anyway. Why would they? We could just go to the cops—game over."

He saw her still shivering. Opening his coat he said, "Okay to share some warmth?" As soon as he said it, his awkward meter pegged.

She hesitated and eyed him. He sensed the same awkwardness in her. Finally, she said, "No. I'm good." She crossed her arms. "We don't have many options left." She apparently thought it was best to pick up the conversation where he'd left off.

"We have to go back to the only leads we have. Hope and your father," he said.

"Whatever. This part is your call. I'll have my chance when we're done."

Eli's eyes caught hers, and they stared for a split second. It was as if their eyes were either magnets and they fought to look away from each other, or they couldn't stand to look at each other. Eli couldn't read her. Then they both broke it off, looking around the doghouse.

"I'm sorry about this." Immediately Eli wished he wouldn't have said that.

They shared another awkward moment. "I'm good. Let's go," she said and stood.

Eli wondered how long this alliance would last. Especially with her.

CHAPTER 30

AS ELI HEADED back into Tulsa, the snow had stopped. He glanced at Sarah sleeping beside him. She looked peaceful. Innocent. Maybe there *was* something between them that neither of them could admit. If he'd learned one thing over the years, it was that life has to run its course. Battling against that was a recipe for unhappiness. You had to take what life gave you. And how you faced it, how you experienced it, not any outcome or destination, was the key to happiness. The lifeforce drawing him to Sarah flowed strong. His heart felt something from the beginning, but because of the obvious complications, it couldn't happen. He pushed that bad idea aside and focused on his mission.

Pulling off the freeway and onto the surface streets, he wished whatever they may have didn't have to be tested so soon.

Sarah stirred and sat up. The dim lights from the dash gave her face a warm glow. "We getting close?"

"We're on Yale Avenue. Be there in five or so," he said gently.

She reached for her phone. "I'd better give Mom a heads-up." She pecked a brief text to her mother.

Eli knew the way. He'd been there several times for small political fundraising dinners during his tenure at Blackwood. The unspoken rule was: if you were invited, you contributed. The dinners were well controlled, and the envelopes never touched the candidates' hands. They were discreetly dropped into a priceless antique bowl near the door.

With each intersection they passed, his focus narrowed. His grip on the wheel tightened while the feeling of not being enough tried to resurrect itself from the deep recesses of his memory. He hadn't seen the Blackwoods since Lucian had suddenly fired him.

This would be a cage match, hopefully not to the death of the combatants. Eli hoped that the growing bond between him and their daughter was stronger than the repulsion he had for Blackwood.

He pulled up to the gates at the entrance to the Blackwood estate. A brick guardhouse was unoccupied, but the cameras, call box, and remotely powered gates did the work of a security guard, he assumed from a central monitoring room inside the home.

Sarah nodded toward the call box with its embedded camera. Eli pushed the button. A woman answered.

"Can I help you?"

"Hey, Mom. It's me," Sarah called out from the passenger's seat.

"Hi, dear," Ruby Blackwood said through the speaker.

The gates groaned and opened.

Eli pulled through and began the short trip along the winding cobblestone driveway that split the five-acre property in half. They circled around the huge, aerated concrete pond, and pulled to the long, elegant entry at the front of the house. The home looked massive. A wide tile walkway bordered with rough-cut granite led to the well-lit entrance to the Tudor Gothic–style home. Multicolored brick, granite, stucco, and painted wood beams adorned the exterior. A thick slate roof held at least five chimneys.

When they exited the truck, he made sure the Glock was hidden under his sweater. He didn't want to see the Blackwoods, and certainly if he did, he didn't want them to see that he was armed. At least not at the start of their conversation. Eli swallowed his reluctance when Sarah walked side by side with him to the door.

"Don't worry. I'll explain everything," she said as her mother appeared through the windowpanes in the enormous front door.

Ruby opened the door, gave Eli a cursory glance, and hugged Sarah. "This is a wonderful surprise," she said, obviously ignoring him.

Sarah held the embrace a little longer, giving him the sense it had been a while since they'd been together. "Hi, Momma." When Sarah pulled back, she pulled Eli's elbow, moving him closer. "Mother, you remember Eli."

Ruby Blackwood was a formidable woman. Even in her early sixties, her presence commanded respect. Framed by her deep-blue cashmere sweater and black stretch pants, her features looked a little more hardened than when Eli had last seen her more than three years ago. Her silver hair still glowed and flowed to her midback. She clearly paid attention to her fitness, and her makeup made her skin appear perfect as if she had none on at all. Her eyes still had the fire of a woman half her age, and Eli had never seen eyes so blue. They looked like jewels.

Ruby smiled and dipped her head. "I do. How are you, Eli?"

Eli didn't know if she understood how loaded that question was. "I'm doing okay."

"Come inside. It's freezing out there," Ruby said, crossing her arms.

Eli followed Sarah inside. He'd always felt like he'd entered a time machine in the Blackwoods' home. The hand-carved millwork, exposed wood beams, and gold Victorian frames hearkened back to the decor of the early twentieth-century mansions built in the heart of Tulsa. He remembered when this modern version had been finished just eight years ago. It was the talk of the town.

They passed the sitting room, den, and study on the way into the cavernous kitchen. There was no sign of Lucian. That was both good and bad.

Ruby circled to the far side of the black soapstone island. Sarah took one of the six stools on the other side facing her mother. Eli waited for Ruby to sit, but she didn't.

She eyed him. "I'll just stand," she said with a smile. She looked at Sarah, who pulled out the stool next to herself. He sat down and folded his hands in front of him.

"So how is Santa Monica?" Ruby asked Sarah.

"It's lovely. This time of year, it's a little cooler and it's been rainy, but we need the water."

"How about work?"

Eli perked up, wanting to see how Sarah would handle this with her mother.

"It's going well. It's building the case one brick at a time."

"You know I can't help you with that."

"I do. I wouldn't put you in that position." Sarah glanced at Eli, then looked her mother in the eyes. "I'm not here for that anyway. We're here because we have a problem with what Dad may be doing outside of work."

"Oh God. What did he do now?" Ruby's expression turned sullen.

"Don't worry. It's not that," Sarah said.

Anger flashed across Ruby's face, and she cut her eyes to Eli, then back to Sarah. "I won't tolerate another. He knows that."

"It's about a friend of Eli's. He's missing."

Ruby seemed to relax. She looked at Eli with concern. "Missing?"

"Yes, Mrs. Blackwood. He's definitely missing. We think someone has taken him."

"It's Ruby. And what do you mean, you think?"

Eli was surprised by her sudden warmth and concern. He didn't feel like he needed to kiss the ring anymore. "His daughter has relayed much of the information and she's not all that reliable."

"Who is this friend?"

"Jim Munro," Sarah said.

Ruby's attention drifted toward the ceiling. "Munro. Munro.

I know him." She eyed Eli. "*Oh*. His daughter. That piece of you-know-what is working with Lucian." A light seemed to go on somewhere in her head. "I get it. You think they're in on it together."

Eli had always thought she was smarter than Lucian.

"Where is he tonight?" Sarah asked.

"You're in luck. He's coming home soon. Said he has to meet with Winchester here for a few minutes, then he'll grace us with his presence."

Eli and Sarah shared a worried look. Eli guessed he was getting an update from Winchester about the events that had just occurred in Hominy.

His phone vibrated in his pocket. He pulled it out to check the caller. When he saw the name, he clenched his teeth and showed it to Sarah. Standing, he said, "Sorry ladies. I've gotta take this." He turned and headed for the study.

CHAPTER 31

WHILE CONNECTING TO the call, Eli walked down the hallway to the study but said nothing until he was securely in the room. Suddenly surprised, he stopped dead in his tracks. The walls were lacquered mahogany and held a large collection of firearms: pistols on one wall and rifles on the other. They were all locked behind glass. He understood where Sarah had gotten her proficiency.

"Eli? Eli," Hope said on the other end.

"I'm here. What do you want?"

"Where have you been?"

Eli didn't think it was a good idea to answer directly. "Checking out a few things."

"Like what?"

He closely examined the long rifle perched in its rack behind the glass. "What do you want?"

Hope ramped up the concern in her voice. "I want to find my father and we're running out of time. Where are you?"

It was as if nothing had happened at Nora Perry's.

"Here in Tulsa."

"Where exactly?"

Eli wondered if he was being set up again. "What do you need?" he said loudly. He heard footsteps in the hallway and Sarah entered the room, questioning him with her eyes. He waved her in, pointed to his phone, and shook his head.

"I need to see you," Hope said. There was now a cry in her voice.

"Why?"

"I need to tell you something. I can't tell you on the phone."

Eli looked at Sarah and wagged his head. He kept silent.

Now Hope was in a full cry. "You said you'd help me. You promised. My father promised too. Said you'd help me. He said you were the only one. His best friend."

Eli couldn't shake the image of Jim. His conscience nagged him. Jim cared about Hope, but there was nothing there in return. Lizzy had said as much. He looked at his watch. It was already almost nine-thirty. He needed to see Blackwood tonight. There was a still a possibility Hope wasn't involved.

"I can meet tomorrow morning at eight." He needed a public place. In the open. Just in case. "The Gathering Place. On the footbridge over the river."

"That's too late. It can't wait. Come now. It's urgent."

He didn't want to believe her. Either way, he had to meet with Blackwood. It was Saturday night. He'd need a busy venue. "I'm following a lead. Once I finish here, I'll head to the Riverfront. Meet me at the bar on their deck overlooking the river. I should be there by eleven."

"No! Come now. I'm at Dad's."

Hope hung up.

Eli looked at his phone like it had bitten him. "She hung up on me. Wanted me to meet her at her father's," he said to Sarah.

"You trust her?"

"Hell, no. I don't know when she's telling the truth or lying. I'm assuming everything is a lie until I can prove otherwise. She said she had something for me about her father. Couldn't do it over the phone."

"Maybe you should—"

"I'm home!" Lucian's voice yanked Eli back to that afternoon three years ago. He hadn't seen Lucian since he'd slinked out of the office after he'd proclaimed Eli could never run a company and fired him. Eli tucked his phone away, let his anger rise, and readied to face the man who had ended his career—and may have kidnapped his friend.

CHAPTER 32

AFTER ELI HEARD Lucian Blackwood close the front door, Sarah stepped into the hallway. Eli couldn't see Lucian, but Sarah stood erect, framed by the millwork of the study's doorway, appearing ready to face a storm. Eli heard Lucian's briefcase hit the floor with a thud.

"Sarah?" Lucian said softly, his tone tender and welcoming. Then, as if suddenly reminded of the proxy fight, he thundered, "What the hell are you doing here!"

"It's still my home," Sarah said. She held her ground facing him in the hallway.

"No, it's not. Not since you started this crap."

Sarah crossed her arms. "You started it. I'm just finishing it."

"Get out."

Ruby stormed down the hallway from the kitchen. "She stays," she said from just behind Sarah. "And you'd do best to calm down unless you want to lose half your shit."

Sarah gave her mother a wide-eyed smirk. Apparently, her mother's salty language was unusual. Despite Sarah's grin, Eli could still see pain in her face. He moved to the study door, then stepped next to her in the hallway, hoping the shock and anger about his presence would move Lucian's focus to him.

Instead, Lucian relaxed and calmly said, "Good evening, Mr. Scott."

It was like he'd expected Eli. Like he'd invited him to his home himself. Did he know he was here already? Was it some kind of misdirection to gain advantage?

Six inches shorter than Eli, Lucian wasn't physically intimidating. And now that Eli saw Lucian for what he was, he held no dominion over him. In the most sarcastic tone he could muster, Eli said, "Nice to see you too, Lucian," landing the mockery like a right hook.

Lucian didn't take the bait. He picked up his briefcase. "What brings you to my home?"

"We need to ask you a few questions," Sarah said.

"You can talk to my lawyers about those questions."

"It's not about the proxy battle. It's not about the company."

Lucian appeared intrigued. He walked to them and stopped. He motioned into the study with his briefcase. "We can talk in here if you'll let me by."

Eli stepped aside, then he and Sarah followed Lucian inside. Ruby stopped at the door. Lucian set his briefcase down, removed his long black coat, draped it over the side of his desk, and sat down in the high-back desk chair. He extended his arms and crossed them in his lap. It was an odd position he'd always assumed when he faced questions while Eli was at Blackwood. He'd done it when he'd fired him. Lizzy had said it was probably a manifestation of his insecurity and his desire to distance himself from the people and situation he was facing.

"Have a seat," he said, directing Eli and Sarah to the two chairs on the other side of the desk. He looked at Ruby standing in the doorway. "Can you give us a minute, please?"

Ruby folded her arms. "I think I'd like to hear this."

He shook his head then looked at Eli. "Ask away."

Eli decided the direct approach might shake Lucian. "Did you have anything to do with the disappearance of Jim Munro?"

Lucian calmly looked left, then right, then focused on Eli. "No. I didn't know he was missing until now." His face was limp. Expressionless. Eli suspected a lie.

"You don't know anything about it? Nothing?" Sarah asked.

"No."

"What if I ask Bart that question?" she asked.

"I can't speak for him, but I'd assume you'd get the same answer." This time Lucian smiled.

Eli wanted to catch Lucian off guard to see his reaction again.

"Do you know Abena Williams?" Eli asked.

"Who?" Lucian looked genuinely surprised.

Eli decided to change tactics. "Are you familiar with the leases you recently acquired in Osage County?"

Lucian raised his brow. "That's confidential. You know that." Then a devilish grin crossed his face. "Oh. Wait. That's right. You wouldn't know that... since you were fired and no one would hire you."

The below-the-belt punch hurt. It was intended to demean him. The shame gremlins rumbled, but Eli held them at bay. "I chose not to work some two-bit job, and you had to pay me not to compete with you. Didn't matter, you still tanked the company." Eli did his best to smile.

Lucian's eyes widened and his jaw muscles flexed. Eli's counterpunch had hit pay dirt.

"The leases?" Eli repeated.

"Yes. I knew about that."

"Why did you acquire them?"

"I'm not going to tell you that." Lucian folded his arms across his chest and stared back at Eli.

Eli suspected what he heard wasn't the truth. Lucian didn't lie as well as Hope. Eli held Lucian's stare but said nothing. Sarah remained quiet too.

Lucian unfolded his arms and stood. "We done here?"

"If you're involved in that man's disappearance in any way, *we're* done," Ruby said. "You two can stay in the south guest quarters. He'll leave you alone." She turned and walked back to the kitchen.

Eli stood, holding his ground. "For now." He heard the front door open. He assumed Winchester was arriving to meet with Lucian. The door closed, but Eli's skin tingled when he heard *two* sets of footsteps coming down the hallway. He looked at Sarah, who shrugged. They both turned and faced the doorway.

A tall man appeared in the doorway. He looked like a rat: his face and nose were long, and his squinty eyes found Eli first. His dead-eyed stare softened to a humorous grin. He looked to his left, and Hope Munro joined him in the study doorway.

CHAPTER 33

ELI FELT A nuclear heat race up his body and accumulate in his face. He realized he was snarling at Hope. Then he suddenly felt unstable, like the ground beneath him had liquefied. The uncertainty wracked his brain.

He launched himself toward the door. "What are you doing here?" he yelled. Winchester slipped his hand under his coat. His expression turned dark. Eli stopped a few feet away from Hope.

Hope greeted the advance with a pleasant smile. "Good evening, Eli."

Eli had to question his recollection of the last few hours for a second. She had just said on the phone she was at her father's house and he had to come now. Her father's house was twenty minutes away. Did she not know he'd see it had been a barefaced lie? She obviously knew where he was. Was it an attempt to lure him away? Away from the Blackwoods? Away from Sarah? Was that why Winchester was here? To do something about Sarah? He glanced over his shoulder to check his positioning relative to Sarah and Winchester. He stood directly between them. He estimated the time it would take to get to his Glock under his sweater. He ignored Winchester, turned back to Hope, and put his hand on his hip to cut the time in half. He remembered what Lizzy had said about a sociopath snapping. He didn't care.

"You said you were at your father's."

Hope rested her hand on her cheek. "No, I didn't." She put both hands out to the side, palms up, and cocked her head. "I said I'd meet you there. But you refused. That's fine. I didn't think you'd be here."

Eli was sure she'd said she was at her father's. But a discomforting uncertainty remained. "You said you had something to tell me about your father?"

An air of superiority enveloped her. "I don't want to get my client involved in personal matters."

"He already knows," Sarah said, stepping next to Eli. "And don't believe anything that snake standing next to you says."

"Miss Blackwood," Winchester said, smiling.

"Go climb back under your rock. Takes a lot of nerve to stand next to the daughter of the man you kidnapped."

"You haven't changed," Winchester said.

"Coming from you, that's a compliment," Sarah said.

Eli noticed Winchester looking past him at Lucian. Subtly, Winchester nodded and pulled his hand from under his coat.

Lucian picked up his briefcase. "I just learned that your father is missing. I'm sorry to hear that. Anything I can do?"

"Thanks, Lucian." Hope nodded at Eli. "He's supposed to be helping me find him. Sorry if they were bothering you."

"You don't need to apologize for me," Sarah said.

Hope ignored Sarah. "Happy to speak with you in private, Eli."

"You can use this room," Lucian said. "I need to speak with Bart in my office." Lucian pushed around Sarah, gathered Winchester, and headed down the hallway toward the back of the house. Hope waited for Sarah to leave. Sarah looked at Eli.

"I'll see you in a minute," he said.

"I'll be with Mom in the kitchen." As Sarah left, she paused, looked at Hope with disgust, then headed down the hallway.

Hope stepped in and closed the door.

Eli decided to minimize the confrontation until he'd heard what she had to say. "What's the new information?"

"Thanks for helping me. You meant a lot to my father and your help means the world to me."

Eli was amazed at her misplaced charm. "Go on."

"I received another message about the ransom to my Signal account. Now they want the process to make it *and* the sample. Same deadline. Same location."

"What kind of sample?"

"They didn't say."

Eli assumed if she was telling the truth and they wanted a sample, it would be some kind of material. It would have to be extremely valuable to Blackwood to orchestrate its theft.

"What else?"

"Said it's part of Dad's work in green energy."

Eli immediately thought about batteries again.

"There's a hole in their logic," he said.

"How so?"

"They asked for the sample, whatever it is, and they asked for the formulation, but they said nothing of the inventor. If the inventor is still alive, they can easily duplicate it or testify that they were the original inventor."

Hope thought for a second, then said. "Guess that means it's my father. He's the inventor. They already have him."

"Then they can't let him go. What's the point if they do?" Eli was sure his logic held. He'd caught a flaw in her lie. Either she was lying to protect Lucian, or she was only protecting herself.

"I can tell you don't believe me. But I love my father." She looked ready to cry again. "We're almost out of time. Let's just get that invention or sample and get it to them by tomorrow night."

She shook her head and turned away. "I've gotta go." Hope turned and left via the front door.

Eli headed to the kitchen to see Sarah. Hope was clearly lying about some things. But she seemed genuine about her father, however Eli knew not to trust his gut. Maybe she was the one being used and Lucian Blackwood knew how to do that. He had always been a master manipulator. There was no question Jim was gone, and the same three questions were still unanswered. Where is Jim Munro, who took him, and why was he taken?

CHAPTER 34

AS ELI WALKED down the hall toward the kitchen, he thought this was a strange milieu. He was in the inner lair of the man he most despised in the world. The man he suspected of kidnapping the person he most revered as a father figure. A man whose daughter was an unabashed liar. Layered on top of that were the remnants of past relationships rising from the darkness and challenging his undeniable attraction to Sarah. It was more than physical. It was deeper than that. Far deeper. The doubts were there, and they couldn't be from more different worlds. She was an environmental, social, and governance warrior who despised the industry to which he'd dedicated most of his life. And, in the end, she was still Lucian Blackwood's daughter.

He entered the kitchen and both women went silent. Ruby was preparing a couple of grilled cheese sandwiches and had a pot of tomato soup simmering on the burner of the large induction stovetop. Sarah stood next to her mother, leaning against the soapstone island with her arms folded. Her deep blue eyes found his, penetrating his defenses. It made him feel invincible and gentle at the same time.

"Anything new?"

Eli looked at her mother. Her back was turned, but he wasn't sure if he should expose her to any liability with the new information. Sarah saw that and nodded.

"She said there was another disappearing encrypted Signal message. It said that there was some type of invention. In the green energy space. I think it's some kind of material. It said to bring the sample and the formulation to the drop tomorrow night."

Sarah raised her brow. "Green energy? That ties with Jim's work."

"I know. But that was it. Nothing else."

"So no proof at all?"

"Unfortunately, none."

Sarah wagged her head. "Do you believe what she's saying?"

"I can't tell. I assume she's lying most of the time. Saying whatever gets her what she wants."

"I can't be in the same room with her. I've seen her half-truths mutilate the facts. I don't trust her at all."

"I'm with you. But she's telling the truth about her father. I verified that he was missing firsthand."

Ruby finished the grilled cheese sandwiches, plated them, and ladled the soup into the shallow white bowls. She turned and delivered them to the two placemats that were set up on the island.

"You two need to eat. Sounds like it's going to be a long twenty-four hours." She lifted her apron and wiped her hands. "The only thing I'll say is don't trust any of them." She looked at Sarah. "That includes your father." Untying the apron strings, she pulled it off, folded it, and dropped it in a drawer. "The guest quarters are already set up. You have a good night. If you need me, text me. I'm locking my door. Goodnight, dear." She headed for the hallway but stopped and turned back and did her best to smile. "Goodnight, Eli. Nice to see you again." She left the kitchen. Eli heard her ascend the stairs then a door close and lock.

Sarah took one of the chairs. Eli took the one beside her. The smell of butter and melted cheese triggered his hunger. They both dug in.

"Is there really an invention or do you think it's a ruse?" Sarah asked.

"It's impossible to tell. I have to think about why she would be lying. She only says anything if it serves her interests without regard for anyone or anything, or if it gives her a sense of control over someone by manipulating them."

"Psycho."

"Antisocial personality disorder is what my friend calls it."

"She a therapist?"

Suddenly Eli felt himself pulling back. The gremlins again. Shame about therapy. He remembered what Lizzy had taught him. He knew where that feeling came from now. He let it wash over him then mustered the courage to open up to her. He'd trust Sarah. "Yes. She was my therapist for a while."

"And you still see her?"

"Yes." Eli waited to see Sarah's reaction.

"Good for you both. Can she help us with Hope?"

Eli was elated. No judgment at all. "Yes. She's already given me her professional advice."

"We might need more help if Hope has that antisocial disorder."

"Sociopathy," Eli said.

"Well, that makes me feel better." Sarah laughed at her own joke. Eli did too.

They finished their dinner and put their dishes in the sink.

"This can go a couple of ways," Eli said. "Either it's just as Hope has relayed and some clandestine third party has Jim and is ransoming him for some green energy invention, or…" Eli hesitated, trying to read Sarah's expression and weighing his next words carefully.

"Or what?" she said.

"Or your father is behind it all."

The words seemed to hit Sarah harder than Eli had thought. "I hope not," she said. "I know I'm hitting him pretty hard in the proxy battle, but that's just money. If he's behind a kidnapping,"—her eyes drifted to the hallway where her mother had gone—"that's a whole different level of consequences."

"I know that's a lot more complicated for you. I'd understand if you need to step back from that angle."

Sarah made sure she made eye contact. "No. I appreciate you saying that, but it goes where it goes. I promised to find your friend if you help me with the proxy fight. All I ask is that we do everything we can to protect my mother from this mess."

"Done. But I need to sort through all this information from Hope again. See what's most likely true and what's most likely a lie."

"Do you need to meet with your therapist?"

"Lizzy."

"Great name. Can she help?"

"Yes. I think I should try before it gets too late." He looked at his watch. It was just after ten-thirty. "Let me see if she's still up."

Eli sent Lizzy a text. She responded immediately. They agreed to meet at her office. "She'll meet me at her office in thirty minutes."

"You be safe. I'll stay up and let you in."

"Are you safe here?" he asked.

"Yes. They wouldn't dare do anything here." Sarah started to leave the kitchen but stopped and faced him. "You know. I can't believe you were an oilman. Working for my father." She shook her head and left the room.

Eli wasn't sure what she'd meant. He knew she was an environmentalist. He was still an oilman. He had many friends in the business who were good people. Most had families and had as much or more concern for the environment than the general public. The warm sensation he'd felt toward Sarah cooled, and he wondered how wide that chasm between them really was.

CHAPTER 35

SARAH LEANED AGAINST the plush pillows on the sitting room window seat. She curled into it and pulled the cozy throw over her legs, being careful not to spill her chardonnay. She took a gentle sip and watched Eli's taillights disappear into the darkness. She wondered why she felt so different. The house was eerily dark, the haunting shapes and statues only visible in the diffuse light from the dim hallway path lighting. She heard the heater kick on, clicking rhythmically as if it were counting down each precious second they had left.

Eli made her feel safe unlike any other man she'd known. He was strong and capable, yet compassionate. She thought she trusted him. But his goal was to rescue Jim Munro. And if not for the promise Eli had made to her, he'd destroy her father to do it. She was trading her father's freedom, if not his life, to help Eli based on the word of Hope Munro, who was a notorious liar, and as far as Sarah was concerned, the most despicable human being she'd ever known.

She took a bigger gulp of her chardonnay and gazed around the dark room. Her eyes fixed on the piano in the corner. She remembered sitting next to her father in their old home so many years ago as a child. It came rushing back like yesterday.

It was a fresh Saturday morning. Snow had fallen and she was stuck inside. Her father, normally at the office on Saturday mornings, surprised her when he walked into the room, placing his fists on his hips and looking inspiringly toward the heavens.

"Super Daddy!" she cheered. She ran to him, and he picked her up. He waltzed with her, spinning and dipping across the room. She giggled and her innocent soul didn't have a care in the world. They sat at the piano and played her favorite melodies from the Care Bears cartoons.

Suddenly, her mind fast forwarded to the most terrible day she'd ever had. It was the first teacher in service half-day of junior high. Her mother had gone to California to visit her brother, Sarah's favorite uncle, who was dying from pancreatic cancer. After the short bus ride to her house, she found the door unlocked. Her dad was home. She was so happy he'd left work. She scurried through the house looking for him, hoping to secure a rare lunch date with her dad. She became worried when he wasn't in his office and headed upstairs. Then she heard them. It was a laugh she'd never forget. The bedroom door was cracked open. She peeked inside. Her father was in bed with a young woman she didn't recognize.

She began to quiver, frozen in place. She started to cry and tried to turn and run. But she couldn't move. Her life was collapsing before her eyes. Finally, she was able to turn away and drag herself down the hallway sucking back the tears.

"Sarah?" her father called.

She turned and watched him buckle his slacks as he tried to catch up with her. His eyes went dark. "What the hell are you doing here?"

"I only had half a day," she cried. She looked around him. "Who is that?"

He checked over his shoulder. Seeing nothing, he grabbed Sarah by the arm and dragged her into her room, slamming the door.

He wagged his finger in her face. "Don't you say anything to your mother. You hear me?"

"But Daddy..."

"Shut up!"

"If you say anything, you'll be responsible for killing your mother. You hear me! And you and I will be through."

His words cut straight through her. She thought her heart would beat right out of her chest. That was the end for her. The end of trusting any man. The beginning of battling every day to try and feel good enough about anything.

She forced herself out of the memory, turned away from the piano, and gazed out the window. She felt the wetness on her cheeks and wiped it away, finishing the remaining half-glass in one guzzle. After clearing her head with a deep exhale, she set the empty glass on the floor.

The evidence against her father was building. The sadness of that truth weighed on her. It was as if it were that day again. But she wasn't thirteen anymore. She was a thirty-three-year-old strong, smart woman. She was in a man's world, having to prove herself at every turn. Her boss was watching, her job on the line. The one thing that stood between her and success was her father. If he's guilty, so be it.

Her phone vibrated beneath the blanket. She picked it up and checked the caller. It was after eleven at night. No one called that late. The name sobered her instantly.

Ellen Trice was one of her father's board members. She was not much younger than Sarah's mother. Ellen's father had given her the day-to-day responsibilities for their very successful human resources and payroll company based in Tulsa. She and Ellen had known each other most of their lives. She'd been very kind to Sarah and her mother. Ellen's father and Lucian had both inherited their companies. They were on each other's boards until a stroke forced the older man to relinquish his seat to his daughter. With the proxy fight ongoing, Sarah knew this was a risky call.

"Hi, Ellen. Everything okay?"

"Yes, hi, Sarah. This isn't an official call. I'm calling as a friend."

Sarah sat up. "Okay?" she said, not hiding her pensiveness.

Ellen cleared her throat. "I have a suggestion for you."

"Ellen, I'm not sure we should have this conversation."

"Well, I'm having it. Hear me out." Ellen paused, and Sarah heard her take a deep breath. "This is ridiculous. You going against your father can only hurt your family. I feel like we know each other well enough that I can say that. Believe me, I know how our fathers can be. But I have an offer."

"On behalf of the board?"

"No. This is from me."

"Ellen, I appreciate the call, but I don't need to hear your offer."

"Look, Sarah. There's something you don't know about. You'll lose. And I imagine that those good ol' boys in California will drop you from their club and treat you like a leper in a second. Instead, we have a relationship with a hedge fund that will make you portfolio manager and partner immediately. They're based in San Francisco so you can stay in California."

There it was. Her bribe. She was correct that it would feel better to sidestep this whole mess and leave it to implode on its own. But Sarah knew right from wrong. She had a conscience, something her father had lost a long time ago.

"Thanks for the call, Ellen. I know it wasn't easy. I also know it wasn't coming from you. I wake up with one person every day. Myself. And I'm liking that person more and more each day. So please tell my father and your board to take that offer and..." Sarah decided not to go there.

"Goodbye," Sarah said. She tossed the phone onto the blanket. She was now betting everything on an oilman she hardly knew. A man who was determined to find the truth by relying on a sociopath. A man she'd have to trust.

CHAPTER 36

ELI PULLED NEXT to Lizzy's SUV. He was eager to get Lizzy's advice about Hope's latest revelations. But something else made him pause. Something that felt like an invisible headwind pushing against him. He wasn't sure what that was about, but he didn't have time to find out. He shoved it aside and stepped out of the truck.

The yellow hue from Lizzy's office windows spread across the thin layer of snow. The threat of more snow had kept the Saturday revelers to a minimum and traffic had been light. As he trotted to the front door, the frigid air stung his nostrils and each breath hung in the air. The door opened and Lizzy stood there wrapped in her thick Pendelton Harding pattern sweater.

"Hey, Eli. Long time no see," she said, smiling as he stepped inside. She closed the door.

"I'm sorry about this," he said. "I need more of your great insight."

"You've been a great client." She waved him into her office. "And besides, if this helps you find Jim, I'm so happy to help."

The relaxing sound of trickling water filled the air. Eli appreciated that she'd turned on the fountain, knowing the effect it had on him. Faint light emanated from the small side-table lamp next to her chair. They assumed their usual positions facing each other in the plush king chairs. She leaned back, crossed her legs, and folded her hands in her lap. The soft light reflected in her eyes and sparkled in her short, dangling earrings, contrasting her dark buzz cut. She looked like she'd been out with friends earlier, but she seemed comfortable, and that relaxed Eli.

"Okay. What's up?" she said.

"I need help with Hope Munro again. But first, I need to update you on what's going on. I'll keep you out of the details, but there are some things you need to know."

"Okay. Go on."

"When Hope left in the limo, it was a limo owned by Blackwood."

Lizzy's mouth dropped open. Then she said, "They're working together?"

"Yes, they are. She claims they are only working on a proxy battle his daughter has launched against the company."

"I saw that online. She's some environmental hedge fund activist. That can't be comfortable for their family."

"That's not the worst of it."

Lizzy looked at him and waited for the big reveal. "Pray tell, young man. What's the worst of it?"

"I've joined together with his daughter. We're helping each other."

Worry lines appeared in Lizzy's forehead. She looked stunned.

Eli felt the headwind turn into a gale. "Wait. There's more."

Lizzy winced. "Lay it on me."

"Everything led to Blackwood. To Lucian. We're staying at his house right now."

Lizzy looked like she'd jumped into the path of an oncoming locomotive. "What?"

"I know," Eli said, shaking his head. "I know the dangers."

She reached over and grabbed her pad and pen. "Let's unpack this." She made a few notes then looked back up at Eli and smiled. "When you tie a knot, it's a good one."

Her humor relaxed him a bit.

"Okay. Let's start with Hope," she said.

Eli nodded. "She said she received another video. The ransom demand. The next step is crucial if it's true. I know not to trust her, but she has given me more information and has done some things I need to sort out. I need to know how much of what she's told me is most likely true, if anything."

"I'm not surprised you are confused. Don't worry about that. That's one of the trademarks of people who have a conscience and have to deal with sociopaths who have no conscience whatsoever."

She looked away in thought, then leaned forward. "This is the most important thing I'm going to say, Eli. Do not assume she has any emotional tie to anyone or anything. She's a cunning predator who can study her conscience-bound victims and manipulate them with no regard for anyone." She leaned back in the chair. "You have more people involved now. You may not be her only target."

While that made sense, he hadn't thought about Sarah or Lucian being targeted by Hope. Now, he thought about what she'd said. "Both of them?"

"Both of them are a possibility. She can't distinguish between good and evil. There is no such thing in her world." Lizzy wrote something else down. "Now, you must remember, our conscience can blind us to her manipulation. Your empathy, your desire to see good in others, to make the world a better place—she'll take full advantage of that. For example, the pity play we talked about last time. It's a manipulation to make you drop your guard."

"What about sorting through what she has told me?"

"In addition to what I've told you before, remember, she's not bound by conscience like you are. She'll exploit it. She'll lie to get you to surrender control. Manipulate people to take away any perceived advantage she thinks someone has in order to gain what they perceive is superiority."

Eli realized he'd been manipulated. But he still didn't know how to weigh what she told him. Assuming everything was a lie was a recipe for his failure, and probably Jim's death if the threat was true.

"How can I weigh what she says? Even if it's not an absolute determination of truth?"

"It's a dangerous game. They fool professionals like me all the time. But I understand that in this situation you're going to have to handicap it, as I mentioned before." She took a deep breath and gazed at Eli for a few seconds.

The anticipation got the best of him. "I'm ready."

"Don't commit to climb that tree until you see how tall it is." She gave Eli a gentle smile, then leaned her elbow on the arm of the chair and rubbed her chin. "Here's a few more things you can do to handicap what she says as a lie." She started a count on her fingers. "First, when she appeals for sympathy to have you feel sorry for her, look for a lie. Like I said, pity disarms suspicion in most with a conscience. Second, when she turns on the charm and seems fascinating, genuine, even saintlike, she's probably lying. She's proficient in acting out emotional reactions and using facial expressions or body language to appear as if she is like you and me. More so than even professional actors. Remember, she doesn't care about anyone. It's only manipulation. Third, frustration will incite anger and or rage. That's the most dangerous one, though. If you confront them—prove a lie they told—they can deny, deny, deny, or lose control. They are very impulsive and don't care who they hurt.

"Finally, remember at all times that they only want predatory success. Controlling or winning is more compelling than anything. They can destroy anyone who they perceive as a competitor in whatever contest they think they are in. If they perceive someone as better or ahead of them, they'll do anything to take them down a notch or destroy them." Lizzy hesitated. "And remember… the tantalizing gaze of a predator is the last thing its victim sees."

Eli rifled through his interactions with Hope. He'd seen all those behaviors.

"You okay?" she asked.

"Yes. Yes, I am. Just taking it all in. She's lied a lot, then."

"No surprise, right?"

Eli acknowledged her with a nod.

"Now. Blackwood," Lizzy said while jotting another note.

Eli felt the tension rising in his throat "I had to go to his home. It all led to him."

"I can see the anger in your eyes," Lizzy said.

"I want to destroy him. And if he's behind it, make him pay."

"Whoa. Remember what we talked about a few sessions ago. Before this thing with Jim. You saw him as an authority figure. When he fired you and told you you'd never amount to anything, you believed him on some level. You need to see him for who and what he is, then keep the emotions in check."

Eli thought back to the session. "Okay. A narcissist whose opinion carries no weight with me."

"Correct. And what he did meant nothing about your worth. He triggered that old childhood pain, but you know how to handle that now. And it's not revenge. That could get you in trouble."

That was the closest thing to a scolding Lizzy had given him. He realized it was good advice. He decided to deal with Blackwood intellectually. Just like Hope. "You're right, of course."

Lizzy's mouth stretched into a tight smile. Eli knew that meant a personal question was coming. "So, tell me about Sarah."

An electricity shivered through him. He felt flush but breathed through it. Hiding it. Then he realized Lizzy knew him too well. "I don't think I've met anyone like her. I think we connected right away. I can't believe we did, considering the circumstances."

"Don't worry about that. You sound a little unsure."

"We come from different worlds. She said something about that tonight."

Lizzy leaned forward again. "That's a good thing to remember. Think about her relationship with her father. At some point there may be a line she won't cross with you or for you. After all, he is her father." Lizzy gave him a knowing look. "Do you remember what happened in your past? You passed on the women who were the kindest to you. That didn't match what you thought of yourself back then, so you didn't trust them. Instead, you got entangled with women who were flawed in some way. You subconsciously thought you could change them. To work out that stuff from your childhood. And you fell for them quickly.

"She's an environmentalist and Blackwood's daughter. Those are powerful forces. Flaws? Only you know. I think you need be careful."

The reality hit Eli squarely. He'd been focused on finding Jim and had started to fall back into his old habits. He was already reading more into Sarah's interest than it probably meant. "Man. You are good."

"Why I make the big bucks!" She laughed.

Eli checked the small digital clock behind Lizzy. "I've kept you too long," he said, standing.

She stood. "Come here."

He did and she hugged him. "Stay safe and stay strong. Trust your intuition, control the emotions, and ignore those damn gremlins."

"I will."

CHAPTER 37

ELI PULLED TO the Blackwoods' gate and rolled down his window. The frigid air sent a shiver through him and electrified his senses. Lucian Blackwood and his henchman lurked somewhere on the estate. He cautiously eyed either side of the entry, looked through the frosted iron gates and down the winding cobblestone ahead, and wondered what they were plotting. Despite her ongoing battle against her father, Eli knew Lucian would be livid that Eli had connected with his daughter. Lucian had proved to be a stealthy vindictive man, and it was only a matter of time before he struck back.

He reached out and pressed the button on the call box.

"Hi, Eli. Glad you're back. I'll meet you at the front door," Sarah said.

It was surreal pulling up to the Blackwoods' gate and hearing Sarah's welcoming voice through the speaker. A defenseless warmth radiated from his heart again. Exposed and vulnerable, he didn't trust it. He'd exercise caution if he sought to connect with her heart again. Lizzy's advice had been spot-on. Always had been. Despite his pensiveness, he let the feeling run for a bit.

"Looking forward to it," he said as the gates opened.

He drifted down the drive in the darkness until he reached the guest spaces near the front entry. Checking the Glock under his sweater, he scanned his surroundings, then exited the truck and made his way toward the front door. He could see Sarah's silhouette through the windowpanes in the door. The image sparked an anticipation he'd hadn't felt before. He fought to maintain his vigilance until he reached the door.

Sarah opened the door, stepped forward, and surprised him with a hug. She was soft and warm. She'd changed into clinging loungewear made from jersey material. She pulled back as if recognizing something different. She stepped back, looking surprised herself, and headed down the hallway.

"Follow me," she said.

She led him through the entry, past the dark kitchen, and, when the hallway split, they went to the right up a few stairs. That brought them into a room that was half kitchen and half den, with a huge TV on the wall and furniture that looked tartan. Then she led him directly into the bedroom. Eli's head spun when he saw the one king bed, but he did his best to control it. It didn't work. Then he saw the sofa cushion stretched across the window seat. A pillow at one end with a folded sheet and blanket. Sarah stopped and turned to look at Eli. She waited.

His awkward meter ramped up again. He pointed to the window. "Thanks for doing that. I'll go get ready for bed." He wasn't sure if he saw a glint of disappointment in her eyes or if it was a look of *what else did you expect?* He only knew he needed rest.

Eli sat next to Sarah at the kitchen island. It was just after four in the morning. They'd both awoken early and headed to the kitchen. Eli fought the urge to think about what came next. To have this develop into anything, they both had to survive the gauntlet that led to Jim. And that gauntlet probably went through Sarah's father.

"Eli," she said. "What did Lizzy say last night?"

"She gave me a way to better handicap Hope's lies." He left out the part about Sarah and her father.

"Yes. Treat everything she says as a lie," Sarah said.

"I get that. But that's not quite what she said."

Eli saw Sarah's body tense a bit.

"What did she say?"

"There were a few behaviors that may indicate she was most likely lying. Turning on the charm, playing the pity card, or playing the blame game."

Sarah looked at him as if he were Mr. Obvious. "That pretty much describes her."

"I know. Most of the time. She also said she's dangerous to people like you and me because we have a conscience—care about other people."

"Danger?"

"Yeah. She knows how to manipulate us—or at least thinks she does. She can also snap."

"How lovely."

Eli saw her relax again. He shifted so he could look directly at her. "I've gone through my interactions with her thinking about Lizzy's tips. First, Jim is missing. That's a fact I've verified. When she told me he was kidnapped and she'd received a video, I wasn't sure if that was the truth or a lie. But I verified it. The second thing she said was that she hadn't deleted clips from Jim's security system and didn't know Abena Williams when I showed her the image. That could have been a lie. Finally, not knowing about her father's request for security and the meeting in Hominy could all be the truth. But she lied again and went to Abena William's apartment without me. The biggest lie of all was when she didn't tell me she was working with your father."

The mention of Sarah's father made her look away. She stared at the ceiling, her fingers massaging her temples. "That means he *could* be behind it all. He could have told her to cover up their arrangement. He could be using her to get whatever it is that he wants. His business is failing. He could be after that green invention because it's worth more than what he has left in the company."

Eli kept his eyes on her. "We'll see where it goes. If that's the case, we'll keep your mother out of it."

"She doesn't deserve this."

"Neither do you."

"But I can take care of myself."

"I know. I'm certain of that. But I want you to know I'm in this with you. Until the end. Like I promised."

She turned to Eli. "The end is what I'm worried about," she said.

They both turned back to their food. Eli wondered about the end. What it would look like. His phone vibrated on the counter. He picked it up. It was an alert from the alarm system at his home. The front door had been opened. He opened the alert and shot up from his stool.

"What? What is it?" Sarah asked.

"The cops just raided my home."

CHAPTER 38

ELI KNEW THE police raid changed everything. They'd issue statewide bulletins. That further limited his options. The pressure ramped up and his focus narrowed. Everything else fell away except his mission. The crisis had deepened. It was a place where he'd always been at his best. He touched his Glock and got comfortable being a wanted man.

It was just after four and the cold predawn air penetrated his sweater. He stuffed a few things into the back seat. Through a cloud of his condensing breath, he watched Sarah hug her mother at the front door of the mansion. He jumped inside the truck and started it, his hands seeking the warm air from the vents. Sarah ran down the steps. She wiped a tear from her cheek and hopped inside next to Eli.

She held a piece of paper in front of her that had a few numbers written on it. "Got it."

"Are you sure no one knows about it?"

"Mother assured me there is no traceable connection."

"I'm sorry," Eli said as he pulled from the parking spot and headed down the drive.

Sarah reached for his arm and squeezed it. "No need for apologies, Eli. You had nothing to do with any of this."

Eli realized she was right. Sarah's support didn't waver. There was no question she was on the same team. At least on this matter. He focused on the road ahead. "I want to tell you how much I appreciate your support, especially considering what you're risking."

"I get the sense that you and I are cut from the same cloth," she said, looking straight ahead.

"How so?"

"I've had a rough parental experience. And I've kissed a lot of frogs. Call it women's intuition, but I get the sense you've had similar experiences."

"The women I've kissed wanted to make me a frog." Eli laughed at himself.

She nodded and gave him a sly grin.

"How long to Grove?" Eli asked.

"Should be less than ninety minutes. And that's taking the back roads."

"You know the way? We have to put the phones in this Faraday bag Butch gave me. Can't be tracked inside it." Eli handed her the bag, and she dropped hers inside with his.

"Done," she said tossing the bag into the glove compartment.

"Great. You know, I'm thinking either Hope or Darnell Williams got the Tulsa Police involved."

"How's that?"

"When we were first at Abena's, I was careful not to leave prints at her apartment. From what I saw, Hope's were all over it. I did the same when I met Darnell there. So, either Darnell got too suspicious about me or Hope made up some lie."

Sarah shook her head. "Doesn't surprise me. You know my father is connected. The city, the police, he could make her prints disappear and they could blame you."

Eli knew Lucian was politically connected. His tentacles reached deep. Eli saw firsthand how Lucian peddled his influence. Campaign support, creating special tax entities around the buildings he developed, and getting jobs for part-time politicians, city officials, and their families. He'd butted heads with Eli more than once on those issues.

"There is also Darnell. His mother has been missing for three days."

Sarah glanced at Eli. "I guess that could be the source."

"Once we get there, we need to come up with a plan to find her. That gets me off the hook."

"If she's alive." Sarah looked as if she wished she hadn't said that.

Eli hoped she was alive. If Abena was dead, all bets were off. There would be no one to clear him. "I hear you. We also need to figure out how your father is tied into this."

Sarah face turned stoic, and she looked down the dark road ahead. "I know."

Eli was certain it had to be difficult for her. After all, like Lizzy had said, Lucian was still her father.

She rode silently for a few minutes, then said, "My father never leaves any paper trail. Anything he wants done, he does it verbally through Winchester. You probably noticed that."

"I did. It took me a while to figure it all out, but once I did, I don't think I was a welcome addition to the team. He had a lot of people on his executive team who just went along with him. I lost respect for them. But that's behind us. Sounds like we need to focus on Winchester."

Sarah scrunched her nose. "That will feel like doing a septic tank inspection with our bare hands."

"I've got a few people in mind who don't mind getting their hands dirty."

"The NLBs?"

Eli laughed. "The NLBs."

"They seem like great people."

"They are. I wish you got to meet them without all this going on."

"Hoping I will."

"Me too." Eli wondered if they'd ever get that chance.

ঌ

Eli took the Grove exit and thanked God that Butch had a TollTag in his truck. It was 5:30 a.m. and still dark as they wound their way down the two-lane Highway 59 toward Grove. At this hour, traffic was nonexistent, but more snow had fallen here. He carefully guided the truck down the snow-packed road. Sarah slept peacefully in the passenger seat. Fencepost after fencepost clicked by, until he spotted the well-lit high-arching span over the Neosho River arm of Grand Lake that descended into town.

Eli had spent many summer days at the sixty-mile lake with Butch and their friends. The deep water was a cool respite from the summer heat while the consistent summer winds challenged their boat-docking skills. It was always a good break for their mental health. But in wintertime, the town was reduced to a small town near the Arkansas border. As far as Eli was concerned, the smaller the better.

Descending the far side of the bridge, Sarah woke up. She gently massaged her face and sat up in the seat.

They passed the Tractor Supply and a tire store.

"Hasn't changed much," Eli said.

"Never does. Always has a small-town feel until you get to the other end of town and see the Walmart and Lowe's."

"Ah, the necessities," Eli said, grinning.

"Turn right up here," Sarah said.

Eli drove down the country road. The trees along the road got thicker and the houses fewer.

"Then left here," she said.

They wound through the woods until they came to a small set of gates between two short stone pillars. She gave him a four-digit code that he entered on the keypad. The gates parted with a groan. It was pitch-black ahead. As Eli pulled down the street, he spotted three large houses on the left and one large newer stucco-and-brick home with a detached garage and guest quarters on the right.

Sarah held a piece of paper up to the dash lights and pointed to the house on the right. "I think this is it."

"Wow. Your mother has a friend with good taste," Eli said.

"Not a friend. She just saved her allowance. It's her private hideaway. She comes up here to get away from my father. He doesn't know about it."

"Nice," Eli said, as he pulled in front of one of the two garages attached to the house.

Sarah got out, looked at the paper again, and punched in a code on the keypad next to the door. The door rolled up, and she waved Eli inside. He pulled the truck into the bay and noticed a new BMW sedan on his right. He got out. Sarah met him at the door.

Eli pulled his Glock from its holster. "I'll check it out first. Just in case."

Sarah nodded.

Eli stepped into the tiled entry that led to a great room with the kitchen and island on his left and the den on the right. He felt Sarah behind him. The first shades of dawn gave the room a muted yellow hue. Expansive plate-glass windows opened to the back porch and deck, which held a pool. He moved to his right and cleared two bedrooms connected by a bathroom. Then he headed past the kitchen, walked past a formal dining room on the left, and cleared the small sitting area on the right. He then headed into the primary suite. Finally, he backtracked and left Sarah in the den, as he ascended a set of stairs to a large loft area with two bedrooms off the back of it.

"All clear," he said as he came back down.

Sarah flipped on the lights. The place was sparkling. Eli opened the refrigerator. It was fully stocked.

"I like how your mom rolls."

"She was pretty awesome even before my father. She said she was the number-one real estate agent in the state five years in a row."

"Nice." Eli walked to the sliding glass door to the back deck. "I need to check the layout outside," he said, opening the door. Stamped concrete decking surrounded the large pool and was supported by a stucco retaining wall. The backyard sloped down to a dock that held a boat on a lift and two jet skis, all covered with tarps. Eli walked back in, then across the breezeway that connected the guest quarters and other garages. He cleared the guest quarters in seconds. When he returned to the main house, Sarah had opened a laptop on the kitchen table.

She pointed to the screen. "You have to be careful. The news picked up the story. You're all over the media."

He sat down next to her and put his Glock on the table. "Expected that. Anything about Jim?"

She made a few clicks and checked a few pages. "Nothing."

"Then we have a problem."

CHAPTER 39

ELI WATCHED SARAH as she set the table for them. Realizing they were both famished and there was nothing they could do until daybreak, Eli had volunteered to make breakfast before they sorted through the challenges ahead of them. Bacon crackled in one pan while he gently scrambled a few eggs in olive oil in the other. The aroma caused his stomach to grind in anticipation. But something else was stirring from a place he couldn't quite identify. It wasn't fear, but it felt like a close cousin. Maybe it was uncertainty. Then he realized he'd felt it before. He and Lizzy had rooted it out of the deep dark place that had hid it from his conscious mind.

Sarah sat at the table with the laptop in front of her. Sipping her coffee, she glanced at him and smiled, returning her attention to the screen. She looked beautiful. Eli recognized that her warmth and trust had triggered him. Her kindness and her support caused the gremlins inside to tell him to distrust her. They had painted Eli as that not-good-enough kid. He'd run from such kindness in the past, drawn to women who treated him more like a flawed child. In the end, those attractive but condescending women had been disasters.

Eli closed his eyes and quickly reminded himself that that was old stuff that belonged to his lying, belittling father. Eli was indeed the man Sarah saw, and she deserved his trust in return. He banished the thoughts from his mind and took a deep cleansing breath. He looked at Sarah again and absorbed the warm energy between them. He finished cooking, plated their breakfast, and joined her at the table. He hesitated before he spoke, entering new territory for him. Sarah looked up from the laptop.

"I want you to know, I'm so grateful that I met you. Not just for your help finding Jim," Eli said.

"I was just thinking the same thing," she said, her eyes glistening.

He leaned over and they kissed. The sensation felt strange and wonderful at the same time. Lizzy had been right. He sat back down, and they both dug in.

"There's a bigger problem than me being wanted," he said.

"Hope?"

Eli was happy they were on the same page. "With me on the run, my access to her has been cut off. With the phones in the Faraday bag, she can't call me, and I can't call her. She's been the only conduit for information from the kidnappers."

"I'll solve the communication part of this when I get those things on the list in town," she said. "I checked and the Walmart had prepaid smartphones."

"The need to connect with her would go away if your father were behind it and just using her."

Sarah put her fork down. "I know. I just find it hard to believe he'd go that far. Kidnapping? Maybe it's the other way around."

"You think Hope is behind this?"

"It's a possibility we have to consider."

"I know. But it's not as likely that she has the connections that it would take to pull this off."

"Maybe. But her ability to lie without any remorse or consideration for anyone might allow her to manipulate someone into using *their* resources," she said.

"Your father?"

"Him and Winchester." Sarah looked certain.

Eli knew she was struggling with the possibility of her father's involvement in Jim's kidnapping. He'd never seen Lucian manipulated the entire time he worked for him. But he had to consider the possibility. "I get that. It seems to me that we need to start with Winchester, then. If he's clean, your father will be cleared. Then we would focus on Hope."

"Makes sense."

Eli looked at his watch. It was just before seven. "Today is the day. We have thirteen hours until the ransom drop if Hope told the truth. We don't have any invention, don't know where Abena is, and aren't sure who's behind all this."

"Is it possible neither Hope nor my father are involved?"

"Yes. But if that's the case we would need to focus on the invention and finding Abena, then get to that ransom drop." Eli realized their dilemma. "We have to do both. Find Abena and check out Winchester. It's the only way."

"Makes sense. But how do we do that and get to that lease north of Hominy by seven tonight?"

Eli had to think about that one. The last clue related to Abena was in Hominy. The car was in the bay beside the wrecked makeshift lab. The thugs at the lab wouldn't have been there if they'd already gotten the invention. Another possibility hit him like a freight train.

"Jim might have destroyed that lab in Hominy. That could be why he'd wanted security for a meeting there. He didn't want them to get it. Maybe Abena went to the lab looking for Jim after she left my house. That's why her car was there."

"Okay. Then where is she now?"

"Maybe stashed somewhere in Hominy or nearby. Somewhere where Jim would have told her to go if something happened." He thought for a minute. "Where would Winchester keep anything he didn't want anyone to see?"

Sarah stared across the kitchen, thinking. "His house. He wouldn't leave it at the office."

"Do you know where he lives?"

"Yes. He lives in Bixby. A small horse ranch."

"Okay. That's not far from your father's house."

"Probably fifteen minutes away."

"Okay."

They finished breakfast and cleaned up.

Sarah pulled the keys to the BMW from the kitchen drawer.

Eli turned to Sarah. "You go get the things we need in town. I'll work on the angle about where Jim would tell Abena to go around Hominy if she got in trouble. Meanwhile, we'll go after Winchester first."

"But you can't be seen in the Tulsa area."

"I don't intend to be seen. And if I am, I have the feeling I'll be dead."

CHAPTER 40

ELI KNEW THIS plan had to be flawless and quick. He was on high alert with a laser focus on detail. It was as if he were preparing to do a house to house with his old Marine squad. After Sarah had returned from town, they'd gone through her haul together. She'd done a great job getting the items from Lowe's and the local Walmart. The duffel bag fit perfectly inside the large cardboard box, and the tape, paper, and lettering mimicked typical delivery labeling. Standing at the island with the long box in front of them, Eli grabbed one of the burner phones and dialed Butch's secure line.

"Hi, Mr. Popular," Butch said. "The cops were here earlier. Hope you're safe."

"I am, my friend. No worries."

"That's good to hear. What's up?"

"Need some help again."

"Go."

"I've gotta get into a house. Probably max security. Looking for a place to hide handwritten documentation or receipts that may provide some clue to where they may be holding Jim. Guy's name is Bart Winchester. Bixby."

"I know of that asshole. His digital footprint is clean. Checked him out when we saw Blackwood might be involved," Butch said.

"I'm looking for any documentation or notes that he probably keeps."

"Got it."

"Can you get me in?"

"When?"

Eli checked the time. It was already 8:35 a.m. "Be there around ten."

"Okay. I'll meet you at the parking lot at the back of the strip mall behind the pizza joint at Memorial and Regal."

"Thanks, man."

"You're a hot item in town, so I hope you have a good disguise."

"Copy that."

"Hey. I won't copy that because I want to avoid looking anything like you right now!"

"Funny. See you at ten."

Eli hung up.

"All good?" Sarah asked.

"Yes. Now I gotta call Hudson."

Sarah smirked. "Tell him I said hi."

Eli chuckled as he dialed and nodded.

"Hey, Hoss," Hudson said.

"I need you to check something out for me."

"You know you're a wanted man?"

"Yes. I always wanted to be wanted," Eli said.

Sarah scrunched her nose at Eli.

Eli rolled his eyes and smiled back.

Hudson chuckled. "Don't spur that bronc unless you have eight seconds in you."

Eli laughed. "Good one. Can you check the area around the old area office for anything that would indicate Jim stashed Abena Williams nearby?"

"Ain't no hill for a stepper."

Eli looked at Sarah, who was watching him. "Sarah says hi, by the way."

"Tell that filly hi back."

"Call me back on this number if you find something, but not before eleven this morning."

"Busy schedule?"

"Let's just say I need to stay focused."

"Okay. Got it," Hudson said. "And Eli?"

"Yeah, Hudson?"

"Be careful and remember to punch through them."

"Thanks, man."

He hung up. "Hudson's on it. Let's pack up and go. We'll need to take the BMW. Hand me that medical mask."

Sarah pulled one from the old box on the counter. "Good thing Mom kept these after the pandemic."

Eli stuffed the mask in his back pocket, grabbed the box on the island, tucked it under his arm, and headed toward the garage. "Remind me to thank your mother."

Eli pulled into the parking lot behind the strip mall wearing a medical mask, baseball cap, and sunglasses. He was sure he looked like a guy who was sick and just coming from his kid's soccer game. It was just before eleven. Eli spotted Butch's black Suburban. He pulled next to it and Sarah rolled down her window. Eli waited for Butch to roll down his dark-tinted window. He wanted to confirm he was inside and alone. Butch rolled down the window halfway, smiled, gave Eli the finger, then rolled it back up.

Sarah shook her head. "You guys did get past junior high, right?"

Grinning, Eli shrugged. "Let's go."

Eli got out and pulled the shipping box and a safety vest from the back seat. Sarah left the car and climbed in the back seat of the

Suburban. Eli gave her the box, then climbed in the front passenger side and closed the door.

"How are you holding up?" Butch asked.

"I'm good," Eli said. "Butch, this is Sarah Blackwood."

"Blackwood?" Butch glanced at Sarah, then gave Eli a *what the hell* look.

"She's good, man. We're on the same team."

Butch looked in the rearview mirror. "So, how are you, Sarah Blackwood?"

"Just keeping it one hundred," Sarah said.

Butch turned back to Eli and handed him a sketch on a piece of paper. "Here's the layout." He pointed to a rectangle at the end of a long driveway. Two smaller rectangles were set on a square court on the right side of the house. "The house is here. Shop is here. And a small, three-stall stable is here. Gate here, at the entrance to the driveway. We've been able to hack the security system and override the code for the gate, and I have a Wi-Fi jammer here."

"Where's Winchester?" Eli asked.

"He's there. But looks like he's getting ready to go somewhere. Packing his truck with a few items. Looks like firearms and a cooler."

"Good. Anyone else?"

"No. But when we jam the Wi-Fi and disable the security system, he'll be able to tell on his apps. We don't know if he has anyone who could respond before *he* can get there."

"If he's getting ready to go to Hominy, he may stop at my parents' house," Sarah said.

Butch threw Eli a nod. "That gives you ten minutes if he responds from there. Can't tell you if anyone else is closer, so plan on seven or less," Butch said. "We'll need access to his computer, so when you get inside,"—Butch handed him a small device with a USB male end—"stick this in one of the USB ports. Takes less than fifteen seconds. Pull it out when the screen shows it completed."

"Less than seven minutes to search all three structures, download the data, find wherever he stores his documentation, and get out," Eli repeated, the compressed timeline pressurizing his body. It sounded like a lot when he'd said it out loud.

Still studying the paper, Eli nodded. "He probably has a safe, too." That added two or three minutes itself.

"Can you handle that?" Butch asked.

"Think so. One of the guys in the squad showed us how to open them."

"Unless it's a high-end deal," Butch said.

"If that's the case, I have a drill and scope. If it's harder than that, I'm toast."

"More like dust," Butch said.

Eli looked at Butch. This time he wasn't smiling.

Butch nodded to a white panel van three spaces away and handed him an earpiece and a key fob. "Here's the keys to the van over there and your coms."

Eli turned back to look at Sarah. He wanted to see her one last time before he left her again. She looked worried. "See you soon," he said, as optimistically as he could.

She forced a quivering smile. "Hopefully not too soon."

Eli knew what she meant. Failure was not an option.

CHAPTER 41

ELI WATCHED BUTCH'S black Suburban turn into the residential area on the left ahead of him. This was one time when he was thankful for Tulsa's urban crawl southward. Continuing through the intersection, the landscape immediately transitioned into ranchettes: Parcels of land that had resisted urban development but were subdivided from the larger ranches that had existed south of town. He anticipated what was ahead. He wasn't afraid. He'd learned long ago that fear could paralyze at just the wrong moment. Anger was another thing altogether. It could be forged by purpose into a cold, calculated determination to prevail. To make Winchester and Blackwood pay for what they'd done. He donned that mental armor and continued south on Lewis Avenue.

Butch and Sarah would be concealed on the side street half a mile away from Winchester's property. If a response came from the north, they might be able to warn him, but from the south, east, or west, he'd be on his own. As their location faded in the rearview mirror, he felt alone, like an astronaut shedding his final booster.

The white van still had the new car smell, and it traveled smoothly down the asphalt road. To the left, he could see the white three-rail ranch fencing marking the perimeter of Winchester's tiny ranch. Ahead in the distance, he spotted the red brick house centered on the pastureland.

He heard Butch's voice in his ear. "In position. Winchester is confirmed to be gone. Good luck, buddy."

Eli knew the communication was only one way. Still, he said, "Thanks, Butch." He didn't need any of the affirmations he and Lizzy had developed over the year in this situation. This was one of his strengths. In crisis, he shined. He had less than five minutes to find the office, download the files, find the safe if there was one, and break into it. Any delay would increase the likelihood of being caught. That would mean the end of any chance of finding his friend. Maybe the end of his life. The last part didn't bother him so much. For some reason, he was never afraid of death—until he thought about Sarah.

As he approached the brick entry gate on his left, he pulled between the long wing walls supported by large stone topped piers. Each held a large carriage light. He rolled down the window. The camera lens embedded in the call box stared back at him. For show, he waited at the gate and feigned a conversation. Butch remotely opened the gates.

"Disabling the alarm and Wi-Fi," Butch said.

Here we go. Eli set the countdown timer on his watch.

The road led to the huge gravel parking area between the house, the shop, and the stable. He looped around the perimeter of the parking area, passing the shop and the stable. He pulled the van adjacent to the front walkway, pointing it toward the gate. He adjusted his mask and safety vest, checked his Glock, got out, and pulled the box from the sliding door on the panel van. The north wind had picked up, and the biting cold stung his cheeks. He walked to the front entrance of the home. The brick entry sheltered him from the wind and provided cover. The double doors had large windowpanes that covered most of the door, giving Eli a clear view of the hallway inside. Satisfied no one was home, he examined the lock and pulled the tools from his vest. He was inside with the box in seconds.

Setting the box on the floor, he slowed his breathing and listened. He heard the wind gusting against the house. He ripped the box open and pulled out the duffel. The layout was as suspected. The hall led to the living room. To the left was the kitchen and a den. To the right was another short hallway. Eli spotted the office doors on the right side of the hallway and the double doors that led to the primary suite on the left. The entire house was filled with handcrafted thick, light-stained oak millwork. Sponge-painted hues of forest green covered the walls. The floors were dark-gray slate. The color scheme made it seem darker than it was. More threatening, too. He slipped down the hallway and entered the office. It was smaller than he'd expected. A large desk faced a window at the front of the house. A laptop sat in the center of the black blotter.

Eli set his duffel on the floor and opened the computer. Producing the USB device from his pocket, he slipped it into the port on the side of the computer. He checked his timer. *Three and a half minutes left.* He listened again. This time he heard a faint whining from the back of the house, like something or someone was in distress. He grabbed his Glock and headed toward the noise. He followed it into the kitchen and through the den, then saw a brown labrador shivering at the back door. He checked his watch again. *Three minutes fifteen seconds left.* He looked at the dog, then back at the office. *Dog didn't pick this asshole as his master.*

Trotting back to the office, he saw the progress bar on the screen hit 100 percent complete. He pulled the USB device free, grabbed the black duffel, and headed for the back door. The dog looked up at him, eyes kind but sad. He pulled the door open and pet the dog as he came inside, wagging his tail. Eli stepped outside and closed the door.

Eli sprinted around the freeform pool and across the side yard, hurdled the fence, ran across onto the gravel parking area, and stopped at the entrance to the shop.

"Still clear. Get out soon," Butch said in his ear.

Pulling out the prybar, he broke open the steel door and went in. Two pickup trucks, one black SUV, and a large ATV occupied the bays. Along the back wall was a large gun safe. Eli inspected the floor as he made his way back. No sign of a floor safe. Once at the gun safe, he began softly manipulating the combination lock. He had it open on his second try. Inside, it looked like an arsenal. But he found nothing that looked like a notebook or documents. He wanted to take the weapons so they couldn't be used against him. But there was no time. He slammed the safe shut and headed for the door.

His watch vibrated. The two-minute warning. He wasn't sure he'd make it. He shoved the door open and ran across the gravel to the three-stall stable. The sliding double doors were ajar. Eli stopped just short of the opening. With his back against the door, he inched closer to the opening, then looked inside. The gray floor was spotless. The three stalls on the left were empty. Judging by the smell of hay and manure, the horses had been there recently. The storage areas on the right held the requisite supplies, saddles, and equipment. He stepped inside.

Immediately to his right was a small office. He opened the door. The walls were paneled with rough knotty-pine tongue-and-groove planks. Two large cabinets were suspended above the floor on either side of the window. No sign of a wall safe. A sink with a cabinet underneath occupied the wall to his left. The floor was smooth, gray concrete. He quickly went to the cabinets beneath the sink and opened them. Other than the plumbing and a few bottles of cleaner, it was empty.

"Time to get out of there," Butch said.

Eli looked at his watch. *Thirty seconds.* They had guessed seven minutes at the outside. He was already there. He noticed the right cabinet had a few chips in the wood between the bottom panel and the frame of the cabinet. Placing his hand in the center of the panel, he put his weight on it, then released it. It clicked and opened. Pulling it up he found the floor safe. An older one. He checked his watch again. *Thirty seconds late.* He slowed his breathing and gently began to manipulate the combination dial. Click by click, he deciphered the three-digit combination. Finally, he opened the safe.

Lifting the lid, he found banded one-hundred-dollar bills. Lots of them. Beneath the cash, he noticed a black leather ledger. He reached in, moved the banded bills aside and pulled the ledger from the safe. Halfway out, he felt cold steel against the back of his head. It shoved his head down as a voice said, "Drop it."

Eli recognized Winchester's voice. He knew what happened next would determine his life, no matter how short it was, from this point forward. He pushed fear away and dug deep for focus. His Marine squad had drilled on this, building on their hand-to-hand combat training. They'd had the time, and they'd collectively known any edge could be the one that saved their lives. They'd used every resource they could to get good at escaping the scenario of a gun to the head or back.

Eli raised his hands. "I'm sorry. Please don't kill me."

"Stand up. Slowly," Winchester said, still pressing the gun against his head.

As Eli stood, he knew that was all he needed.

"Hands behind your head."

He couldn't let himself be cuffed. Swinging his head to the left, he spun, raising his elbow high, and trapped Winchester's gun hand in the crook of his elbow. Eli followed through with his right hand, driving it hard into Winchester's elbow. Winchester grunted in pain, and the gun fell to the floor. But Winchester recovered faster than Eli anticipated, throwing his left elbow against Eli's head. Ignoring the pain shooting through his skull, Eli kicked the gun to the far corner and came over the top with a crushing right to Winchester's cheek. Winchester staggered back, gathered himself, and charged Eli. Eli patiently waited and coiled his frame. He spun away from Winchester's path and drove his right fist into his jaw when he passed. He crashed into the back wall and slumped to the floor.

Eli brushed himself off, picked up the gun, ejected the shell and the clip, and put it in his belt. When he bent down to pick up the ledger, he heard the door swing open behind him, and before he could turn, he heard a thud as a silenced shot rang out, splintering the paneling on the back wall.

Eli spun and faced the door, drawing his Glock. He saw another man on the floor in the doorway, bleeding from a gash in the back of his head. Then Sarah stepped over him, holding a shovel.

"You're late, cowboy."

CHAPTER 42

LUCIAN BLACKWOOD ANXIOUSLY watched the dried leaves race across his driveway from his office window. He'd gotten the alert on his watch from the front gate. Winchester was returning after he had sped away responding to a break-in at his ranch. It was the first time Lucian was grateful that Ruby was so involved in the Baptist church and nowhere to be found.

Winchester's black pickup skidded to a stop, and he exploded from the cab and marched inside. Lucian glanced at the Glock that sat next to his parka on his desk. Hearing Winchester's footsteps on the stairs, he grabbed the Glock and returned it to the drawer. He'd never win a gunfight with Winchester and his men, and he doubted Winchester would hurt his meal ticket.

The door swung open without the customary knock, and Winchester barged in. Blackwood immediately noticed Winchester's swollen face and knew the news couldn't have been worse. It felt like a seismic shift in his world, an earthquake that could crumble what was left of the Blackwood dynasty that had been built by his father. The earth was opening to swallow him. His wealth was vaporizing, along with his influence, as his oil company had been crippled by a long string of failed investments. Accelerating his own fall was the fact that he'd pledged his stock to secure loans to invest in a plethora of nonenergy investments, all of which were failing and heading to a margin call that would be the death knell to his stock holdings in Blackwood Energy. It would also destroy what was left of his reputation and power. The only hope was the green invention Jim Munro had promoted as the holy grail of electric cars, a multimillion-dollar—if not billion-dollar—creation.

"What's the damage?" Lucian asked Winchester.

Winchester looked as if he would choke on his own words. "The ledger. Scott and your daughter have it."

The words felt like a chainsaw cutting off his legs. His face on fire, he yelled, "The ledger? Are you some kind of idiot?"

Winchester's eyes narrowed on Lucian and his jaw muscles twitched. "I'll get it back. It's coded. They won't figure it out."

Lucian knew that look. And he knew what it meant for Sarah: a fatal one car crash, an accidental fatal fall, or an airtight suicide. Winchester was a master of his craft. He'd eliminated threats, and based on the look in his eyes, she and Scott were next.

He couldn't believe it was coming to that. Sarah and he had been so close when she was a kid. She'd called him "Super Daddy" when she was four and had proudly shared every soccer trophy with him until she was eleven. Then Ruby shared his other indiscretions with her and everything changed. She'd only told Sarah half the story, leaving out the part about her mother's refusal to meet his needs. Ruby had abandoned her wifely duties and biblical responsibility to her husband. He'd been forced to find solace and satisfaction with others.

Still, Sarah hated him and everything he did for them for the remainder of their lives together. She'd polluted Lucian's son's view of him until he didn't want anything to do with his father or his business. And now she was on a full-frontal attack on Blackwood Energy at the worst possible time.

He remembered what Hope had said earlier. *You're so insightful and decisive. You've done a great job so far with the rebuilding. I probably didn't even need to say that. You're always one step ahead of us. You know that. The new image you're building, your legacy, and monetizing that green opportunity, all have to happen this week or all your hard work will be destroyed.*

Lucian looked away. Hope had been right at every turn. He'd held his daughter's ESG attack at bay by following Hope's advice. Eli Scott was the problem. He'd be powered by revenge. That's how Lucian would be if he were Scott. Stop at nothing to destroy Blackwood Energy and Lucian himself. He'd been a pain in the ass since he'd hired him. Lucian had been fed up with his diversity bullshit, valuing employees' input on decisions that affected them *before* Lucian made them, and focusing on that crap he called value-driven leadership. Eliminating him would be more fun than it was to fire him.

But Sarah was problematic. Winchester crossed his arms and awaited Lucian's instructions.

"What about the cleaning woman?" Lucian asked.

"We don't know where she went after the lab in Hominy," Winchester said, rubbing his puffy cheek.

"We need the formulation," Lucian said. "After Munro destroyed and cleaned out that lab, she's the only one who might have it."

"You think she had anything to do with developing it?"

"Hell no! She's a fifty-year-old female janitor. And she's a…" Lucian hesitated and remembered Hope's coaching. "Black."

Winchester shook his head.

Lucian continued. "She's just a mule. Someone Munro was exploiting to steal and carry the information."

Winchester glanced at his phone then back at Lucian. "It's already after noon. We gotta clean this up now. You have to publicly disclose everything this week to reverse your spiral or you're done."

For the first time in his life, Lucian felt the crushing grip of his own guilt. He knew Winchester was an ask-for-forgiveness-not-permission fixer. It had always preserved Lucian's deniability. But he couldn't let that happen this time. "Find Scott and Sarah. Do not kill them! Then find this janitor."

"Sarah won't be coming back here," Winchester said.

"I don't care. Just get them."

"What about the ransom drop tonight?" Winchester asked.

For the first time in Lucian's life, he'd have to get his hands dirty. He'd witness Eli Scott's end at the hands of Winchester and his men to ensure his daughter's survival. After all, Scott was the problem, and once he had the invention under his control, he'd end Sarah's efforts to destroy him. Lucian reached for his jacket and shrugged it on. "Keep it," he said walking around Winchester and toward the door. "And I'm coming with you."

CHAPTER 43

ELI HELD THE ledger in his hand, cupped between his fingers and his palm, like he was carrying a book down the hall in high school—except he wanted to crush it. The ledger held the key to the leverage they needed. It would be the catalyst for Lucian's downfall. He and Sarah had taken the van and followed Butch back downtown. There was no time to go through the ledger. They'd spent their time checking the van's mirrors for any sign of a tail. Once downtown, Butch had carded them into the private executive garage beneath his office building. After they parked the vehicles, he'd given the card to Eli and had taken the van to be "dealt with."

Eli now stood in the corner of Butch's office and scanned the overcast sky, wondering if Jim Munro was out there somewhere, alone, terrified, or accepting of his death. Eli was certain Jim was thinking of his daughter. He'd been assured by Lizzy that Jim's daughter wasn't thinking about him. It wasn't hard to believe.

He noticed Sarah's reflection in the window and turned in time to see her return to the office, two cups of coffee in her hands. She looked different. Then he realized she was still the same, but how he felt about her had changed. She'd saved his life.

He raised the book in his hand. "Ready to go through this?"

He detected a reluctance as the corners of her mouth turned down ever so slightly. "Yes. I guess we should."

They met at the round table tucked in the corner formed by two floor-to-ceiling windows. She handed him his coffee.

"Thanks seems so trite after what you did back there," Eli said, waiting for her to sit in the opposite chair.

Instead, she dragged the chair around the table and sat next to his chair. "You would have done the same for me. I get the sense you would have done the same for most people."

Eli sat next to her and felt her aura warm him. "That's nice of you to say. I would have definitely done it for you." He smiled. She did the same and squeezed his forearm.

He slid the book between them. "Here we go." He opened it to the first page.

Each line was dated, but everything else was gibberish. It was in some alphanumeric code Winchester had used to conceal each entry. Eli drifted his index finger down the page line by line, giving his interpretation of each. The first three lines were the same code. The dates and times corresponded with the attacks on Eli, Hope, and Butch, and the attack in Hominy at the makeshift lab. With each line, Sarah nodded, but the softness in her eyes disappeared, and the tension in her jaw hardened. Eli knew somewhere deep inside her, hope about sparing her father was dying.

Eli's finger stopped on a line—the line where the date coincided with Jim Munro's disappearance on Wednesday night. His finger quivered and he realized he was pressing hard into the page. It wasn't conclusive, but it meant a high likelihood Lucian had ordered Jim's kidnapping. A dark energy filled him. At that moment, he wanted to extract as much pain and suffering from Lucian as humanly possible. Some would call it vengeance, but it was a step beyond that.

"Eli?" Sarah's voice pulled him out of his obsession.

He could see the struggle in her eyes. She'd recognized his visceral reaction, and he could see it hurt her. "I'm so sorry." He reached over and cupped her hand between his. "I was just thinking about all the pain this has caused."

Sarah's eyes glazed with tears, but she didn't let them fall. "I know this may implicate my father in this. I have to be sure, and while I wanted to take control of his business because I know that would hurt him, I don't want to kill him."

Eli warmed her hands in his. "I get that. I can't stand what he's done: to you, to me, and to Jim. But I understand he's your father. It's just an emotion I'll deal with. I'll take control of what my actions will be. We can't guarantee how he'll be treated under the law, but I can assure you, I care about you and what you need. I won't kill him."

She couldn't speak and just nodded, forcing something between a grimace and a smile. She pulled her hands from his, dabbed one eye with a curled index finger, and fluttered through the remaining pages. She turned to Eli, sighed, and said, "There's enough here to shortcut the proxy battle."

Eli leaned back. "It also gives us leverage."

"If Winchester and his men don't get to us first."

"He knows we have this. Winchester saw it. As long as we do, it's a risk for them to hurt or kill us. Buys us some time."

"We only have six hours left. Do you think they'll follow through?"

"Yes." Eli leaned forward and focused on Sarah. "They need whatever this invention is. They still have Jim and could kill him. No telling what Winchester could do."

Eli's burner vibrated in his pocket. He pulled it out. "Hey, Hudson."

"By god, we found her," he said in his thick Oklahoma accent. "Even a blind squirrel finds an acorn every now and then."

"Where?"

"There were two sides of a duplex, walking distance from the old area office, rented at the same time. About a week ago. For three months. The manger said the guy paid in cash. Ten grand. Said to keep it quiet. That matches what you said Jim pulled out in cash last week. Right?"

"Yes. Is she there?"

"Guess so. I haven't seen her. There ain't no garages on the units and the driveways are empty. It's either empty, someone dropped her off, or she walked there on foot."

"Thanks for finding her. Can you keep an eye on the place? We can be there in an hour."

"Already done. Be careful. Sounds like you're catchin' 'em faster than you can string 'em."

"That I am! See you in an hour."

Eli hung up. Sarah stared at him. "Hudson thinks he found Abena. We gotta get to Hominy. If we find Abena, I think we find out about this invention—any maybe Jim."

"What if she's not there?"

Eli had avoided thinking about that alternative. He knew what it meant.

"Then Jim is a dead man."

CHAPTER 44

ELI CHECKED THE equipment in his duffel, glanced at Sarah beside him under the tailgate of the black Suburban, and adjusted his cap. The small executive garage was empty; it felt like an ice box and smelled like concrete dust and stale exhaust. Following Eli's lead, Sarah had borrowed a cap from Butch's collection in his office hoping it would cover her short blonde hair. She looked sporty with the hat on, but she was laser-focused as she went through the items in her bag. The longer he looked at her, the more the conflict twisted his insides into a knot. He wondered if he could keep the promise he'd made to her.

His phone vibrated in his pocket. He pulled the burner out and checked the caller ID. It was Butch.

"You got what you need?"

"Yes. Just loading up." Eli smiled at Sarah.

"Good. I got some bad news," Butch said.

"What's up?"

"Hope Munro just called me. Said she needed to talk to you right away. She was crying. Said she's been contacted again. Wouldn't tell me anything more."

Sarah stared at Eli. He just wagged his head, covered the phone, and said, "It's Hope again."

She rolled her eyes and headed for the passenger seat.

Eli closed the tailgate, then trotted to the driver's door. He opened it, slid inside, and started the truck.

He put the phone back to his ear. "I know we can't trust her, but did she say how I could reach her?" Eli asked.

"Said you had her number."

Eli hesitated and looked at Sarah. "Did *you* believe her?"

"Yes. But after what Lizzy told you, I'm not sure."

Sarah was shaking her head.

"All right. We're headed out now. I'll touch base with Hudson when we get there."

"Copy that. Be safe,"

"Thanks, man."

Butch hung up. Eli pulled from the spot and headed out of the garage. The day was gray and it looked like it could snow again any minute. Eli prayed it wouldn't. They couldn't spare the time.

He turned onto the city street.

Sarah looked as if she were holding her breath. Finally, she let out a deep sigh and said, "What did she say this time?"

"She wouldn't tell Butch. Wants to tell me directly. Got another message, I think."

"We're going to have to hear what she has to say, aren't we." The disgust on Sarah's face said everything.

"Afraid so. Sounded like she was upset."

"Get out the Oscar."

"I hear you. Still, I have to call."

Sarah turned away and stared ahead.

As he wound along the surface streets that led to I-244, he dialed Hope's number.

"I'm so glad you called," Hope said, her words garbled by her sobbing.

Eli remembered Lizzy's warning about how crying would only

make the likelihood of a lie higher. Crocodile tears. "Butch said you were contacted."

"Yes. But we have to meet in person. I can't say this over the phone."

Eli wanted to choke her through the phone. "You're kidding me. I know you're working for Blackwood and Winchester. Why should I believe you?"

"Oh, God. Oh, God, no." She bawled for a few seconds, then continued. "I love my father. He's the only one who ever understood me." She sobbed again. "I took the Blackwood job before any of this happened. Blackwood's been forcing me to finish my work on the proxy fight. Do you think he's involved? With my dad's kidnapping?"

He eyed Sarah who just stared back at him. "I think you know the answer to that," he said.

"No, Eli. You said you'd help me. Dad said you were the only one to trust. Please just meet me. After, you can do what you want. Please, God. Please."

Sarah caught his attention. She shook her head *no*. He looked at the clock on the dash.

"I only have a minute. You'll have to meet me at the Gathering Place. On the bridge to the boathouse. You have ten minutes to get there. Then I'm gone."

Eli hung up, spun the SUV around, and headed toward Riverside Drive.

"You're kidding me!" Sarah said.

"I have to do this. Trust me."

"It's not you I'm not trusting. It could be a trap."

"It's a cold Sunday. Nobody will be there. If someone is, I'll see them. I'll mask up and have on my sunglasses."

"What do you expect to get?"

"A clear conscience. If she's telling the truth about any of it, and I ignore it, I couldn't live knowing I had a hand in Jim's death."

Sarah looked as if she'd acquiesced. "I understand."

Eli drove down Riverside Drive at the speed limit. He was at the park in four minutes, and after making a U-turn to head back north, he pulled into a parking area with an immediate exit back onto Riverside. He shoved the shifter into park.

"Stay here," he said. "Keep the engine running. If anything happens, get out of here and call Butch. He'll know what to do."

"I'm going with you," Sarah said.

Eli shook his head. "I need you here. In the driver's seat. Just in case. I can't risk both our lives, especially with her track record. I'll be right back. Give me five minutes from now, then go."

Eli opened his door. Sarah opened hers.

She came around to his side of the car and kissed his cheek. "Be careful. And hurry back." She climbed into the driver's seat of the idling SUV.

Eli made his way along the pathways through the trees and into the open-lawn areas of the park. While the surgical mask warmed his cheeks, his eyes watered in the frigid wind. Standing at the top of a hill, he could see both snow-covered lawns, the two pathways into the area, and the entrance to the bridge. The light snow from last night remained, and only one set of footprints led from the path on his left onto the bridge entrance. The park was empty, as it always was on his winter runs on bad weather days. He carefully made his way along the line of trees, eyes constantly scanning the area, until he approached the entrance to the bridge. He spotted Hope in her long black winter coat at the center of the bridge. She was alone.

When he walked up, she turned to face him. Her eyes were red, and her pink cheeks were tear-streaked.

"Oh, thank you!" she said. She sniffled and wiped her nose with a Kleenex from her coat pocket.

"Okay. Tell me what you received."

"The video showed my father. He looked much worse than before." She started crying then sucked in a few sobbing breaths.

"They said to bring the formula, the sample, the inventor, and the ledger." She reached out and grabbed his arm. "Ledger? What do they mean ledger?" She sobbed again. "Eli, he looked so much worse. They're going to kill him. Do you know about a ledger?"

That was it. Blackwood and Winchester were behind it. He made no effort to hide his disgust. "Anything else?"

"No," she wiped her face with the back of her hand. "That was it."

"Okay. I'm going to go. You stay right here until I'm out of sight." Eli turned and walked away.

"Where are you headed?" she called out.

Eli looked at her over his shoulder. "Stay here." He kept walking in the snow.

"But how will I reach you?"

"You won't. I'll reach you if I need to," he said, trying not to yell.

"What about the meeting tonight? It's just a few hours away. Do you have everything?" she yelled.

Eli stopped and turned. He didn't trust her. With anything. "I'll be there."

He turned and headed back toward the Suburban.

CHAPTER 45

AS ELI TROTTED up the hill, carefully retracing his footprints in the snow, he saw him. A lone police officer was coming uphill from the center of the park. He was tracking Hope's footprints. Moving through the tree line, Eli slowed his movements, hoping to buy a little time before the officer spotted him. He knew he had the advantage for now, since he had the uphill position on the slippery snow-covered hillside. But that advantage would be erased in a split second with the officer's radio. Eli kept moving up the hill along the tree line, and when he reached the walking path on the other side of the trees on the way to the parking lot, he saw Hope walking toward the officer.

Speeding to a run, Eli looked back just as Hope met the officer. They argued for a few seconds, then, reluctantly, Hope pointed up the hill in Eli's direction. The last thing he saw before he disappeared down the path was the officer reaching for the mic clipped to his shoulder. Sprinting now, he burst through the tree line, slid to a stop in front of the Suburban. Grabbing the hood with his hands, pulled himself around the front of the SUV, and jumped into the passenger seat.

"Go! Go!"

Sarah shoved the vehicle into reverse and spun the tires, backing out of the space. Then slamming the shifter into drive, she swung the fishtailing SUV onto the ramp down to Riverside Drive.

Checking her mirrors, she said, "Who's after us?"

"The Tulsa Police."

"Shit. I knew it was a trap."

"I don't think so. They may have just followed her tracks in the snow. Didn't look like it was a setup. Keep it around the speed limit. The cops won't know what we're driving."

Sarah slowed down. "What did she say?"

Eli knew this would ramp up the conflict between them. He thought about how to say it but then decided to be open and honest. "She said that she got another video. It said the meeting was still on but to bring the formula, the inventor, and the ledger."

Sarah took her eyes from the road and looked at Eli. "Ledger?"

Eli saw her connect the dots in her mind. He hated the sadness filling her eyes.

"He's behind it, then," she said. "No question."

Eli just nodded.

She stared ahead as she maneuvered the SUV through the side streets. After a few moments, she said, "We don't have an invention, a formula, or its inventor."

"That's why we're going to Hominy."

"But were almost out of time. Maybe I need to confront him."

Eli knew who she meant but asked anyway. "Who?"

"My father." Sarah stopped at the intersection. To the left was the ramp toward Hominy; to the right was the route back into town. She turned and faced Eli. "Winchester won't do anything without him. That is, as long as he's paying him. Maybe I can convince him to shut it down."

"He'll just deny it. He already did. We can't burn the time. Take the ramp to I-244 and let's get to Hominy."

"Maybe I can convince him."

Eli could see the struggle in her shifting eyes. "Look. If we find

Abena, maybe she directs us to this invention. We'll at least have that. Your father has taken things this far. Lied to you. He tried to take me out. We can't risk Jim's life. We've gotta get there with something." Frustrated, Eli looked away, then turned back to her said, "You don't have to do this. You've done more than enough. I can drop you at the Mayo and go myself."

She held her gaze on Eli, her eyes vibrating now. A flash of anger ripped across her face. She snapped her head forward, yanked the steering wheel to the left, and gunned it up the ramp toward Hominy.

CHAPTER 46

ELI SAT QUIETLY in the passenger seat and stared at the darkening sky. It could snow any moment, and that was the last thing they needed. It was after two with only five hours left until the ransom drop. Every minute counted now. They had to talk to Abena and see if she could tell them about what she and Jim had done.

He'd traveled this road hundreds of times as a young engineer, heading the other way, from Hominy into Tulsa, to get a taste of "civilization." In his youth, that had been defined by asphalt rash and McDonalds. But he'd learned the country ways and had come to love its people.

As Sarah drove in silence up Highway 99, dry warm air screamed from the dashboard vents. She'd been quiet since the intersection in Tulsa. Her expression hadn't changed: intensely staring at the road ahead with distress radiating from her face. Eli had filled the time trying to figure out where he'd gone wrong. What he'd said, and what he *should* say now. It felt familiar. He'd done something wrong. Worse yet, it was as if he hadn't measured up in some way.

Then, a conversation with Lizzy came to mind. They'd been working on that very sensation for months. Not being enough. Trying to figure out how to *make* someone happy. Trying to *make* someone like him. Trying to *read* someone else's mind and say or do just the *right* thing. He'd realized then, with Lizzy's help, it had always been a fool's game. He'd backslid into that mindset again.

Eli closed his eyes. He hadn't realized the setup when it happened at seven years old, but he recognized it now and told himself he was *always* enough. He opened his eyes. Realizing silence was the coward's way out, he said, "Are you doing okay, Sarah? I get the sense that you're in pain, and I hate to see that."

She blinked her eyes several times, then sighed. "I guess it's that you know what's going on between me and my father. I think you understand why I feel the way I do. He's my father. And yes, ever since I was a teenager and realized what he'd been doing to my mother, I hated everything he'd done. But before that, when I was just a kid, he was my dad. He did things with me. We were close. Yes, I'd like to take away his power and control over the company and see him be held accountable for what he's done. But there's a part of me that loves the part of him that loved *me*. And that's why I don't want him physically harmed. I feel like I'm sacrificing that to help you. And I think I just realized that I know nothing about why you want me to sacrifice so much to make him pay?"

Trapped between wanting a deeper relationship with Sarah and his steadfast commitment to save his mentor, Eli sensed this was one of those moments in life where being open was necessary, but he had to let go of the outcome. Sarah's reaction was her right. They were her feelings and not something to manipulate or control. Whether she wanted the same thing he did would be up to Sarah. He'd learned, with Lizzy's help, that being open was a way to live life more deeply. She'd told him that intimacy actually broke down into four words: *In to me see*. She'd said that it took courage to be open and accept whatever may come. But relationships, deep loving relationships, were built on that. It had been the one thing that stood between him and the loving partnership he'd sought. He'd had a parade of failed relationships. He didn't want to let this chance slip away.

"I hear you. I appreciate everything you're doing. I respect how you feel, and I will do everything I can to keep your father, and especially your mother, from getting hurt. As far as my commitment to risk everything to help Jim, despite his daughter's lies, I owe him my life. All of it."

"Can I ask why?" she asked, still looking down the road.

For the first time in his life, since he'd sorted out his feelings with Lizzy, he jumped off into the unknown. "Jim was always the father I never had. It was because of something that happened when I was seven years old." He told Sarah the story he'd told Lizzy about his mother's suicide attempt.

When he finished, Sarah glanced at him. "I'm so sorry."

"Thanks," Eli said, He kept his eyes forward, but he was back in another moment from his past. "Then, eleven years ago, my mother was diagnosed with aggressive brain cancer. I spent four weeks in the hospice with her. My father refused to go with me. He said it was too painful. I was furious. I learned later that he'd already taken up with someone else. But Jim sent me to my mother's side. Told me to take as much time as I needed. He said it wasn't vacation time and I'd still get paid. He could have been fired for doing that. But he knew how important it would be to me. The last moments I spent with her, she told me I was a good boy. Just as if I was that little boy again. I was thirty-two years old. But she was apologizing to that little boy. Because of Jim, I was there for her.

"Jim mentored me at work from the beginning and has been like a father to me. I am who I am today because of him. So I'd give everything to help get him back. And Lizzy has helped me put all of that into perspective. Another kind human being who helped me."

Sarah kept her focus on the road, her eyes said she understood. She put her hand on his thigh. "I didn't know, Eli. I'm so sorry you went through all of that. Guess we have a lot more in common that I thought."

Eli sighed. It felt as if he'd just taken off a lead jacket. "I appreciate you." He covered her hand with his.

He noticed they were entering the town of Cleveland, fifteen minutes south of Hominy.

Looking to her left, Sarah slowed the SUV. A Highway Patrol car sat idling in the gas station parking lot.

"You think they're looking for us? Hope told them?" she asked.

"There's no telling what she said to them. I don't know that it was a setup—she seemed genuinely surprised. She's fooled me before, though."

They continued north on the highway and the state trooper stayed put. But Eli didn't feel relieved. Every minute closer to Hominy was a minute closer to the end—another outcome he might not be able to control.

CHAPTER 47

AS THEY DROVE into Hominy, snow began to fall. The wind had picked up. The heavy veil of snow blew sideways across the road. Sarah leaned forward, peering through the thick flakes, headlights and fog lights on, looking for the one stop sign that marked the block before the turn into town. Eli knew getting to Abena wouldn't be easy. She'd be scared and on alert. Jim had been taken, and she'd be next. They didn't want to draw any attention to her either. Blackwood and his goons knew the area. He was certain they'd been searching for her, too.

Sarah gently rolled the heavy SUV to the stop sign. "Turn left here?"

"Next block. Then turn right a few blocks down Main."

The snow was heavy now and visibility was down to ten yards. The outlines of the buildings on either side of Main Street were barely visible, and Eli strained his eyes to see them. "Okay. Turn right here." Eli heard the accumulating snow crunching under the tires as Sarah turned onto Hudson's street. "Go about four blocks. Their house will be on the right. A white picket fence."

"White?" Sarah chuckled. She was leaning over the steering wheel now, searching the right side of the road. They were moving at a crawl. "Not sure we'll see it in this whiteout."

Eli spotted the fence and the faint outline of the two-story house. The light-gray siding was nearly invisible in the storm. "Right here."

Sarah turned the Suburban into the wide driveway and pulled next to the old red-on-white pickup. The small carriage lights on the wraparound front porch glowed in the blowing snow.

Eli turned up the collar on his jacket. "Okay. You ready?"

Sarah pulled the hood up on her jacket and glanced at Eli. "No. But let's go."

Eli looked up at the weather. "Leave it running," he said. He got out quickly. Shielding his eyes against the pelting snow, he waited for Sarah at the entrance to the walkway that led to the porch. The snow found its way down the back of his neck, but he refused to shiver. Eli heard the crisp snapping of the barely visible OU flag in the front yard as it flapped wildly in the wind.

Together, they walked through the snow to the front door. Just as they got there, it opened.

Hudson was dressed in a black sweatshirt and jeans with the same oil-smudged OU ballcap pushed back on his head. "If this was rain, I think the animals would start pairin' up," he said, grinning and inviting them in with his hand.

Eli let Sarah enter first, and he followed her.

"Around to the right, young lady. In the kitchen," Hudson said.

They walked through the small entry and immediately into the tiny kitchen. The smell of warm coffee and cinnamon rolls filled the air. At the small maple table in the corner, Sonny stood, scraping his thick legs against the underside of the table. Sherry had her silvery strawberry hair pulled up into a tight spiral. She removed a baking sheet full of rolls from the oven, then she set them on the stove.

"Nice to see you again, Miss Sarah," Sonny said. Sarah hugged him, and Eli and Sonny bumped fists.

"Sarah, this is Sherry, my better three-quarters," Hudson said.

Sherry wiped her hands on her apron and offered one to Sarah. Sarah shook it.

"Nice to meet you." She glanced at Hudson. "I hope he hasn't been like this the entire time." She leaned close to Sarah and whispered, "I told him he was funny forty years ago. Big mistake."

Sarah chuckled.

Eli went to Sherry and hugged her.

"So good to see you. Wish it was under better circumstances," she said.

"I just play it as it lies," Eli said. "I'll take seeing you any way I can get it."

"Okay. Let's sit down and work this out real quick before we have a foot of snow," Hudson said.

"I'm going to get these ready," Sherry said, moving to the stove and grabbing a bowl of icing.

The rest of them sat at the table. Hudson had a drawing showing the layout of the complex already on the table. Sherry delivered cinnamon rolls and coffee. The warm coffee and glazed hot cinnamon rolls drove the remaining chill from Eli's bones.

"This is what we know," Hudson said. The sketch showed a dozen buildings around a circular court. Hudson pointed to one to the right, at the entrance to the complex. "These are the units we think she's in. These are one-story, stand-alone duplexes. You can see this one is visible from the others in the complex, but with the weather, probably only this one across the street and the one next door can see it. I didn't see any movement. No car. No tracks in the snow when I was over there earlier."

"Lights?" Eli asked.

"Not many windows, but I didn't see any." Hudson pointed to the road leading to the complex. "We should take your rig, and park it here. Sarah, Sonny, and I will hang back. You need to go in on foot. Don't know who's watching. You can get around the curve and to the front door here. Don't know how you'll get in. If I were her, I wouldn't answer the door."

"I've got a prybar in the car," Eli said.

"Be careful there, cowboy. She might have a gun," Hudson said.

"I'll go with him," Sarah said.

Everyone at the table looked at her.

"Now who's the tree full of young owls?" she said, half smiling. "He needs backup close by. A lookout, too."

"No," Eli said. "Too dangerous."

Sarah looked directly at Eli. "Are you forgetting what happened at Winchester's?"

Hudson and Sonny shared a curious look, then stared at Eli.

"You've got a point," Eli said. "She can handle it, guys. We'll get Abena and text you to bring the car around when we're ready."

"All right. But if anyone else shows up, we're coming fast," Sonny said.

"Just don't spook her," Eli said.

Eli wasn't sure if Abena would cooperate. She'd known Jim had been taken, and if she knew about the invention, she'd know she was a target. But she'd come to his home once seeking his help. The only problem was the news that he was now a suspect in her own disappearance. While she would know that wasn't the truth, she'd be scared. If there was any doubt about Eli in her mind, she could be trouble, and they were running out of time.

CHAPTER 48

RIDING IN THE back seat of the Suburban, Eli closed his eyes and controlled his breathing. He focused on the task ahead. He'd done this many times before, but not with his mentor's life hanging in the balance. He hoped Abena was there. She held the key to Jim's rescue. Perhaps she knew about the invention. He guessed she did. Finding out what her role had been in acquiring it could also help in identifying its inventor. She could have the sample and the process to create it or know where it was. That all led to Jim, and with less than four hours left until the drop, there were no other options. If she wasn't there or didn't have the information, Jim would be killed.

Reviewing his mental checklist, he knew precision mattered. He was confident in the things he could control. Minimize risk, anticipate obstacles, and improvise. His heartrate slowed and he opened his eyes. He looked at Sarah next to him. She stared straight ahead, but it wasn't confidence he saw. It was worry. She tapped her foot lightly on the floorboard. He reached across and squeezed her hand. She nervously smiled at him. He calmly nodded. "We've got this."

Hudson drove through the backstreets with caution. The snow wasn't letting up and the last thing they needed was to end up in a ditch. The driving blizzard would provide additional cover, and Eli's risk assessment improved just a little. It was 3:35 and the sun, wherever it was, had moved lower in the winter sky, ushering in an early dusk. As Hudson slowed the Suburban, Eli checked his Glock and reached behind him for the prybar. Sarah checked her gun and tucked it back under her jacket, pulling the hood over her head. As Hudson pulled to the side of the road, Eli tugged his cap lower.

Hudson turned and hooked his arm over the back of the front seat. "Okay, kids. You're on. We're here and ready. We'll keep watch and wait for your text."

"Thanks, Hudson. Thanks for everything," Eli said, patting Hudson's arm.

"Yes. Thank you both for everything," Sarah said.

"I feel like we're at the Emmys," Sonny said to Hudson.

"Then you better thank your momma," Hudson said.

"Okay you two. We'll see you in a minute," Eli said. He nodded to Sarah to open her door. She did and got out. Eli slid over and stepped out into the snow.

"Eli," Hudson yelled over the storm. "Remember, there are two ways in. We can only watch one."

Eli nodded. "Sarah's got that covered." Eli closed the door.

The wind had stiffened, and snowflakes pelted his face, forcing him to squint. Shielding his eyes with his forearm, he trudged through the deepening snow with Sarah right behind him. The wind whistled in the branches of the scattered trees, but their footsteps were muffled by the snow. He followed the bar ditch on his right around the turn to the entrance into the complex. He spotted the single pole streetlight at the entrance that gave the falling snow a yellow tint. The outline of the first duplex appeared ahead on their right. He paused, and Sarah stepped next to him. He checked the visibility to the other adjacent units. He could barely see their silhouettes. If a person were at their front doors, he'd never see them. He couldn't even see their front porches. He pointed to the front door of the unit.

"We'll go straight to the front door." He pointed to the road that disappeared into the blizzard. "You'll have to watch that roadway in."

She nodded, and he started for the duplex. The snow was deep enough that he couldn't distinguish the walkway from the rest of the yard. He made a beeline for the small light he assumed marked the front door. The cold was numbing his hands. He hoped he could still handle his gun. Once at the front door, he stopped. Sarah turned, putting her back against his, and scanned the unguarded roadway into the complex.

Leaning his ear against the door, he listened over the low growl of the blizzard. He covered his other ear. No radio, no TV, no noise at all. "Here we go," he said over his shoulder. He pounded on the door. "Abena Williams," he yelled. He heard a metal-on-metal sound. Maybe a rifle being cocked. He stepped to the left to avoid a gunshot blast. Reaching behind him, he moved Sarah with him.

He pounded again. "Miss Williams. It's Eli Scott." He hoped that familiarity was a good thing and the bulletins on TV hadn't made it negative. He listened for a few seconds. There was no movement he could detect. He raised the frozen prybar in his left hand. He turned and tapped Sarah on the shoulder. He showed her the prybar. She spun and stood behind him and placed her hand on his back. He felt her other hand higher on his back, probably holding her gun.

In one fluid motion, he thrusted the prybar into the jamb just above the latch and ripped the door open. Dropping the prybar, he grabbed his Glock and stepped through the doorway. It was dark inside other than a small fluorescent light tucked in the hood of the stove. He moved to the middle of the entryway. The storm still howled in the open doorway, muting any sound from inside. He scanned the kitchen on the right and a small living room on the left. "It's clear," he whispered to Sarah behind him. As he moved into the kitchen, he heard Sarah close the door. He stopped and listened again. A hallway to the right of the kitchen led to what he assumed were the two bedrooms Hudson had mentioned in the floorplan. He worried what he might find there if Blackwood's people had gotten there first.

Then, he heard a faint shuffling, as if someone were adjusting their position. He pointed down the hallway then raised his fist shoulder high. Sarah stopped. He moved slowly down the hallway and reached the first bedroom door. It was open. He cleared it quickly, then moved to the last bedroom door at the end of the hallway. The door was closed but not latched. It was the last hiding place. He was sure he'd heard a noise. Easing the door ajar, he peeked through the crack between the door and jamb. He spotted a reflection in the bedroom window of a person crouched behind the door holding a rifle.

He rammed his shoulder into the door and spun, reaching behind the door and grabbing the barrel of a rifle. The gun fired, stinging his hand. He yanked the gun away and targeted the person behind the door.

"Don't kill me. Please," a woman pleaded in what sounded like a British accent.

Eli flipped on the light. Abena Williams cowered on the floor with her hands raised over her head. Sarah rushed down the hallway and stopped in the open doorway. Eli holstered his gun. He reached down and helped Abena to her feet. "We're not here to hurt you. I'm Eli Scott."

"I know who you are," Abena said, lowering her hands, her eyes wide. She wiped tears from her smooth black skin. "Who the hell is this?"

"I'm Sarah Blackwood."

Abena's eyes grew wider, then narrowed on Sarah. "I'm not helping any Blackwood!"

CHAPTER 49

ABENA WILLIAMS LOOKED at Eli with crossed arms. Eli's heart raced, knowing that he was looking at the one person who could lead him to Jim. The smell of mildew and grease permeated the cramped unit. The storm's chill leaked in around the aged windows. Her smooth dark ebony skin glistened in the kitchen lights. Her high cheekbones, almond eyes, and lack of visible wrinkles belied her fifty-year-old age. A colorful headwrap hid all but glimpses of her dark hair. She shifted her eyes from Eli to Sarah and back with a look of concern. But it wasn't the wrinkled crow's feet, creased-brow concern. It looked effortless, as if it were her resting face. Her eyes glistened with intelligence.

Eli knew they had to alleviate her concern. "Miss Williams, like I said, we're not here to hurt you. It's exactly the opposite. We're here to help you and find my friend Jim Munro."

Her eyes widened on Eli. "You say that, Mr. Scott, but you're a wanted man," Abena said in her staccato British accent. "Wanted for questioning in *my* disappearance." Then she focused on Sarah. "And you're a Blackwood. Your daddy is a racist, and according to Jim, behind this whole mess."

Eli wanted to be gentle but firm with her. They were running out of time. "Think about it, Miss Williams, you of all people would know if I was involved in your so-called disappearance. I didn't take you. I even met with your son."

Abena's eyebrows shot up. "My son? You talked to Darnell?"

"Yes. I did."

"How is he?"

"He was worried. But he was fine when I talked to him. He helped me. He found me through Professor Gregory."

"You know Professor Gregory, too?"

"Yes. He was very kind. He and Professor Perry helped us find you."

Abena nodded toward Sarah. "Then why are you working with her?"

Sarah shook her head. "If you get online and check, you'll see that I don't agree with my father on anything. Especially his view on race. Right now, I'm battling him and his board for control of the company for those very reasons," Sarah said.

Eli pointed at Sarah. "She *volunteered* to help me find you and find Jim."

Abena cocked her head and gave Sarah a silent side-eye. Then she slowly nodded. "Okay." She uncrossed her arms and looked at both of them. "Call me Abena. Why are you here?"

Eli holstered his gun. "We need to know what you were doing with Jim. It may help us find him."

"We have a deadline of seven tonight," Sarah said.

Eli tried not to flinch, but he wished she hadn't said that. The added pressure wouldn't help.

"Deadline? For what?"

Eli decided since the cat was already out of the bag, he should be honest with her. "His kidnappers asked for an exchange. Jim for whatever the invention was that he had and its inventor."

Surprise and fear spread across her face. Her eyes widened.

"What is it, Abena?" Sarah asked.

Abena remained quiet. She looked down at the floor, deep in thought. Her lips parted, then her eyes found Eli's.

"That's why he destroyed the lab," Abena said.

"Who destroyed the lab?" Eli asked.

She appeared as if she'd just solved a riddle. "Jim destroyed the lab so they couldn't get it. He knew they were coming for him."

"Who was coming?" Eli said.

Abena sneered at Sarah. "Her daddy."

"How did you end up here? We saw your car at the lab in the old shop," Eli said.

Abena nodded. "Yes. After I helped Jim destroy everything, I went back to Tulsa. Someone was at my apartment, so I went to find Jim. He wasn't there. He'd talked a lot about you. So I went to your house, but you weren't home. I had nowhere else to go. Jim told me to come here if anything happened. Come here and wait. So I parked at the shop and walked here."

"Wait for what?"

"I assumed for him. But you said someone has him." Abena turned to Sarah. "Your daddy has him."

"Abena," Eli said, "Do you know anything about an invention?"

Her eyes said she did. She hesitated. "It's a renewable organic replacement for a rare earth metal in a lithium battery."

Eli knew that battery technology was rapidly developing. But sourcing the rare earth metals required was costly, not to mention the environmental and human cost of their mining. "What metal?" Eli asked.

Abena cocked her head again. "Do you know anything about the DRC?"

"A little. The Democratic Republic of Congo," Eli said. He'd decided not to mention what Darnell had told him and see if their stories matched.

"I know it's full of those metals you talked about for batteries," Sarah said. "But it's a mess how they mine them."

Abena nodded in agreement. "I am from the DRC. Came here with my parents as a child." Abena's attention drifted off to another place and time. "Before that we worked in those mines. It was terrible. I saw some of my friends break their backs, their spines get crushed. We worked knee-deep in poison. Mothers, fathers, children—they got sick. Some got cancer. Some died. Still, we worked to make enough money to eat. We didn't see any of the money people pay for their expensive electric cars.

"But my parents got me out. Out to America. Here for a better life. They worked hard so I could go to school. Ever since the first day I worked in the mine, I wanted to learn how to stop it. I studied math and chemistry and biology in high school. Started at Oklahoma State in biochemistry. But then they got sick and died. From working in the mine."

"Abena, who's the inventor?" Eli asked.

She ignored him. "I went to work at the University of Tulsa. The only job I could get. Cleaning the laboratories. I had Darnell and then his father died. But I kept going. On my own. I got to see them work. I got to see the students' notes. I got to know Professor Gregory and Professor Perry. I read textbooks. Then I collected the old equipment."

Eli knew where this was going. "Abena, you didn't steal the invention. Did you?"

"Steal. No. I've never stolen anything in my entire life. My parents were good people. Even as poor as we were, we all knew that would be wrong."

Eli looked at Sarah. She looked stunned. She'd reached the same conclusion.

"Who's the inventor?" Eli asked, again.

Abena proudly pulled her shoulders back. "I am. I developed an organic renewable compound that replaces cobalt in the lithium-ion battery."

CHAPTER 50

ELI RUBBED HIS forehead in an effort to relieve the pressure that had immediately erupted. News he thought would be Jim's salvation now grew into a dilemma that signaled Jim's demise. A myriad of emotions boiled inside. The plan he'd had now was no longer a plan. There wasn't a world where he'd turn over any human being, let alone a fifty-year-old single mother, to Blackwood in exchange for his friend. She'd created something that would save thousands of men, women, and children. Even Jim would kill that trade. He'd rather die.

Snapped from his disappointed trance by a gust rattling the living room window screen, Eli raised his head and settled his gaze on Abena. She looked terrified. She hadn't reached the same conclusion. "I won't let them get you," he said. "That won't be part of the deal." He felt better, but her shifting eyes and quivering chin said she didn't.

He glanced at Sarah. She seemed to be doing another calculation. The guilt of her father now seemed unbearable. Eli saw her tilt her head back, take a deep breath, and maybe accept her father's fate.

"We need to see if we can get the sample and procedure for your invention," Eli said.

Abena shook her head. "I don't have it. I gave the digital files to Jim. We destroyed everything else."

Eli felt his hope deflate. Stunned by what he'd heard, he looked at Sarah.

"What was in those files?" Sarah asked.

"The formulation, the process, a diagram of the bench scale design of the pilot test, videos demonstrating the results of the tests that showed that this formulation performed better than any other published demonstration. Everything."

"What did Jim do with it?" Eli asked.

"I think he took the files and compressed them. Then he said he made a copy and destroyed the hard drives and deleted the information in the cloud."

"Only one copy exists then?" Eli asked to confirm what he'd heard.

"As far as I know."

"Any idea where he may have put it?" Eli asked.

"He held on to it. He was going to bring it up here to a meeting on Thursday."

"Here?" Sarah said.

"Yes. The plan was to come to the makeshift lab and run a demonstration."

"For whom?" Eli asked.

"Jim had made arrangements through an investment banker to have their client meet us at the lab."

Eli's hope flared again. "What bank?"

"I don't know. But it was one of those fancy ones in New York."

"That narrows it down to at least twenty," Sarah said.

"And their client?" Eli suspected he knew the answer.

"Jim didn't know at first. But later, on the way up on Wednesday, he found out it was Blackwood. We both panicked. He knew what that meant. It wasn't good. He called the banker and said the deal was off. But he was worried that Blackwood's people would find him. Try to steal it."

Eli knew that without the data, the only chance to save Jim was to find him before the meeting. He checked the time. It was already 4:17 p.m. They had less than two hours to find him.

"How did you find Jim in the first place?"

Abena looked confused. "What?"

"How did you meet?" Eli asked.

"Oh. Jim had done quite a bit for the Greenwood District. He'd helped several Black-owned businesses, donated scholarships, and spent time with young Black businessmen, mentoring them. I had heard his name and seen him in the area and a friend of mine introduced us. He said he was heavily involved in alternative energy and one thing led to another."

None of the information provided any clues to Jim's location now. Sarah turned to Eli. "You said that both his cars were at his house?"

"Yes," Eli answered. He knew that meant either Jim never started on the trip to Hominy Wednesday night or he took another car.

Eli turned back to Abena. "Do you know if Jim made it up here on Wednesday night?"

"No. I didn't hear anything after we destroyed the lab and the data to keep it out of Blackwood's hands." Abena turned and stared at Sarah.

Eli's heart sunk deeper into the darkness engulfing it. If Jim had never left Tulsa, that was where he was taken. He could still be there. It was at least an hour away. Probably two hours in this weather. While it was a long shot, Eli had one last question.

"What kind of car was Jim driving Wednesday when you destroyed the lab?"

Abena dropped her head to think. She covered her lips with her fingers, then removed them. "I think it was his black Range Rover."

Eli felt a smile drifting across his face. He turned to Sarah. "He only owns a Lexus sedan and a Ford Bronco."

"Rental?" she said.

He reached in his pocket for his burner. "Rental. We need to get out of here. Butch may be able to trace the rental car."

He texted Hudson to come get them. He looked for a response. The longer he waited, the tighter his muscles became. After a minute, he texted again. He didn't get an answer.

"Hudson's not answering," he said to Sarah.

"The storm?" she said.

"Maybe. What's the number for your burner?" Sarah checked her phone and gave it to Eli. He texted her.

"Got it." She shared a worried look with him.

Eli texted Sonny. Again, no answer. The sinking feeling in the pit of his stomach grew. "Something's wrong," he said, zipping his jacket up.

Abena and Sarah stared at him.

"Let's go," he said. "We gotta get out of here."

Sarah zipped her jacket. "Abena. Where's your coat?"

"In the closet."

"Let's get it. We don't have much time."

Abena headed for the front hall closet and started to put on her coat. "Is someone coming?"

Eli walked to the front window and peered out into the storm. He couldn't see beyond the porch. It was a whiteout. If Hudson and Sonny hadn't answered, trouble was already here. He just couldn't see it.

CHAPTER 51

ELI STOOD TO the side of the living room window and hooked the drapes with his fingers. Gently pulling them away from the window frame, he created a thin opening. Darkness had arrived and the snow, only visible in the porch light, was now horizontal, interrupted only by violent gusts. The screens rattled continuously. Someone could be waiting just beyond the porch. He would never spot them.

Turning away from the window, he examined Sarah and Abena waiting in the dimly lit hallway. Abena had a full-length black wool coat, but Sarah only had the hooded windbreaker. His jacket was just as thin as Sarah's but minus a hood. With Hudson and Sonny unresponsive, he had to assume the worst. That thought hit him hard. He swallowed his growing sorrow and thought about Sherry. He had to get to her. Another gust rattled the duplex, and he knew they'd only have minutes before the deadly grip of the storm would overcome their bare hands and thin clothing.

"We need to move. To Hudson's house. I have to get to Sherry and be sure she's okay. Then we'll see if we can use their truck," Eli said.

"You think Hudson and Sonny are gone?" Sarah asked.

Based on the look in Sarah's eyes, Eli thought a response wasn't necessary. He didn't want to upset Abena any further and subtly shook his head.

"Abena, do you have any other sweaters or jackets?" he said.

She nodded and ran into the bedroom. She returned with a thin sweater and another windbreaker. "Put them on," Eli said to Sarah. Both seemed to realize that Abena's clothing would be too small for Eli. The concern was written in their faces as Sarah stretched the tight sweater over her body and shrugged on the two windbreakers.

Eli pulled the Glock from his belt. "Keep your hands covered. I'll lead us out. Sarah will be behind Abena. Stay very close and hold hands if you must. We can't get separated in this. We'll head straight to Hudson's. We can't see them, so they can't see us." He went to the front door, grabbed the deadbolt, and asked, "Ready?"

Both women nodded. Eli opened the door. The gust nearly knocked him over. The snow hit him like a sandblaster. The roar of the storm was all he heard. Raising his free arm to protect his eyes, he stepped out on the porch. Abena grabbed his jacket. Battling the constant wind, he moved slowly off the porch and into the calf-deep snow. The wind ripped at his jacket. The snow stung his face and bare hands. He moved carefully but crisply through the drifts in the general direction of Hudson's. He couldn't feel his feet, but it didn't matter. He wouldn't know if he was on the street or in the grass even if he wasn't numb. Suddenly his foot slipped forward down a steep slope. He pulled it back and stopped, feeling Abena behind him. He assumed it was the bar ditch and turned parallel to the slope.

"Everyone okay?" he yelled as loud as he could. Abena tugged on his jacket. He turned back. She nodded. Through the snow he spotted Sarah with her arm protecting her eyes. Hands and feet now numb, he continued on. He could barely feel the cold Glock in his frozen hand. Finding a target and pulling the trigger would only be reflex instead of feel.

A metallic thud stopped him in his tracks. He looked ahead in the direction of the sound, pointing his shaking Glock toward the sound. He held his breath but heard nothing. Taking a few more steps, he heard it again, twice, as if it were driven by the gusting storm. Now it was much closer.

He cautiously took a few more steps into the darkness and ran into the grill of the black Suburban. He scanned the area with his gun and noticed the dangling sideview mirror banging against the car. Turning and gathering Abena and Sarah, he yelled, "Wait here while I check the car." They both nodded. He took Abena's hand and leaned her against the hood. He grabbed Sarah's arm. "I'll be back."

Still shielding her eyes from the snow, Sarah said, "I've got her."

Feeling his way along the fender, he felt bullet holes in the sheet metal. As he made it to the driver's door, his mind wanted to block out what his eyes would see. Raising his hands, he felt for the door handle. His hand hooked it, and he stopped. He held his breath again, listened, then, fighting off the driving snow, scanned front and back of the vehicle. Satisfied they were alone, he reached into his pocket, pulled out his phone, and turned on its flashlight.

The window was shattered. The seat covered with blood. The windshield had several bullet holes on both sides. The passenger seat was bloodied, and the door was ajar. He shined the light on the ground. The snow had already covered his tracks, so any tracks around the SUV would be gone. Any bodies would be frozen and buried. He turned with his flashlight and scanned the snow ahead and to the right of the SUV. Based on the implied trajectory of the bullet holes, the attackers' bodies would be there. Nothing. If there weren't bodies, they'd taken them along with his friends. He dropped his head. A gaping void opened inside him. He thought about Hudson and Sonny and all the time they'd spent together that had forged their friendship. There wouldn't be any more. His eyes were already watery from the blizzard, but his vision blurred further. He remembered Lizzy's advice, and leaned into the sadness, then breathed and pushed the devastating emptiness away. He replaced it with seething anger and refocused on the mission. He raised his head and went back to Sarah who hugged Abena against the hood, protecting her from the cold.

"They're gone. But we can get inside for a minute and warm up."

He led them to the back door of the SUV and opened it. They climbed in. He slammed the door shut. The wind whistled through the bullet holes in the windshield and snow blew in through the shattered driver's window. The butcher store scent of blood Eli remembered from his missions swirled in the frigid air. Sheltered from the wind, they huddled together warming themselves.

Abena was staring at the front seats and sobbing. Sarah leaned forward and looked around Abena at Eli. She had a look of determination Eli hadn't seen before. "We'll get them," she said.

"We can't stay here much longer. They may be back," Eli said, then blew into his cupped hands. "We've gotta get to Hudson's and check on Sherry."

Sarah rubbed Abena's shoulders. "You almost ready?"

Abena wiped her cheeks and nodded.

"Here we go," Eli said and opened the door.

The trek to Hudson's took half the time it had taken to get to the Suburban. Still, Eli shivered hard, and his hands couldn't feel a thing. Reaching Hudson's picket fence, Eli stopped and peered through the snow. The porch lights were still on, glowing yellow in the fading snowfall. The front door was closed. Perhaps a good sign. Reaching the steps to the porch, Eli turned and said, "Wait here."

He ascended the snow-covered steps. Positioning himself beside the door, he tried the knob. It turned. He heard someone rack a shotgun.

"Sherry. It's me," he yelled, not sure if it was her.

"Show yourself," she yelled from inside.

Eli nearly collapsed at the sound of her voice. Gently, he opened the door, peeked around the door jamb, and spotted Sherry pointing the shotgun at him.

"You alone?" she said.

"Just have Sarah and Abena with me."

She broke down the shotgun, and with sadness in her eyes, said, "Hudson?"

CHAPTER 52

ELI LOCKED EYES with Sherry and his determination morphed into intense sorrow and guilt. What started out as helping Jim's daughter had become a failing endeavor that had already taken two of his best friends and brought a wrenching guilt that deepened with every second he saw Sherry's pain.

"They were attacked. There was nothing in their car. It was shot up pretty bad. Blood on the seats," Eli said.

"They weren't there?" Sherry said, a tinge of hope in her eyes.

"No," Eli said.

She set the shotgun in the corner of the kitchen. "Then they could still be alive."

It was a statement and not a question. Eli let her hang on to that even though he'd seen the car. The chance they survived that attack was near zero.

Eli thought about Blackwood and the logic behind the attack. If they were going through with a ransom drop in less than two hours, why attack? The only reason that made sense was that they thought Eli already had what they wanted. Rather than honor their own deal, they tried to take it. They didn't know he didn't have anything. He forced himself to refocus. The only option now was to find Jim *before* the meeting. It's not like Blackwood would cancel the meeting due to the weather. He still desperately needed Abena's discovery. But the storm would play to Blackwood's advantage. It would provide cover for their movements, ground any aircraft, and result in a much slower response should the authorities respond.

Sarah and Abena peeled off their coats, dropped them on the back of the wooden kitchen chairs, and sat down. Eli stood against the kitchen cabinets, his arms folded. Sherry poured hot coffee for them.

"Okay, Abena, can you think of anything about where Jim might have been taken?" Eli asked.

"No. Other than it had to be Wednesday night."

Sarah leaned back in her chair and her eyes brightened. "Wednesday night after you all destroyed the lab?"

Abena dipped her head.

Sarah looked at Eli. They both said in unison, "The rental."

"The rental was nowhere to be found in Tulsa. At his house," Sarah said.

"And that could mean he was taken while up here," Eli said. "Who left first, Abena? You or Jim?"

"Jim."

Eli pulled his phone out. "You keep watch. I'll call Butch."

The women headed to the windows at the front and back of the house. Eli pulled out his burner. His hands tingled as they thawed. He clumsily dialed Butch's number.

"Hey, cowboy, cops were here again," Butch said. "Stay away. You snowed in up there?"

"Hey, Butch. Worse. Here with Sherry. Hudson and Sonny are missing."

"Shit. I'm on my way!"

"Wait. Need your help. Jim had a rental car on Wednesday. They track those things, don't they?"

"Yup. They can if they want. Need me to find it? My guy has

a way into their GPS tracking. All I need is the make and model. There are only a few companies here in Tulsa."

Eli gave him the information. "Ping me back if you get a hit. Look at last Wednesday and its current location. Gotta be quick. We're out of time."

"Got it. What about Hudson and Sonny?"

"I don't have much hope, but I could use the extra help."

"Say no more. I'll get a few NLBs over there and I'll head up right away."

"Thanks, man."

"Hang on. Just got a text from Jimmy Mac. Says Sonny carried Hudson, both wounded, to his house. Phones compromised and they'd killed the one of the attackers before they'd fled. Sonny says sorry. Rushing them to Cleveland Hospital now."

Eli dropped his head in relief. "Thank God."

"You let Sherry know, and I'll let Renee know about Sonny."

"Will do." Eli ended the call.

Eli thought about Blackwood. He understood what Sarah wanted, but Lucian Blackwood needed to pay for this. He went into the living room where Sarah was looking out the window.

"Storm's letting up," she said.

"Good news. Sonny and Hudson are headed to the hospital. We need to be ready to move. Butch said they can track the rental."

"What about Sherry?"

"I'll let her know. Butch is on his way here, then he and the guys will take care of her. Someone will be here to protect her in a few minutes."

"And Abena?"

"She stays with us. Might need her to help find Jim."

Sherry walked into the room, her eyes hopeful. "I thought I heard Hudson's name?"

Eli hugged her. "He's headed to Cleveland Hospital with Sonny and Jimmy Mac. Someone will be here soon to get you there." Sherry sobbed against his shoulder.

Eli's burner vibrated. He pulled back a little and smiled at Sherry. "He'll be okay. I know it," Eli said. She nodded and wiped her eyes. "Sorry, I gotta take this," he said. "It's Butch." She nodded again and he took the call.

"It's me," Butch said. "We have the last GPS location on Wednesday at 9:07 p.m. between Hominy and Pawhuska just off Highway 99. It goes dead there. Nothing after that."

"Text me the location."

"Will do. I'm in my four-by-four Cherokee. Be there in less than an hour. Stan is on his way to you. Lives in Hominy. Should be there any minute."

"Okay. Thanks, Butch."

"You going after the bastards?" Butch asked.

"Yes."

"Be careful. Happy hunting."

Butch ended the call.

Sarah eyed Eli.

"Rental GPS disabled Wednesday night *north* of town," he said.

"North?" she said scrunching her nose. "That's the wrong way."

Eli thought Jim would have headed south, back to Tulsa. "Does Blackwood Energy have any other assets in the area?" he asked.

Sarah thought for a few seconds. "You know, I remember seeing in our proxy fight that they had bought a warehouse with a small pipe yard to support the ten wells they had planned on the leases west of Wynona."

"Where?"

"South side of Pawhuska. Along the highway." Sarah turned her head to the side as if prying more from her memory. "They haven't permitted the wells yet, so the warehouse might still be empty."

She turned and pulled the side of the curtains and looked out. She grabbed her gun from its holster. "Someone's coming."

"One person?"

"Yes. Is that your man?"

"Short and stocky. Cowboy hat. Bowlegged?"

"Yeah. He's got a rifle."

Eli headed to the front door. "It's Stan."

He opened the door.

Stan stomped the snow from his boots, removed his hat and shook it, then entered. Leaving his rifle just inside the doorway, he hugged Eli. "Hey, old boy. Great to see you. Sorry it's for this shit."

"Great to see you, Stan. Sherry is in the back. We're gonna get going."

Stan turned back to Sarah, raised his hat, put it on, then tipped it once. He grabbed his rifle and headed to the back of the house.

"He looks tough," Sarah said.

"He is." He walked back to Sarah. "I think we head to Pawhuska. In this weather, it will take thirty or forty minutes in Hudson's four-wheel-drive pickup."

"You think Jim's there?"

"I do. It's our only shot now. If we have to, we can get back to the lease outside of Wynona in twenty minutes, but we don't have anything to exchange."

"If my father is there, let me handle him. Don't hurt him."

Eli remained silent, not knowing what to say. There were no guarantees now.

"You promised."

She was right. He had promised. "That was before Hudson and Sonny."

They stood there for a moment locked in each other's gaze. Eli felt the bond between them melting. He stayed quiet. Her father had nearly killed his friends. He couldn't promise.

Sarah's eyes narrowed on him. She remained silent for a moment, then looked away. "Okay. I'll get Abena," she said as she left the room.

Sadness grew inside him as he watched her leave. Eli knew there was a lot riding on his instinct that Jim was in Pawhuska. But he trusted his twisting gut. As he retrieved his coat, his determination grew. He'd save Jim, then help Abena recreate her discovery that would save thousands of women and children. He'd keep Sarah safe. He hoped she'd understand what he had to do. He didn't want to fail her. To do all that, and have any chance at a life with her, he'd have to survive the night.

CHAPTER 53

ELI WRESTLED THE wheel of the old pickup as it plowed through the snow on Highway 99. The deep tread he'd seen on the mud and snow tires when he'd spun the front hubs to lock it in four-wheel drive gripped the roadway. His fingers thawed, and he flexed them on the wheel. The snow had tapered off, and confident in the truck's traction, he gave it more gas. He glanced at the clock on the display. It was five-thirty. They'd burn thirty minutes getting to Pawhuska and another twenty getting to the exchange before seven if they didn't find Jim. With no data files and his unwillingness to turn over Abena, he knew this was a long shot; the silence inside the cab said Sarah and Abena agreed. But he was out of options, and this was the best and only lead they had.

Sarah sat in the passenger's seat staring straight ahead. Eli wondered if he'd crossed the line by backtracking on his promise not to kill her father. Abena sat between them, her eyes fearful and wandering. As the air blasted from the vents and warmed, the smell of crude oil thickened. Years ago, it had been Hudson's work truck.

Eli's optimism swelled with each mile closer to the warehouse. Jim had gone north of Hominy, then disappeared. He wasn't at the doghouse. That only left one other place Blackwood controlled. The warehouse. "Anything else about this warehouse?" Eli asked.

Sarah leaned forward and looked around Abena. "Only that they paid a pretty penny for it. It's probably newer."

Eli knew he'd have to fight his way in and out. "When we get there, I'll go in alone. Can't risk you guys being taken or hurt."

Sarah returned her attention to the road ahead. "Well see once we get there."

Her voice had gone flat. There was no longer a connection. A tinge of regret arose from his heart, but he shoved it away and pressed on through the snow.

Twenty minutes later, Sarah called out, "Turn here."

There were no tire tracks in the deep, freshly fallen snow ahead.

Eli guided the truck between two gas stations onto Highway 60, using the stop sign as a guide for the edge of the road.

"The warehouse will be two miles ahead on the left," she said. She pulled out her pistol and checked it.

Eli wanted to argue, but he figured it was pointless. He'd already done enough damage. He'd tangle with Sarah when they got to the warehouse. Then, he had another idea. A manipulation that would trap Sarah, forcing her to stay. "Abena, you'll stay here. I'll leave it running and point it toward the street. Any sign of trouble, drive away and go to the highway patrol office back where I showed you south of town off Highway 99."

She looked at Sarah, terrified. "Are you leaving me?"

Sarah leaned forward and gave Eli a dirty look. She'd realized what he'd done. "No, I'll stay with you."

Eli felt the air in the truck between them thicken. He'd put another nail in the coffin of their relationship. He didn't like doing it, but it was necessary to protect Sarah and Abena.

Minutes later a large warehouse, with a flat-white finish, appeared on the left. It was well lit, and the large parking lot was empty. When they reached the turn into the parking lot, there were no tire tracks into the entrance. Eli made the turn and looped through the parking lot in the virgin snow. There were no vehicles, but they could still be parked inside the closed loading bays. He pulled to the side door, grabbed the prybar, and said, "Wait here."

As he opened his door, Sarah opened hers and circled the truck. They met at the front of the truck.

"I'm sorry," Eli said.

She shook her head and continued on to the driver's seat, slamming the door.

Eli noticed the security camera above the door. At this point, it didn't matter. His body tingled in anticipation of finding Jim inside. He pried the door open, pulled out his Glock, and went inside. The warehouse was dark, other than a few dim lights along the walls. As he cleared each section, his optimism bled out. The warehouse was empty and the office was dark. He dropped his gun to his side and stuck the prybar under his arm. He sighed, dropped his head, then looked at his watch. It was already 6:10 p.m.

His disappointment swamped him. He'd just wasted an hour. Maybe the last hour of Jim's life. In the darkness, he looked up to the roof. "Sorry, Jim." Now, it all came down to the meeting at seven, and he had nothing he was willing to trade.

CHAPTER 54

AS ELI DROVE south, back through the drifted snow on Highway 99, he battled the steering wheel, dread building in his heart. He was close to failing on all fronts. Once again in his life, he didn't measure up. He had little leverage, and Jim could be dead in less than an hour. Eli knew his own chances of survival were low. While dying didn't scare him, a devastating regret of never having experienced the love of his life clawed at him from the inside. He'd had a chance with Sarah, but to keep her safe, he had to go against her wishes and let her go. He tried to retrieve the bulk of Lizzy's good advice, but it was pointless. All he thought about was that he'd never see Lizzy again, either. The only bright spot was Abena. If he kept her out of this, maybe she could save all those children. He decided there was only one thing to do. Get angry and get focused.

"Sarah, I need you to promise you'll get Abena out of here."

"You can't go in alone," she said.

"Abena's work comes first," he said, tersely.

Sarah leaned across Abena, gritting her teeth and said, "You'll be outnumbered."

Eli stared ahead. "Been there, done that."

Abena turned to confront Sarah. "I can't let your father get this. I plan to use it for the people of the DRC. I want to stop the killing of my people. Children in particular. I'll license it and create a fund for the people in the artisanal mines who lose their jobs when this works. Your father isn't driven by that. He'll try to make as much money for himself as he can."

Eli saw Sarah get the point. She knew Abena was right.

"Are you sure it works?" Sarah asked. She looked hopeful, but Eli wasn't sure if it was for her father or the children of the DRC.

"Oh, it works." Abena turned to Eli. "My bench test showed charging time drops to less than five minutes for a five-hundred-mile trip. It's easy to scale."

Sarah leaned forward, looking at Eli again. "What about my father?" Her tone sounded like she was talking to a stranger.

Eli responded in kind. "He won't be there. Lucian never got his hands dirty. It will be Winchester and his thugs."

"You have no leverage," Sarah argued. Eli glanced at her. Her eyes softened. "It's a suicide mission."

The sadness in her eyes stirred his heart. Despite her anger, she still cared. "They don't know that. I have enough to stall or distract them. I assume you can't shut down the proxy fight on your own?"

She wagged her head. "I can't. The senior partners in the firm have to do that."

"Then this is the only way. He won't be there. I'm certain." Eli said. "I'll go in. See what's what. If I can get Jim freed, I'll do it. If not, I'll tell them we can recreate it."

Abena shook her head. "That will take time. I must get the equipment, make the test samples and batteries, then run the tests."

Eli wagged his head, once. "Again, you won't have to do it. I just need to make them think you will."

"What if they kill Jim?" Sarah said.

Her comment made Eli angrier. He took a breath and waited to respond. Let the rage attached to that thought subside. It didn't. Then he said, loudly, "I'll kill as many of them as I can."

Sarah leaned back into the seat. She stared straight ahead. Anger, fear, and disappointment silently mixed across her face. Abena looked terrified again and stared straight ahead. Eli glanced over his shoulder at the gap between the seat and the back of the cab. The soles of a pair of steel-toe work boots were wedged behind the seat. An oil-stained Carhartt jacket hung in the far corner. He returned his attention to the snow-covered highway. No one spoke until they reached the turn in Wynona.

At least three sets of tracks turned in from the south, coming from Tulsa. Eli slowed the truck and turned down the county road. He followed the tracks down the right side of the road. The oncoming lane back was pristine snow—no tracks returned.

"Looks like the meeting is on," Eli said.

"I can't let you go in by yourself. That's at least three vehicles," Sarah said leaning forward and looking at the tracks ahead.

"We don't have a choice. I won't risk your life and that of a single mother who's trying to save a bunch of kids." Eli slowed the truck. "With that many vehicles, they'll have lookouts. I'll have to walk in. I'll turn around up ahead at the next county road. It's only a quarter mile in from there."

"Dressed like that?"

"No. There's boots and a coat behind you. I need to check the toolbox in the bed. I need to make a distraction." He nodded toward the glove box. "Check to see if there is anything I can light a rag with."

Sarah opened the glove box. She dug under some papers and pulled out a pack of cigarettes with a lighter stuck in its wrapper. She held them up.

"Hudson told Sherry he'd quit," Eli said, grinning, until he remembered about Hudson and Sonny.

"Glad he didn't," Sarah said.

Eli reached the intersection, turned the truck around, and stopped in the lane heading back to the highway. "They can't see you here. If anything looks suspicious or you don't hear from me in the next thirty minutes, get her out of here."

Sarah scowled and looked ahead. Then she reached behind her and handed Eli the boots and the coat. He opened the door, slipped on the boots, and pulled the coat over his jacket. He checked his Glock, stepped out into the snow, and looked back into the cab. He saw Abena. A tear ran down her cheek.

"Mr. Scott, you be careful. And thank you for protecting me."

Eli smiled and gave her a two-fingered salute. Abena smiled nervously.

Sarah opened her door and got out. She slogged around the front of the truck through the deep snow. She stopped facing Eli. She was stoic. She looked as if she wanted to say something. Eli certainly did. Be he wasn't ready to say what he felt. The invisible force holding him back had returned. Neither spoke until the silence became awkward.

"If I don't see you again, I want you to know you're an exceptional woman," Eli said. It wasn't what he wanted to say, but he had to say something.

Sarah hugged him. "Come back to us," she said. She released him and stepped into the truck.

Eli went to the white, rusted toolbox that stretched across the truck bed just behind the cab. He opened it. The tray was full of tools. He slid the tray aside and searched the storage below. It was there. Right where it should be. He thanked Ravenel Energy for the company's focus on safety first and pulled the fire extinguisher from the box. He grabbed a rag from the bottom of the box, then reached over to the tool tray and pulled out a wire cutter, box knife, and a coffee can full of bolts. Grabbing a screwdriver, he removed the spare blade from the box knife. He reached behind him and carefully cut the top of his waistband and slipped it inside. He took the wire cutters and clipped the long hose from the extinguisher, dumped the bolts from the can into the snow, and shoved the rag into the can.

He made his way along the side of the truck to the gas tank and jammed the hose inside. He siphoned gas out onto the rag in the can. He looked up at the cab and saw Sarah watching him in the large side-view mirror. He took one last look, then headed across the snow-covered road and disappeared into the woods.

CHAPTER 55

AS ELI MOVED deeper into the woods, he couldn't forget what he was leaving behind. The image of Sarah from the side-view mirror tugged at his heart. It felt as if a strange force was resisting every step he took, pulling him back to her. The snow was deep and that made each step difficult, his legs heavy as he pulled them from the snow. The blackjack oaks still held their brown leaves, each leaf cupping new fallen snow that then fell to the ground as he passed. The smell of gasoline was strong. He covered the gas-saturated rag to keep it dry. The joyous anticipation of finally seeing Jim was buried under the weight of knowing what he had to do. Killing wasn't something he took lightly. It took serious mental preparation. Just as in his Marine training. He pushed Sarah from his mind and thought about what was on the line now.

Abena was right. Blackwood would only want the discovery for the profits. It would also greenwash his nasty approach to the business. Hope could spin it to rebuild his credibility on Wall Street and Main Street. He'd take the profits for himself and let those children and their families starve. He'd kill Abena to secure it. He'd said Eli wasn't CEO material when he'd fired him. That he wouldn't amount to anything. Eli hoped he was about to prove him wrong.

The truck readout had said it was twenty-one degrees. The

thicker work coat shielded him from most of it, and the high boots kept the snow from numbing his ankles. He was moving through the pitch-black forest as quietly as he could. But when he pushed through the low, tangled branches of the blackjacks, the dry leaves crunched and crackled. His hands stung from the cold, and he periodically blew into them, warming his fingers enough to handle the Glock.

Three minutes in, he saw dim light diffusing through the trees. He remembered the lone light on the creosote pole near the entrance to the cleared drilling pad. He'd estimated he'd have to deal with six men besides Winchester. Two at the entrance for sure. Two more at the door of the doghouse and two more inside. He would neutralize them two at a time. That added exponentially to the difficulty of the attack.

When he could see the light through the leaves, he slowed his walk and pulled out his gun. Based on his memory, he'd been traveling due west toward the Blackwood lease. That put him on the east side of the drilling pad. He'd arrive just behind the doghouse, concealed by the woods. If his hunch was correct, he'd have to deal with the two men on the porch to the doghouse first.

Spotting the silhouette of the doghouse, he dropped to his knees. The snow was halfway up his thigh. He wouldn't be able to crawl in. Moving, inch by inch, to the left side of the silhouette, he quietly positioned himself only ten yards from the entrance to the doghouse. The entrance looked like the back of a caboose: an elevated platform covered by an extension of the doghouse roof. Two men circulated around the perimeter. Both had what looked like AR-15s.

In the distance, Eli could see the entrance to the lease. The gravel road entered from his left and a black SUV sat facing the entrance. He noticed the condensing vapor from the exhaust. The two men were inside. That was a mistake he hadn't anticipated. He hoped it was a fatal one. If they had this amount of firepower, Jim was here. He took a moment and calmed himself as his determination grew.

He pulled back and circled to his left around the perimeter of the drilling pad. When he reached the road, he dug into his pocket and pulled out Hudson's lighter, checked it, and stuffed it back in. He secured his Glock in its holster. He moved along the road, away from the drilling pad, until he reached a bend in the road, out of sight of the men in the SUV. In the darkness, he crossed to the far side and made his way through the woods to the start of the gravel pad. The SUV was still idling and shielded his approach from the men at the doghouse.

Eli let out a long breath, filling the frozen night air with a cloud. This had to work. He dropped on all fours, the snow reaching his chest. Still, he crawled toward the back of the SUV. They'd be watching the road ahead of them. He curled around behind the SUV out of view of the mirrors. Crawling through the deep snow and beneath the SUV, he pulled out the wire cutters and snipped the fuel line running from the gas tank. Plugging it with his thumb, he carefully pushed the rag and can underneath the gas tank, just short of the severed fuel line. The engine sputtered. He pulled the rag out and elongated it, making a fuse. He crawled back out from under the car, lit the rag, and bolted back into the woods.

As he retraced his route, the SUV ignited, catching the occupants by surprise. The two men at the doghouse ran toward the SUV. Running now, he raced back to the doghouse, pulled out his box knife, and waited at the door. The first man yanked open the door. Eli grabbed his rifle, turning toward him. With one move, he sliced the man's neck at the vocal cords. The man's momentum carried his dead weight over the rail and into the snow. The second man led with his rifle, pointing it in Eli's direction as he exited. Again, grabbing the barrel, Eli pulled him close. He got an errant shot off, but Eli opened his neck and shoved him over the rail. Hearing the gunfire, the two men trying to rescue the occupants of the SUV turned and began to run back to the platform where Eli crouched. With two precise shots, both men were gone.

Assuming Winchester would use Jim as a shield, Eli readied to go inside. Using the metal door jamb as cover, he pressed his back against the wall adjacent to the door, raised his Glock, and spun into the doorway ready to fire. Shocked by what he saw, he hesitated, trying to make sense of the scene. Eli could see the entire interior. Jim wasn't there. Blackwood stood next to an empty chair. He was half scowling and half smiling. Eli thought about Sarah and didn't fire. In that moment, he felt cold steel press into the back of his head.

"Drop it," Winchester said from behind him—again.

CHAPTER 56

ELI STRAINED AGAINST the thick white zip ties around his wrists. They'd been strung through the vertical supports of the back of the ancient steel chair. He thought about the drillers who probably used it and pulled strength from their cumulative toughness. The doghouse was narrow but long. A set of lockers lined the wall behind him; to his left was a cramped, dented built-in desk. On his right, a long bench ran the length of the room. Winchester sat on the bench still holding the gun on Eli. Blackwood stood in front of him. The asshole had his hunting gear on. Eli prayed that Sarah had heard the shots and taken off with Abena. By now, they'd be south of town and out of danger.

Eli stopped focusing on his restraints. "Where's Jim Munro?"

Blackwood, arms folded, shared a chuckle with Winchester. "Where are the files and the inventor?"

"You don't think I'm stupid enough to have them with me before I see Jim, do you?" It wasn't lost on Eli that now his life depended on a lie, even though Hope was the sociopath.

"Like I told you when I fired you, I think you're stupid enough to do anything."

Blackwood's words triggered Eli's self-doubt, and the shame

demons rattled their cages. He needed their anger, but not their irrational thinking. He shook off Blackwood's barb.

"I need proof of life," Eli demanded.

"And I need to be thirty years younger!" Blackwood shared another laugh with Winchester.

"That wouldn't make you any smarter," Eli said.

"You don't look like you're in any position to negotiate. Now, where are the files and the sample? We know there is a video showing the performance of the product."

"What are you going to do with it?"

"None of your damn business. But I'll tell you anyway." He stood and started to pace back and forth in the small space. "Once I have it, I'll file the patents. Then, I'll license it. Ms. Munro says she can use it to show how I transformed my oil company into a leading environmental company. I won't have to lift a finger."

"So say you. The truth has a way of coming out."

"Ms. Munro has assured me that a lie is just a truth in disguise. That she'll weave a web so tight the truth can't be penetrated."

"Spoken like a person without a conscience."

A strange, curious expression rippled across Blackwood's face. He'd taken it personally. "I sleep fine at night. I'm doing what I have to in order to protect my family and our legacy."

"No matter how many people get hurt or killed?"

"If they live up to their promises, no one gets hurt."

"That's not what happened."

Blackwood looked momentarily confused.

"Where's Jim?" Eli said again.

"On his way," Blackwood said. "Now live up to your end of the deal. Where are the data files, the sample, and the inventor?"

Eli evaluated the situation. Without Jim present, he had no idea if Blackwood would come through. Winchester looked as if he'd pull the trigger as soon as they had the information. He looked like he *wanted* to no matter what happened. Blackwood had surprised Eli by showing up. But he was sure he'd leave and let Winchester finish him. Eli would have to work himself free. Then he could take out Winchester. Blackwood was a coward. He'd wilt once Winchester was gone. Eli carefully moved his two fingers inside the slit in his waistband. He felt the blade between them and slowly pulled it out, turning it toward the plastic cuffs. They'd missed the thin blade when they patted him down. Now, he needed time to cut through the cuffs.

"Give me proof of life, and I'll get what you want."

"You mean what I deserve," Blackwood said, righteousness squaring his shoulders.

"Deserve?"

"Your friend had cut a deal with my representatives but then reneged. Said I wasn't the right buyer."

That news was surprising, but it fit with what Eli had discovered. The banker, the meeting scheduled for last week that never happened. It all fit.

"I need to see him," Eli said.

"I can make him tell us," Winchester said.

Blackwood pondered the offer but then shook his head. "No." He checked the time on his watch. "They'll be here soon."

An alarm sounded in Eli's head. *They* meant there were more on the way. If Sarah hadn't left, she'd be spotted, and that would create a whole other set of problems.

Then his eyes caught a glimmer, ever so dim, just outside the door next to the window behind Blackwood. He wasn't sure if "they" had arrived or if it was someone else. He realized if it were someone else, it would be Sarah. Exactly the wrong move. As time passed the likelihood of it being someone they expected disappeared. Eli could yell, but she'd lose the element of surprise. He couldn't stop her, so he decided to distract them.

He refocused on Blackwood. "Why did you fire me? I opened

up the organization, got ideas flowing, we had a plan for growth. Now you've gutted the company."

He stiffened, taking the bait. "Because you were too stupid to quit. We sent you the signals, but you stayed on. Cost me millions. You'd lost respect for us. That last move of consulting the people affected before I could make a decision sealed it."

"While I still believe in doing that, that particular incident was a setup, and you know it. And I was committed to the people there. The openness just threatened you."

Blackwood's face turned red, and the door behind him swung open. Sarah stepped in and aimed at Winchester. "Drop the gun."

Winchester smiled and dropped the gun too easily.

Eli struggled against the cuffs. He hadn't cut deep enough yet. "Sarah, there's someone else out there!" he yelled.

She turned back toward the door as the butt end of a rifle exploded from the darkness and slammed into her forehead. She collapsed on the ground. Eli stopped struggling. He glared at Winchester. *He'd soon be a dead man.*

CHAPTER 57

ELI WATCHED THE thug step inside and take Sarah's gun. She lay on the floor unconscious, blood dripping from her matted hair. A few drips hit the metal floor. A concussion, but she wouldn't bleed to death. Whether it was a skull fracture or not he didn't know. He was the reason she was here, hurt, bleeding on the floor.

He yanked at the cuffs and yelled. "Leave her alone!"

The man was thick and burly, with tattoos covering his neck and hands. He was missing a finger on his right hand. Ignoring Eli, he pulled a set of zip ties from his pocket, bound Sarah's hands behind her, and lifted her onto the end of the bench. Her head, arms, and legs flopped lifelessly to the bench. Eli saw her chest rise and fall. Blackwood showed no concern. That boiled Eli's blood.

"You good with that?" Eli said, throwing a nod in Sarah's direction.

"She made her choice. She shouldn't have come," Lucian said.

Blackwood's indifference in the face of Sarah's love for her father pissed Eli off even more. Blackwood deserved whatever he'd get. Eli would do what he had to do to save Sarah and Jim, including killing Blackwood, but it would be the end of whatever their relationship could have become. He'd been lonely most of his life, and something was telling him Sarah would be his last chance at love. But he'd give that up to save her.

Jim was on his way. That meant his escorts would add to the mounting odds against getting out of this. He now had two men to take out. Blackwood didn't count. He'd fold once the other two were down. At least Eli hoped that would be the case. Jim's escorts would probably add two more. It was getting crowded.

Sarah's eyes flashed open, and her body jerked. She fought against the restraints then seemed to realize it was hopeless. She righted herself on the bench and blinked her eyes in pain.

She locked them on Blackwood. "Father? You… you need to stop this now."

He shook his head. "It's gone too far," he said. "You've gone too far. I warned you."

"It's been you all along. *You've* taken it too far. This is your life you're throwing away."

Blackwood laughed. "I'm not throwing anything away. I'm *saving* a way of life. The likes of you can't see that. I've spent my life earning my fortune, shaping this town, and it's bleeding hearts like you trying to take it away from me. I've earned this. And I'll get away with it, too."

Eli could see the devastation in Sarah's eyes. Her father's words had done much more damage than the butt end of the rifle. Eli jumped into the fray to get the focus off Sarah. Expose Blackwood for what he was. It might help ease her pain. "You haven't earned anything. You've taken the value of the company and cut it by two-thirds. Your investors are livid. If it wasn't for that good-ole-boy board of yours, you'd be out on your ass." As he spoke, Eli gently continued to move the blade back and forth against the thick plastic.

"That's enough from you!" Blackwood yelled. He eyed Winchester. "Do it your way," he said.

Winchester nodded to the side of beef standing by the door. The thug walked behind Eli and pressed down on Eli's shoulders so he couldn't stand. Winchester rose, wrapped his knuckles in a rag, and belted Eli in the left cheek, snapping his head to the right.

"Stop it!" Sarah yelled.

While the pain shot through his cheek and left eye, Eli slowly turned his head back and smiled. "Just like I thought. You hit like a coward." Eli talked to the pain, made friends with it.

Winchester switched hands and hit him on the right side of his face. He felt a loose tooth as he turned his head back to Winchester and spat on the floor.

Winchester re-wrapped his fist. "Okay. That's just the warm-up. Where are the data and the inventor?"

"Go screw yourself." Eli stared back at Winchester.

Winchester cocked his arm and drove his fist into the bridge of Eli's nose. Pain split his eyes. Blood gushed over his chin.

Sarah shot up, her hands still bound behind her. "Stop him, Father!" The thug shoved her back down.

"Do you know where it is?" Blackwood asked his daughter.

Eli glared at Sarah through his swelling eyes. She was still squinting in pain. "I don't know anything," she said. "If I did, I wouldn't tell you anyway."

Blackwood turned to Winchester. "Again."

Winchester drove his fist into Eli's midsection. All the air left Eli's lungs. His six-pack balled in a knot. With the thug pinning his shoulders, he couldn't bend over in reaction to the pain. He just took it.

"I can do this all day," Winchester said, grinning.

Eli could see the revenge searing in his eyes. Winchester's next punch to Eli's jaw set his head spinning into a delirium. His chin fell as if the earth were opening up and pulling it down. He fought to stay conscious and hold on to the blade hidden in his fingers. He wouldn't leave Sarah on her own with these criminals.

"Please stop," Sarah cried.

Eli struggled to turn his head, unable to lift it. He saw Sarah through the blood in his eyes. She looked defeated. Winchester reached under Eli's chin, lifted his head, and looked into his eyes. "He's about to go."

Blackwood's phone rang and he answered. "Who?" He paused and listened for a moment. "Okay." He ended the call. "We have a special guest. Time to go to plan B."

CHAPTER 58

ELI'S MIND CRAWLED out of the haze. His entire body throbbed. He could barely see through the blood and his other senses were overwhelmed with pain. He dropped his head and closed his eyes to concentrate on what was happening. He wondered what Blackwood was talking about. More specifically, *who* he was talking about. What guest would be unexpected, especially by him? Jim's arrival seemed to be anticipated. It couldn't be him. The known cast of suspects was limited to the people already in the room, other than Hope Munro, and with Jim's arrival anticipated, there was no way Blackwood would have Hope anywhere near here. That left Abena.

As the thug moved from behind him, Eli manipulated the small blade in his fingers and began to cut against the cuffs again. His concentration was fading. It required much more effort than before. It was hard work when he was able to do it. His fingers were fatigued, and the thick cold plastic didn't cut easily with the dull blade. But Eli was running out of time. If he didn't do something soon, he was certain they'd all be dead, including Sarah. Once free, he'd have a chance. People would die. He couldn't guarantee who. The one thing Eli knew for sure was that if Blackwood prevailed, they would all die. Abena would fail. The people in the Congo who'd no longer earn any money in the mines would starve. There would be no fund to support them. He knew Jim wouldn't want that. He would gladly sacrifice his life for all of theirs. Eli thought about the children in the DRC. Some were probably Nathan's age. Eli dug deep, and his determination took over.

Blackwood motioned Winchester to come closer. Winchester went to him and leaned close. Blackwood whispered into his ear. Winchester immediately started to grin.

Blackwood grinned too. "I always knew you couldn't count." He looked at Winchester, and they shared a laugh. Blackwood looked back at Eli. "You missed one."

Terror ripped through Eli when he realized that there was a rover. A man on recon around the perimeter of the lease. With Winchester's obvious military background, that person was probably the most cunning and lethal of the bunch. He knew what he meant for Abena if she hadn't left.

Blackwood turned and walked to the door. Looking over his shoulder at Eli, he opened the door. The cold air flooded inside, and Abena was shoved to the center of the doorway. A massive hand gripped her bicep, her wrists pinned behind her. Even though he'd anticipated as much, the sight of her crippled his heart. Terror bled from her eyes and tears streamed down her smooth skin. Her body trembled, and Eli knew it wasn't from the cold. She kept wagging her head and looking at Eli. Her mouth was going through contortions, driven by the tsunami of fear and sadness Eli imagined was coursing through her, again, because of him.

"Bring her inside," Blackwood said, letting go of the door and walking back into the room.

Abena was shoved into the doghouse, and her captor stood behind her. He was at least a full head taller than Abena. His white face was emotionless, and his eyes efficiently swept the room. At Winchester's direction, he deposited Abena to the bench next to Sarah. Eli was still seated in the chair, his hands bound together through its back. Blackwood and Winchester stood between him and the women seated on the bench. The two thugs took positions behind Blackwood, blocking the door. Eli struggled to saw away at the cuffs. He realized he'd have to go through Blackwood and Winchester to get to the muscle behind them. Getting to Winchester wouldn't be a problem. But the thugs behind him would get off a shot each before he could reach them. He estimated he had a twenty percent chance of survival.

"Get the janitor ready," Blackwood said. Winchester grabbed Abena and she screamed. He yanked her down the bench, stopping her in front of Eli.

Winchester slapped her. "Shut up."

"No!" Sarah groaned, looking groggy again.

"Try that with me, asshole!" Eli yelled.

Winchester grinned. "I'll get to you in a second."

Winchester raised his hand again. Abena cringed. She heaved with each sob, trying to swallow them. As she cried, focused on Eli, the disappointment and resignation in her eyes crushed him. He kept sawing.

"Now," Blackwood walked to Abena and bent down. They were face-to-face. Winchester stepped aside.

"What did you give to Jim Munro?" Lucian asked.

Abena's head wagged faster, but she didn't speak.

Blackwood looked at Winchester. "Hit him again!"

Winchester stepped in front of Eli. The upper cut to Eli's jaw surprised him, and the room went bright white. When his vision returned, the pain ripped through his jaw and ears. He realized he'd dropped the razor blade from the box knife.

"Stop it, Father." Sarah said more clearly. "I'll stop the proxy fight. I'll shut it all down."

Still stooped in front of Abena, Blackwood held his eyes on her and said, "It's too late for that now."

Then Blackwood ripped off Abena's headwrap and grabbed her hair. "What did you give to Munro?"

Eli worked his jaw against the pain, then said, "She doesn't know anything. We thought the same thing."

Blackwell stood and put his hands on his hips. "Then you tell us where the files are."

Eli dropped his head and sighed.

"Again!" Blackwood yelled.

This time Winchester's punch came out of nowhere and landed on his cheek, nearly knocking him over in the chair. Blood sprayed onto the wall.

"Stop!" Abena yelled. "I'll tell you."

"Now that's more like it." Blackwood crossed his arms. "Go ahead."

Abena eyed the goons in the back, then Blackwood and Winchester. "It's an organic, renewable replacement for cobalt. It… it improves performance and lowers the cost of lithium-ion batteries."

"Impressive," Blackwood said, "especially coming from someone like you."

Eli knew what Blackwood meant, and it reenergized his hate for him. Eli let it burn inside him, used it to focus on what he needed to do.

"Where are the data and the sample?" Blackwood said.

She shook her head and looked at the floor. "I gave it to Jim. That's the last I saw of it."

"So, he was lying to us. We'll ask him when he gets here," Blackwood said. "Who's the inventor?"

Abena looked up at him. She didn't answer and her tears streamed harder down her face.

Blackwood slapped her.

Sarah stood and charged her father. After only two steps, the thug slugged her to the ground. He put his foot on her back and pinned her to the cold metal floor.

Eli struggled against the ties and tried to stand. "You bastard!"

Winchester shoved him down and the rover came over and pinned him to the chair again.

Blackwood laughed at Eli then turned back to Abena. "One last time. Who's the inventor?" Blackwood raised his hand again.

"Me!" she blurted. "Me." She bowed her head and cried uncontrollably.

Blackwood started to laugh. He kept laughing and looked at Winchester, who joined in. Then, still laughing, he looked at the two thugs until they joined in. He turned back to Abena. "You expect us to believe that *you* are the inventor? You're a"—he made air quotes—"Black bitch. You're a glorified janitor. A woman who's done that most of her life after she snuck into this country. God knows what you did before that."

Abena stopped crying and locked her eyes on Blackwood. Eli struggled against the rover's pressure, trying to stand. He'd heard enough.

The other thug pulled Sarah from the floor and slammed her back on the bench. Eli locked his eyes on her. Finally, she regained focus and fixed her eyes on Eli. She didn't have to say a word. She'd surrendered any fantasy about her father, and she seemed to be longing for Eli. He dug deep for every ounce of love he had inside. Her bloody mouth turned up and Eli nodded slowly.

Outside, the thud of a car door caught Blackwood's attention. "Now we'll see who can tell who's lying."

Eli had one thought. *Jim's here.*

CHAPTER 59

ELI HEARD THE footsteps on the metal grating getting louder as they approached the door. And odd sense of joy lifted his spirit. He was happy his friend was here. His head and face throbbed. He struggled to see through his swollen eyes. A shadow appeared in the window next to the door.

The thugs looked back at Blackwood, who said, "Let them in."

The rover opened the door and stepped aside. The rush of frigid air felt good on Eli's face. Eli waited to see his friend. Everyone in the doghouse focused on the doorway. Then, Hope Munro waltzed in. She wore a hooded black puffer coat. Her skin looked blazing white against her coat. Her glossy red lips had probably been done in the car. Her hands were casually stuck in her deep pockets.

At first, her appearance stunned Eli. His heartrate doubled and his mind stumbled to make sense of it all. If she was involved all along, what did that mean for Jim? He looked at Blackwood. He seemed to be expecting her.

"Did you bring him?" Blackwood asked.

Hope nodded. "He's in the car." She pulled one hand from her coat and pointed at the thugs with her thumb. "Can these two give me a hand?"

Blackwood raised his head in the direction of the vehicle,

motioning the thugs to help her. The two walked out the door, leaving Eli alone in the chair. Hope followed, leaving the door open. Eli heard them open a car door, then slam it shut. Seconds later, two deafening shots rang out and echoed in the steel room. Moving toward the door, Winchester reached for his gun.

Hope appeared in the doorway, aiming her pistol at Winchester. "I wouldn't touch that if I were you."

Eli looked at Sarah as she sat up. He mouthed *Wait*.

"Put that on the floor," Hope said as she stepped inside and closed the door.

Winchester carefully laid his gun on the floor.

"What are you doing?" Blackwood asked. He started toward her, too.

"Stop right there," she said to Blackwood. Still aiming at Winchester, she said, "Get over there with him."

Winchester stepped next to Blackwood. Blackwood looked as stunned as Eli had been. Eli still wondered about Jim. Hope had just improved his odds.

Hope kicked the gun to the corner and tossed a pair of thick zip-tie cuffs to Winchester. "Put his on first, then yours."

Winchester didn't move.

Hope thrust the gun in his face. "Now!"

Winchester cuffed Blackwood, then himself.

"You pull his tight," she said to Blackwood.

Blackwood used his cuffed hands to grab and pull Winchester's cuffs tight.

"Bring your father in here and let's get this done," Blackwood said. The uncertainty in his voice made Eli start putting pressure on his cuffs. He could charge Hope and end this with her getting only one shot off.

"Dear old Dad didn't make the trip." Her smile looked terrifyingly genuine.

"What do you mean? We need him to get what we want," Blackwood said.

Hope slowly nodded, her deadly glare aimed at Blackwood. "You mean to get what *I* want."

Blackwood looked confused. He tipped his head toward Eli and Abena. "We need him to get the truth out of them."

Hope smiled. "The truth?"

"Yes." Blackwood pointed at Abena. "She said she's the inventor. That can't be the case."

"Why not?" Hope said.

Lucian raised his eyebrows. "Look at her."

"You stupid racist. She *is* the inventor," Hope said.

Eli attempted to pull his wrists apart again. It didn't work. "Hope, where is your father?" Eli asked.

She turned to Eli with great satisfaction on her face. "He's dead."

"Dead?" Eli said. A frigid emptiness filled him.

Hope laughed.

Eli didn't know if she was telling the truth or not. He wanted to assume it was a lie, just like everything else that had come out of her mouth. But something deep inside said Hope looked different. Had he witnessed what the truth looked like for the first time?

She stopped laughing. "He's been dead since before we first met last week."

Hope's words hit Eli harder than Winchester's punches. Still, he wasn't sure it was the truth. He prayed it wasn't.

"What?" Blackwood said. "This is all a lie?"

"I told you. A lie is only the truth in disguise," Hope said.

"How do we get the truth without your father?" Blackwood asked.

"You keep saying we. You're out of this. You never were in it. Now shut up." She turned back to Eli. "This man has the answers. That's why I pulled him in. I had to kill my father to do it, but a girl's gotta do what a girl's gotta do."

Eli believed her this time. His heart shattered. The pain he'd ignored came roaring back, and he felt nauseous. Breathing became nearly impossible. Jim was dead and now he'd risked his friends' lives, along with Sarah's and Abena's, for a lie. He could see what Lizzy had warned him about. Hope had crossed the line. She was impulsive, and the violent tendency had worsened to bloodlust. Killing was the ultimate way to show her superiority over people. She stole everything when she killed them. She'd demonstrated that with the guiltless killing of the two thugs. He assumed she wouldn't stop with Winchester's mercs. He desperately tugged at the restraints.

"Let them go and I'll give you what you want," Eli said.

"Listen to that, ladies," Hope said, glancing at Sarah and Abena on the bench to her right. "He wants to save you from me. How gallant." Keeping the gun on Blackwood and Winchester, she stepped closer to Eli. "I think not. He can't save you. He's not good enough. Look how I've fooled him."

"You've fooled no one," Sarah said. "Everyone knows what you are."

Eli shook his head, hoping Sarah saw it.

Hope took one step back to put Sarah in her field of fire.

"You think you're better than me," Hope said. "But you have a flaw I don't have. Several, for that matter. You're too soft, not quite smart enough, and blind to how your father really feels about you." She kept her gun on Winchester and Blackwood.

"You're right," Eli said. "We all have flaws. But we didn't kill our fathers." He hoped to draw Hope's attention to him. It worked.

As she prowled toward Eli, her bottomless eyes locked on his. "You too? You were the easiest to fool. If I didn't need you to tell me what I need to know, you'd be next. But I have a present for you. One you'll really love." She backed up to the door, opened it, reached out of sight, and pulled a person in through the door.

Eli's heart stopped. It was Lizzy.

CHAPTER 60

THE ROOM INSTANTLY turned frigid, and the smell of gunpowder, mixed with the hydrocarbons permanently forged into the steel walls, seeped into Eli's blood-crusted nose. The terror in Lizzy's eyes, the panicked pulsating breaths under the duct tape covering her mouth, and her outsized eyes made Eli's body quake. He was certain Lizzy knew what Hope was capable of. She'd just seen it firsthand. A tidal wave of worthlessness crashed over him, and self-doubt rose up to choke him. But Lizzy's eyes changed and they locked on him. As if telepathically, his weaknesses melted away. The cloud of self-doubt parted, replaced by angry resolve. His muscles swelled and he subtly leaned forward in the metal chair.

Eli looked around the room at what he'd done. Abena was innocent, just trying to help her family and the world. Darnell would be waiting for her. Terrified, she stared back at him. Sarah had become a victim of her own conscience. She'd touched something inside Eli that he'd never felt before. She'd lost her father right before his eyes. Clearly shocked, she eyed him with a mix of fear and hope in her eyes. He looked back at Lizzy. She'd helped him save and rebuild his life. She seemed to recognize the determination building inside him.

Hope shoved Lizzy between Sarah and Abena. "Have a seat."

"You'll never get away with this," Winchester said flatly. "It was stupid to kill your father. We will track you down. There will be no safe place."

Hope slowly nodded and chuckled. She raised her gun and fired. Winchester collapsed on the floor, blood gushing from his neck. Hope stared at him, a sick satisfaction radiating from her face. He shuddered with his last breath, and she smiled. Blackwood closed his eyes and trembled.

She looked up at her captive audience. "My father mistreated me. He was terrible. I was completely underappreciated." She calmly walked to Abena, pointing the gun at her head.

Abena cowered, panicking and crying. Her eyes shut tight.

"He chose her and her work over me, his own daughter," Hope said.

Eli recognized Hope's sociopathic need for pity. And he could see that one by one, she'd kill them all. He needed to get her closer to him. He'd only get one chance to stop her. He had to be sure he could.

"And yet, here we are," he said. "You still need something. I won't give it to you if you hurt her. You need her. You know that."

She snapped her attention to Eli. She stayed next to Abena, halfway down the bench and ten feet away. "Let's get right to it, then," Hope said.

She took one step backward, stopped in front of Lizzy, and looked back at Eli. "I need you to tell me where the data files are that contain the formula."

"Let them go and I'll do whatever you want," he said.

"You think this is a negotiation?"

"I think you know what this is. You're a smart woman."

Hope seemed to recognize Eli's attempt to manipulate her. "I'll tell you what," she said, pointing her gun between Sarah and Lizzy. "I'll let you pick which one."

Eli looked at Lizzy. She had that look. The look he'd seen many times before in their sessions when she knew *he knew* the answer to a question he had asked. He then looked at Sarah. She wasn't afraid. A toughness emanated from her posture, taut muscles, and unyielding stare back at him. She was ready.

Eli was ready to die. He wasn't afraid. He thought about what leverage he could possibly have that Lizzy clearly thought he had. He glanced back at Sarah. He loved her compassion. Her caring for him and others in her life, even her father. It was the same caring he felt toward others. He thought about Nathan and his mother and how much he cared. Then, the answer flashed into his mind.

Conscience.

It's the one thing that connects us all, Lizzy had said. And it was the one thing sociopaths never had. They'd leverage others' consciences against them. Manipulate them. But he had to get this right. If what Lizzy had told him wasn't true for Hope, he was certain he'd watch them all die. He knew what he had to do even though it would cost him what might be his only chance at love. It would cost him Sarah.

CHAPTER 61

ELI BATTLED THE sadness trying to pull him inside himself. He only needed a split second, and baiting Hope would provide it. But he wasn't sure it would work. It wasn't that he didn't trust Lizzy, it was how—or if—what she'd told him applied to Hope. The only thing he was sure of was that if it worked, his chances with Sarah would be gone. But she needed to carry on. He loved her because he knew she'd carry her family forward in the right way. He looked at her one last time. She seemed confused by his expression, but then he saw her realize something was about to happen.

Lizzy sat there, her deep breathing an effort to stay calm. She cut her eyes away from Hope and shifted her gaze to him. He owed her his life. Now he'd repay her with his. Abena still cried. It broke his heart. She was pure goodness. And her work would literally save the world. At least part of it. He glanced at Blackwood cowering against the wall next to Winchester's body.

Eli just shook his head. Starting his plan, he shook it long enough and hard enough to be noticed.

"What?" Hope said.

"Nothing," Eli said.

"No! Tell me." She walked toward Eli. *Mistake number one.*

Eli put as much downward pressure on his wrists as he could.

The zip ties cut into his skin, but he needed as much force as he could apply. He braced his feet flat on the floor and tensed his thighs.

"Why did you shake your head?" Hope said as she pointed the gun at him. He was getting her to respond impulsively. *Mistake number two.*

He glanced at Sarah one last time. Then, he said to Hope, "I'm just amazed you fell for it."

"Fell for what?"

Eli nodded at Blackwood. "His manipulation."

Hope eyed Blackwood. "His?"

"Yeah. He's been playing you all along."

"No, he hasn't."

"The fact that you don't recognize it proves he's better than you at manipulating people," Eli said.

"Don't listen to him," Blackwood said on the verge of tears.

"Eli. What are you doing?" Sarah said.

Hope pointed the gun back at Sarah. "Shut up." She turned back to Eli. "No. I orchestrated this whole thing. You had no idea. They had no idea. Now, I'm going to win. I'm going to be richer than he ever was."

Eli laughed. "You just made my point. You have no idea. You're here *because* of him. He's far better than you are at this, and he'll end up much richer."

He could see the rage in her eyes as she looked at Blackwood like her prey—her next victim who she thought others saw as superior. She wasn't winning. Eli closely studied her gun hand and her eyes and readied himself. She aimed her gun at Blackwood. Her eyes began to close. The muscles in her hand twitched.

In one movement, Eli shot up with the chair attached behind him, dropped all his weight back into the chair, driving it to the floor, and yanked on the zip ties with all his might. The chair crashed into the floor and the zip ties popped off his wrists. He lunged at

Hope as she fired, blocking the shot intended for Blackwood. The bullet burned into his shoulder as he tackled her. Eli grabbed for the gun barrel and twisted it away from him. He drove her to the floor. But Hope was much stronger than he'd anticipated, and he was weakened by the gunshot wound in his shoulder. They struggled with the gun. Face to face with Hope, he saw the predator's rage in her dark eyes. With their hands locked between them, he tried to wrestle the gun away but couldn't. The gun fired, the force pounding his chest. Eli waited for the pain. It never came. Hope's body went limp. Her eyes opened wide in shock. She stared at him. She seemed to know she was dying, and this time she cared.

CHAPTER 62

ELI COULDN'T HEAR. His ears rang from the gunshot blast and his shoulder burned in pain. He leaned against the wall and slid down to sit on the floor. He pressed on the wound and felt the blood seeping between his fingers. Hope lay on the floor in front of him, a bloom of red growing from the bullet hole in her chest. A larger pool of blood grew from beneath her. The smell of gunpowder hung in the air. Eli watched as Sarah, with her hands bound behind her, pushed into a back-bridge, and stretched her hands under her feet and in front of her. She ran to Eli.

"I got you." She pressed her cuffed hands over his wound.

"The toolbox," Eli said as he nodded to the dented blue box in the corner. "Pliers." Sarah stood and ran to it, pulling out a pair of cutting pliers. She went to Lizzy and cut her free. Lizzy took the pliers and cut the cuffs from Sarah's wrists. Then she did the same for Abena.

Sarah grabbed the red first aid kit mounted near the door and returned to Eli's side. While she dressed his wound, Eli saw her glance at her father. Blackwood was in shock. Eli wasn't sure if it was the realization that his family dynasty was over, or if it was the fact that Eli had saved his life. Sarah glanced at her father. She wagged her head and turned her attention back to Eli.

She finished the dressing. "Are you okay for a second?"

"Yes. Thank you."

She stood and went to her father. Eli thought she was going to hug him, but she searched his pockets and pulled out his phone. Leaving him cuffed, she dialed 911. After speaking with the operator, she put the phone on speaker and returned to Eli.

"They're on their way," Sarah said. "Hang in there." She looked back at her father again. "I can't believe you saved him."

Eli saw gratitude in her eyes. "I didn't," he said. "I saved us."

Sarah smiled, leaned in, and kissed his forehead. Then she looked back at Hope on the floor.

Eli did, too. He thought about Jim. "Help me up."

Sarah did. Eli walked to Lizzy, who comforted Abena.

"Was anyone else in the SUV with you?"

Tears grew in Lizzy's eyes. "No, Eli. I'm so sorry."

With that, Eli felt a gaping hole take up a permanent residence in his soul. Hope had told the truth. Jim, the man who meant everything to Eli, was dead. His eyes filled but he held back his tears. "Are you okay, Abena?" he asked.

"I..." She looked at Hope on the floor. "I think so. If Jim is gone . . . does that mean my work is too?"

Eli hadn't thought about that until now. He turned back and looked at Hope. Her puffer jacket was open. Fighting back his bottomless sorrow, he turned, bent down, and searched her pockets. Then he spotted the necklace. Jim had said stardust connected everyone. It was a lie to help his daughter. It hadn't worked. Lizzy was right. *Conscience connects us all.* It was the one thing they had that Hope didn't. He looked at the starlike necklace around Hope's neck. Hope had said Jim had just given it to her. He reached over and yanked it from her neck.

"What are you doing?" Sarah asked.

Eli didn't answer. Under the crushing weight of the reality of Jim's death, he held up the necklace. He slid the starlike pendant from its chain. It was heavy. She'd said it was made from a meteor. Eli flipped it over and noticed a seam that split it in half. He worked it with his hands but couldn't pry it open. Then he twisted it and pried it at the same time. It sprung open. There, inside, was a small flash drive and a tiny vile filled with dark material. Everyone stared at Eli.

Sarah moved closer to Eli and looked in his hand. "Is that what I think it is?"

Eli held up the vile between his thumb and forefinger. "Yes, it is."

Eli realized what Hope had killed for was around her neck the entire time. He dropped his head and thought about Jim. He must have thought it was the safest place to hide it. Around his daughter's neck. He'd had no idea what she'd do. He'd made the same mistake Eli had. He'd thought she had at least a splinter of conscience. At least enough to care for him. It had cost him his life. A piece of Eli's heart plunged into eternity. Jim was the greatest friend and father he knew. The daughter he'd loved had killed him, and with it, a part of Eli's heart.

CHAPTER 63

ELI RAISED HIS face to the bright sunshine as he headed toward the doors to the modern brick-and-glass building in the Greenwood District of Tulsa. This was a great day. Abena had invited him to see her office.

Sarah had taken the time to work with her, connecting her with venture capitalists and bankers in only two weeks. Sarah had visited Eli in the hospital, and they'd talked each evening by phone, but time with her outside of that was limited due to the deluge of challenges facing her family. Lucian Blackwood was in jail waiting to stand trial for a host of crimes including conspiracy to commit murder, attempted murder, bribery, and fraud. The DA was even charging him for the murder of Jim Munro since he'd hired Hope before the crime and would have benefitted from his killing. They'd uncovered documents to that effect at Hope's house. He would never get out. Sarah was already in the middle of revamping the company, the management, and the board. Eli had a date with her tonight; the first time they'd have meaningful private time together since the shooting three weeks ago. He was a *good* nervous.

Eli entered the building and noted Abena's name on the directory next to the elevator bank. Gratitude filled him, and he looked up and thanked Jim for what he'd done for her. He took the middle car to the sixth floor and headed to the far corner of the building. He turned the corner and saw Abena and Darnell: Abena in her colorful Liputa from her birthplace and Darnell in a crisp blue blazer, standing in front of the glass doors. They'd taped a red ribbon across the entrance. A wave of joy surged through him. He pulled his shoulders back and proudly smiled. Abena didn't wait for Eli. She ran to him, carefully avoiding his sling while hugging him.

"I'm so glad you came." She took Eli by his free hand and headed for Darnell. "We wanted you to be the first."

"First?"

"Yes. Our first visitor. You remember Darnell?" Abena said.

Eli shook his hand. "Great to see you."

"Thank you, sir."

"No need for formality. It's Eli."

"Well okay, Eli. I wanted to thank you for saving my mother. I'd hug you, but it looks like it might hurt."

Eli chuckled. "It might. But what I did is nothing you wouldn't have done."

"I doubt that," Darnell said.

Abena reached down and picked up a pair of oversized scissors. "Would you do us the honor?"

Eli absorbed her happiness. It was contagious. Abena would do great things for the world. He was sure of that. "I'd be honored," he said, taking the scissors.

"Hold on," Darnell said, positioning himself and his phone to take a picture.

Abena held up the middle of the ribbon and nodded to Eli. He positioned the scissors over the ribbon and paused, smiling at Darnell. When Darnell finished with the pictures, Eli said, "Wait. One more." He stepped forward, handed the scissors to Darnell, and took his phone. Abena beamed standing beside her son. Eli snapped the picture. "I want that one," he said.

After Darnell handed the scissors back to him, Eli had both of them help him cut the ribbon. Then they went inside.

"So, how's it going?" Eli asked.

"I've already set up the foundation. The demonstration proved the technology. We've lined up third-party testing thanks to Professor Gregory and Professor Perry. Then it's scaling it."

"When are you headed back to Dallas?" Eli asked Darnell.

"Not for a while. Took a leave of absence to help Mom."

"Good for you."

Abena seemed to be pondering a question.

"What is it, Abena?"

She sheepishly dipped her head. "Did they find out what happened to Jim?"

Sadness reached out from somewhere deep inside. "Yes," Eli said.

Apparently seeing Eli's dour expression, Abena quickly said, "You don't have to talk about it if you don't want to."

Eli fought off the grief and softened his mood. "It's okay. The authorities were able to trace his last movements. He'd been killed in his car at his home. She'd driven him to the Arkansas River, south of town, and buried him in a sandbar. Then she detailed his car at her house and drove it back to Jim's. Luckily, they found him before the spring rains."

Abena frowned and Darnell hugged her. "And what about Blackwood? Did he know?"

Eli shook his head. "Oddly enough, he didn't. Apparently, he thought Hope had taken him but not killed him. She manipulated him too." Eli noticed a wrinkle of worry across her face. He went to her and hugged her. "But still, he helped her. He's going away for life. You'll never have to worry about him again."

Abena looked up at him. "I wanted to ask about Lizzy, but I wasn't sure if that's private."

Eli had to laugh. "She's famous now. It's no secret that I see her. She saved us all with her advice."

“The news said they’re more of them out there—people with antisocial personality disorder. One in twenty-five people,” Abena said worriedly.

“It’s okay. Lizzy tells me there aren’t many like Hope. And there are many more of us than them.”

Eli checked the time. “I’ve gotta get going. I have an appointment with Lizzy. Don’t want to be late.”

“Thanks again,” Darnell said, shaking Eli’s hand.

Abena gently hugged him again. “Thank you for saving the children and families of the DRC.”

“It’s all you, Abena.” Eli said. “It’s all you.”

CHAPTER 64

THE TRIP TO the offices of NorthStar Counseling was enjoyable. It was one of those mid-March Saturdays that made Eli love Tulsa. The hint of spring filled the crisp air, promising a new season of renewal. He drove along Utica Avenue, his window open, and the warm unfiltered sun on his skin and the scent of the blooming dogwoods made everything better.

Anxious about his first appointment with Lizzy since the shooting, he thought about what Lizzy might ask. He guided his car into the parking lot and parked in front of the office. He'd been here many times over the past year and a half but today felt different—*he* felt different. The "brake," as he'd called it, that lead coat that had tempered his joy, was gone. And for the first time in a long while, he felt like he'd found his place in life. That he belonged.

Knowing he'd be asked, he paused and inventoried the emotions he was feeling at that moment. He settled on a few, left the Explorer, and, as he walked to the entrance, enjoyed the playful chirps of the birds hidden in the green-leafed trees. Opening the front door, he heard the pebbled fountain in the corner. Instead of relaxing, his anxiousness grew. Of all his sessions with Lizzy, something was telling him this one required special attention.

Knocking on the doorframe, he waited until Lizzy looked up from her notepad.

"Eli! You look like a man on a mission."

"Mission impossible," he said, forcing a chuckle.

"I think you've already had that one." She stood and Eli met her halfway into the office. She gave him a hug then walked to her chair. Eli took his usual chair facing her.

"How's the healing going?" she said.

"Good. They've got me in PT right now. Should be as good as new in a few weeks. No bone or ligaments damaged."

"That's good news. How are you feeling otherwise?"

"I was just thinking about that."

Lizzy smiled. "I could tell by the smoke coming out of your ears." She opened her notebook and pulled out her pen. "Let's get to it, then."

"First of all, I wanted to say I'm sorry for what I got you into."

Lizzy dropped her pen into the notebook and closed it. "Can you tell me more about that?"

"You know," Eli said. "If I would have listened to you and never trusted Hope whatsoever, none of what happened would have happened. Especially the part involving you."

"So you feel…?"

"Guilty, I guess." As soon as he said it, he knew he didn't feel guilty. "Scratch that. Shame. I feel like I *should have* known."

"Okay. She fooled a lot of other people, too."

"She fooled me." Eli thought about Jim's service. It had been a well-attended celebration of his life. Eli had seen to that. He'd touched so many people's lives. The ceremony had been graveside to accommodate the crowd. But the entire time, Eli had felt inescapable guilt and shame about his death. "Maybe Jim might be alive and none of this would have happened."

Lizzy took a deep breath, then let it out. "I know this may be hard to hear. She manipulated his good heart, his conscience, and that's why he's dead."

Eli thought about it for a moment. Lizzy was more right than wrong. "Maybe."

"Do you know why she was able to fool so many people?"

"Other than being a skilled liar, I'm not sure."

"What's the one thing that everyone had in common, other than Hope."

Eli thought about what they'd discussed previously. "Hope was brilliant, cunning, and manipulative. But she didn't care about anyone."

Lizzy nodded and said, "And you know why she didn't care. Don't you?"

Eli could see where Lizzy was headed. "A conscience."

Lizzy grinned. "And you said you weren't sure. What did everyone else have that she didn't?"

"Conscience." Eli said.

"That's why everyone missed it. She used that trait against us all. Even professionals. You see, we can't comprehend what it's like not to have one. It's nearly impossible to do. She'd spent her entire life learning how to use that to manipulate people. You couldn't believe that she had no feelings whatsoever for her father. Apparently, neither did he."

"No. I didn't. That's my point. I thought there had to be something there. She'd even shown that she did."

"She *learned* how to show it. To people who have a conscience."

Eli knew Lizzy was right. "I get it, I guess."

"You used that fact against her. You remembered what we'd discussed. She had no conscience. No reticence about even killing. Only a predatory lust to be number one. Better than or above everyone she played the game with. When you goaded her into thinking that Blackwood was better, she impulsively tried to eliminate the competition. That gave you the time to save us. The one thing that ties us all together, and the fact that she didn't have it, is the only weapon that worked. I'm proud of you."

Eli felt the shame that weighed his soul down dissolve. The cleansing relief was overwhelming, and he felt like crying but didn't.

Lizzy stood and walked to him, opening her arms. He stood and she embraced him. She whispered, "It's not your fault. It never was. Let that go. It's not yours. It never was."

Flooded with something akin to joy, Eli felt a tear run down his cheek. "I'm so glad you're here."

She pulled back, gently touched his shoulders with her hands, and said, "I'm so glad you're here, too." She turned away, picked up the pad from the chair, and sat back down.

Eli took his seat and wiped his cheek. With one cleansing breath, the shame gremlins were gone.

"What else is on your mind today?" she asked.

Eli didn't have to think about that one. "My date with Sarah tonight."

"Please give her my best. It looks like she's been busy."

"She has. She was able to accelerate the proxy fight, nominate new board members, schedule a shareholder vote, and interview new CEO and chairman candidates."

"That's quite a list. How are you two doing?"

Eli, despite anticipating the question, became suddenly uncomfortable and sat up straight in his chair. "She came to see me each day in the hospital. Then we texted or called each other each day."

Lizzy saw right through him. "How did that make you feel?"

Eli searched for the words and shifted in his chair. "To be honest, for some reason, I got this weird sensation. She didn't have to do all that. I knew she was busy."

Lizzy's eyes widened. "What was the sensation? What did it feel like?"

Eli thought about Sarah. The sensation returned. "It feels like worry."

"That's a man's answer. What's the *emotion*?"

Eli laughed at himself. Lizzy had hit the nail on the head. He dug deeper. "You know, it's fear."

"Okay. Now we're getting somewhere. What do you think you're afraid of?"

"I don't know. I just feel it."

Lizzy put her pad aside and leaned forward in her chair, resting her elbows on her knees.

"Let's try this. Think of the last time you felt this."

Eli ran through his past. He thought about other relationships he'd had. None of them had lasted, but the ones he'd walked away from early felt most like this. "Other relationships felt like this. The ones I walked away from."

"And why did you walk away from them?"

Eli's mind was blank. He tried to force himself to come up with an answer, but he couldn't.

Lizzy leaned back in her chair and waited.

"You know. I don't know."

Lizzy smiled. "Eli, if I told you that trust is the belief in the good intentions and competence of others, what would you say?"

As much as Eli didn't want to believe it, it felt right. "I was afraid because I didn't trust them? That fits. I have no idea why."

"It's the last piece to your puzzle. Think about the relationships you *haven't* had. The ones you rejected."

Eli did. "You're right. They felt like this."

"Let me help you. You rejected those you didn't trust. And you didn't trust them because of that old self-image. Deep down, despite your confidence in your *abilities*, you viewed yourself as that little kid who wasn't good enough. You distrusted the people who were kind to you because they couldn't see that you weren't good enough. It didn't square with your self-image. The ones who treated you poorly you trusted because your unconscious mind said they agreed with that childhood view that you were flawed and not enough. That you deserved to be treated poorly. But that little boy inside wanted their approval, too. Maybe thinking that would change *them*. That kid hoped he could save them like he couldn't save his mother. And if you could, then you wouldn't be that unworthy kid."

Eli went back through his relationships. One by one, they fell in line with what Lizzy said. Like a long string of dominoes falling against each other. The last domino, though, was not what he'd expected. It was Sarah.

"You're right," he said.

"Look, Eli. It's not because you're flawed. No one ever taught you to be deeply known. Vulnerable—but safe inside love. It can be terrifying when you've had to spend much of your life protecting the parts you thought weren't loveable. All you need to do is remember that you're always enough. You deserve to be treated like it. Trust those people. It might be uncomfortable, but if you lean into that, wonderful things can happen."

He thought about Sarah. The sensation was mostly gone. He decided he'd lean in and let it go wherever it went.

Lizzy stood, recognizing Eli's personal revelation. "I think you're ready for that date. Don't let those old childhood beliefs trip you up. She sees a loveable man. Just be *that* man."

Eli stood. "I've said this a thousand times, but I can't thank you enough."

"You're welcome. The only thing I ask in return is that you live the life you deserve."

As Eli headed out the door, he felt as if the weight of the world had been lifted from him. He looked forward to the evening and what might lie ahead.

CHAPTER 65

ELI HAD REMOVED his sling, donned a sport coat, and driven to pick up Sarah at her parents' house. With her father gone, the home had a completely different vibe. Sarah had been late getting home. As she changed, Eli and her mother talked in the kitchen. Ruby Blackwood had renewed energy—an energy Eli had never seen. After exchanging pleasantries, he asked, "How are you doing, Ruby?"

Ruby lit up. "I'm doing well. Sarah has me hopping on the business side, and I've had to deal with Lucian's arrest and incarceration. You know, it's surreal. He's a broken man now. He's cooperating and he'll take a plea deal. He even turned over the remaining Blackwood shares to me. I think with Winchester dead, he knows he has no buffer. He's on the hook for it all."

"That's great," Eli said. He could tell Ruby had something else on her mind.

Ruby paused, gathering herself. Her eyes glistened. "You know the best thing is that with Lucian gone, Cody is back. With Sarah staying here, I have my son and my daughter back.

"I'm happy it's working out so well." She seemed to catch herself and calmed. "I know it wasn't easy. Especially losing your friend. But if it wasn't for you… well, I don't like to think about that."

"That's kind of you to say that," Eli said.

Eli heard footsteps coming down the hallway. Sarah walked into the kitchen dressed in dark pants and a cashmere sweater. She looked stunning. Eli had to remind himself to breathe. "Wow. You look beautiful."

"Thank you. Sorry about the delay," she said. "Are you ready?"

"Yes, I am," Eli said, thinking his tone was too eager.

Sarah's smile sent a tantalizing current through him.

Her mother smiled at Eli. "You kids enjoy yourselves. You've certainly earned it."

Eli headed toward Sarah and offered her his arm. Taking it, she looked back and said, "Bye, Mom. No need to wait up."

Eli felt a comfortable connection to her as they walked to the car. The ride to the restaurant was the best ride he'd taken in a long time. Sarah was animated, engaging, and funny. They traded their favorite funny stories from the oilfield and her life in Southern California.

Eli had picked a waterfront restaurant along the Arkansas River, just across the bridge into Jenks. It was one of those bonus days in the Oklahoma early spring where the temperatures had soared into the seventies. Eli had reserved a table on the waterfront deck overlooking the river. As they took their seats, Eli gazed at the river. The streetlights along the bridge reflected in the dark water. The steady whispering gurgle of the swollen river mixed with the hum of conversations around them. The scent of garlic and butter from the grill stirred his hunger.

Over a Greek salad with grilled chicken for Sarah and a filet mignon for Eli, they caught up with each other's lives since the shooting. Sarah had been swamped by the governance and legal issues in restructuring Blackwood Energy and helping Abena connect with venture capitalists to launch her company. Eli talked about arranging Jim's graveside service and tending to the matters of his estate. The conversation flowed naturally, like the river moving downstream with the spring rains.

"How are you feeling about your family these days?" Eli asked.

"Mother is doing wonderfully. I thought she would. And Cody is back. Even might stick around. I'm trying to get him to take a role in the company again."

"Your brother was good when he was there before," he said.

Sarah nodded then smiled at Eli. "You wouldn't be interested, would you?"

Eli leaned back and laughed. "No. Thanks, but no. I'm done with that. Happy to give you some names. For the board or for operations."

"So, what are you going to do?" she asked.

"I'm figuring that out as we speak."

Eli thought he saw Sarah blush. He shifted the conversation. "And I'm writing again."

Sarah took a sip of her Chardonnay. "Interesting. I never asked what you wrote?"

"I write stories that show people making their way through life's adversities to discover life-changing things about themselves and the world around them."

"I'd read something like that."

"Thank you. I'm also fielding lots of calls for help, too. The media seems to think Lizzy and I are some kind of team."

"What kind of calls?"

"People in desperate situations wanting us to help in some way."

"There were quite a few people that came up to us after Jim's ceremony," Sarah said.

"More of the same."

Sarah paused, as if waiting to jump into a cold pool. Her eyes were soft but sparkled in the lights from the bridge. "Do you miss him?"

Eli, in return, felt like he was edging to the end of a high dive, looking over the edge, into something he'd never tried with anyone. He decided to jump in. "I miss him every minute." He locked eyes with Sarah. "But here's the deal. I feel him every day. Despite being raised Catholic, I'm not much on religion these days." He chuckled at himself. "These days I think it's all about energy."

Grinning, Sarah said, "Spoken like a true oilman." She offered her wine glass and Eli clicked his glass with hers. They both had a drink. Then she said, "I couldn't resist. Go on. Please."

"I think there is an energy in the universe greater than any one of us. I don't think any organized religion has it perfect, but it's out there. I think we have some of that energy inside us, and when we die, part of that energy stays. I feel Jim every day. His energy. And I think that energy connects us all. Maybe it's conscience like Lizzy says—the ability to care for another human being."

Sarah put down her wine and slowly bobbed her head in agreement. "Do you feel that energy in me?"

Her question cut straight through him. He put his wine glass on the table. "I do."

Eli could feel it. It was strong, powerful, and warm. It was something his soul had longed for. It had been instant and unexpected. A mutual spark that kept him warm. They didn't speak for a moment. They gazed at each other as the candlelight flickered in their eyes.

Eli broke the silence, "What about you? What will you do after this? I don't even know what you do when you're not working."

Sarah softly smiled and took another sip of chardonnay. "I exercise. You know, I like to run in Santa Monica. Take Pilates classes. Have dinner with my friends." She leaned forward and whispered, "Sometimes I sneak away to the gun range."

Eli smiled. "What about next steps?"

She took another sip. "It depends… on what my heart says." She leaned back in her chair and rested her gaze on Eli. He offered his glass, and she clicked it with hers. Sarah gently set her glass down. She looked to either side, then folded her hands on the table. Sadness filled her eyes. "It's been very difficult, these past weeks, dealing with the matters involving my father. It's brought up that feeling of being betrayed from my childhood. I know that every daughter thinks her daddy is a superhero, and at some point, they see that he's only human." Sarah blotted her eye with her napkin. "But the twist in my father's story…well it was devastating—such a disappointment…"

Eli reached across the table and cupped her hands in his. "Hey… hey. I get it. I'm sorry you have to go through that again. I want you to know that I'm here—right here for you if you need me."

Sarah leaned back and picked up her napkin again, touching up her eyes. She smiled at Eli, then chuckled. "You know, I have to say, I've never felt more comfortable, closer to anyone than I do with you."

Her comment warmed his aching heart. "The feeling is mutual." Eli looked around the restaurant. "Let's get out of here."

Finished with dinner, they both took their last sip of wine.

Eli didn't want their conversation to end. Because the weather was warm and they'd both been cloistered by their work the past week, he suggested an evening stroll at the Gathering Place. He nodded at the server, took care of the bill, and arm in arm, they headed for the car.

Eli pulled from Riverside Drive into a familiar parking place adjacent to the basketball courts. He met Sarah at the passenger's door, holding it open, then closing it gently behind her. He heard a ball bounce and looked over his shoulder. Dusk had forced the court light on, and Eli noticed a lone boy, maybe twelve years old, standing at the foul line practicing free throws as his frustrated mother stood beneath the basket catching the ball and bouncing it back to him.

"Go ahead," Sarah said, smiling.

"It'll just be a minute."

"That's what he said."

Eli laughed. He trotted around the fence and onto the court. "Hey there. How's it going?"

The tired mother just looked him over. But the boy stopped, stuffed the ball under his arm, and scowled. "Not good."

"Wait a minute," the boy's mother said, perking up. "I've seen you. Online. That story about Blackwood Energy."

"Yes, ma'am," Eli said.

"You saved all those people."

"I had lots of help," Eli said.

The mother looked behind Eli and saw Sarah, her fingers in the chain-link fence, watching them.

"She was there too."

Eli nodded in agreement. "Mind if I show him just one thing?"

"No. Not at all." She sternly looked at her son. "Jeremy, you listen."

Jeremy looked like he couldn't care less about who Eli was.

Eli walked to him. "Listen, man. I've been where you are. I think if you make one adjustment, things will start working for you."

"What's that?" Jeremy said, unimpressed.

"Pull your elbow in. Here,"—Eli put his hands out—"Let me show you."

Jeremy gave him the ball. Eli demonstrated pulling his right elbow in square with the basket. "Like this. That's it. Give it a shot."

Eli gave the ball back and stepped aside. The boy sighed, bounced the ball once, and readied to shoot as Eli had shown him. He took the shot. It went in on the first try.

Eli trotted toward Sarah.

"Hey, mister!" Jeremy yelled.

Eli stopped and turned.

"Thanks!" Jeremy and his mother grinned.

Eli waved. "I gotta get back to that beautiful lady." He turned and trotted around the fence to Sarah.

"Sorry. Couldn't resist."

Sarah smiled again. "No worries, coach."

Eli offered his hand, and she took it. They made their way

through the tree line to the walking path along the river. Venus hovered over the horizon in the clear black sky and the lighted concrete path ahead glowed. Feeling chilly, Eli removed his sport coat and covered Sarah's shoulders. He took her hand in his and their pace seemed to be in sync.

"Thanks, Eli. I wanted to let you know I'm sorry I've been so busy."

They walked up the slight grade toward the bridge. "There's no reason for an apology," he said. "I know what you've been up against."

She looked ahead. "You're very understanding. How are you feeling about what went down? I haven't seen you in person since Jim's celebration of life."

"Thanks for asking. I'm dealing with it. It will take a while. Lizzy has helped me see a few things that might make it easier."

"How's Lizzy doing?"

"Lizzy is Lizzy. Doing well. She's a rock."

"I'm sure glad you sought her advice. It saved my life."

"You know, I just told her the same thing."

They shared a laugh.

It was dark now and they'd reached the pedestrian bridge that stretched across the Arkansas River. The normally quiet spillway near the bridge was roaring with the spring rainfall. Eli led them halfway across the bridge, and they stopped and leaned on the railing. The lights from the Jenks bridge twinkled in the distance. The night sky had become brilliant with stars. They both looked downstream, the lights from the scattered businesses along the river reflecting in the water.

Sarah looked at him. "What you did for my father… I can't thank you enough. I know how you feel about him. It took a lot to do what you did. I know you said you did it for us. But there was no guarantee there would even be an us."

"Didn't want there to be a chance that your father's murder would be the one thing you and I would always remember."

Sarah looked down at the river rushing below them. Eli thought he could see her blushing again. "Always?" she said, still looking at the river.

Eli felt like he was about to jump into the churning water. He remembered his conversation with Lizzy. He found himself smiling. He laughed at himself and looked at the sky. Sarah saw him look up, and she did the same. Suddenly, a shooting star blazed across the sky and flamed out in a split second.

She pointed to the sky. "Did you see that?"

Eli had. He nodded. One word came to mind. *Stardust.* Jim had told Hope it was the one thing that connected them all. But he was wrong. Eli knew what he needed to say.

Eli turned and faced Sarah. She turned and faced him, too.

He took her hands in his. Her eyes were twinkling like the stars.

"What are you thinking?" she asked.

"I'm thinking how tragic it would be to have the one thing you wanted in life right in front of you and never know it."

Sarah smiled. "I see you, Eli. I see all of you."

She leaned in and they kissed.

Eli felt gravity disappear, replaced by vibrant energy between them. The shield that had protected the most vulnerable but precious parts of himself from the cold hard light of day melted away in the etherical warmth they shared. He'd killed stardust but found the one thing he'd wanted for the entirety of his life.

THE END

ACKNOWLEDGEMENTS

As always, this book would not be possible without the help and support of my wife, CJ. Special thanks to Kelly Buck for her expertise in the field of Psychology. Thanks to Keri Barnum for her help and guidance and to all the people behind Mahogany Row Press. I'm grateful for Julie Miller and her wonderful editorial help. Any mistakes are of my doing, not hers. Finally, special thanks to the team at Damonza for another great cover.

If you enjoyed *The Mentor's Daughter*, leaving a review will let other readers know how much you loved it.

I'd be grateful if you helped spread the word by recommending it to your friends and family and posting on social media, too.

To learn more about new books and exclusive content, sign up for my author mailing list and receive a copy of my first novel, *The Sunset Conspiracy* free: http//stevehadden.com or scan the QR Code below.

Keep reading for a riveting excerpt from *The Victim of the System*...The first Ike Rossi thriller...

CHAPTER 1

JACK COLE KNEW they were coming for him next. He waited in the dense shrubs with a vengeful patience. He reminded himself he was here for a reason—one that justified the action. He fought back the dark sensation that this was wrong. *Thou shalt not kill* had been drilled into him at Saint John's. But this was the only way to end it—to be safe.

His hand shook as he gripped the heavy rifle and took aim at the front door of the mansion across the private cul-de-sac. He settled the jitter with the thought that this man had killed his dad.

He leaned back against the tree and braced for the kick. Then, through the bushes, he saw a sliver of light widen as the front door opened. He dropped his head and took aim through the scope. He'd been watching the lawyer's house for days.

The thick door swung open and his target stepped out, closing the door behind him. Jack hesitated when he came face-to-face with him through the scope. Still, he steadied the heavy rifle and squeezed the trigger.

The blast slammed his back against the thick tree. The kick felt stronger than it had when he'd fired it on his first hunting trip with his father, just two months ago. As he scrambled to regain his balance, he saw his prey—the man responsible for destroying what was left of his family—fall against the front door of the red brick home, his white shirt splattered with blood and his face paralyzed in shock. Blood smeared as the man grabbed at the door, apparently reaching for someone inside. Finally, the attorney collapsed with his contorted body wrapped around his large legal briefcase.

Jack stood and froze, shocked by the carnage he'd unleashed. When the door swung open and a panicked woman rushed out, he came to his senses.

In seconds, Jack secured and covered the rifle and began his escape. Halfway down the cul-de-sac, he was sure someone had called 911. As he calmly pulled the red wagon his father had given him on his ninth birthday, he heard the police cars responding. They raced through the expensive suburban homes toward 1119 Blackbird Court.

The two cars turned onto the cul-de-sac and slowed when the patrolmen passed a mom and her children standing in their driveway, gaping at the terrifying scene. At the deep end of the cul-de-sac, the police cars screeched to a stop. Their doors sprang open and two officers swept the area with their guns drawn. The other two rushed to the porch. The woman cradled the man's body, screaming wildly. Blood coated the porch and covered the woman's face and arms.

Jack fought the urge to run and wandered out of the cul-de-sac. Two other police cars and an ambulance raced past. Over his shoulder, he saw the paramedics rush to the porch. Then Jack turned the corner and lost sight of what he'd done—and he began to cry.

SIX MONTHS LATER

CHAPTER 2

IKE ROSSI HATED this place. Not because something had happened here. Instead, it was something that hadn't. It represented failure. A rotting failure that he placed firmly on his own shoulders. While it had been twenty-two years, the wound was as raw as it was on that dreadful day he'd tried to forget for most of his adult life. Now, after years of dead ends, he was here once again to close that wound.

He waited on the hard bench in the massive lobby of the Allegheny County Courthouse flanked by murals of Peace, Justice, and Industry. Despite their ominous presence, he ignored them. He'd never found any of those here.

As 9 a.m. approached, the lobby swelled with people making their way to their destinies. Their voices and the clicks of their best shoes echoed through the massive honeycomb of thick stone archways as they wound up the network of stairs leading to the courtrooms on the floors above. Nameless faces all carried their tags: anger, sadness, fear, and arrogance. Those who were above it all, those who feared the system, and those who just saw money. While he'd always heard it was the best system on earth, he was painfully convinced that justice deserved better.

Three benches down, Ike's eyes locked on a small boy who was crying and leaning into a woman's side as she tried desperately to comfort him. When he recognized Jack Cole from the flood of news reports over the last six months, he didn't feel the prickly disdain that had roiled in his gut as he watched the initial reports on TV. At first, he'd condemned the ten-year-old boy as another killer—one who took the life of someone's parent. But as the case unfolded, he'd discovered the boy had lost his father. The constant wound Ike kept hidden in his soul opened a little wider. He knew what it was like to lose a parent.

According to the reports, Jack Cole's father had committed suicide as a result of a nasty divorce from Brenda Falzone Cole, the estranged daughter of one of the richest families in the country. Jack, a genius ten-year-old, had shot and killed his mother's family law attorney—not exactly what Ike expected from a kid. When he was finally identified in video from a neighbor's security camera and questioned, he shocked investigators by admitting the act.

Claiming he didn't have a choice under Pennsylvania law, the prosecutor was trying the boy as an adult. Jack faced a murder charge. Due to his young age, both sides wanted to fast-track the trial. It was scheduled to start next Monday, just a week away.

The boy looked up and caught Ike's gaze. Despite his best efforts, Ike couldn't look away. Tears streamed down Jack's face, but at the same time, his eyes begged for help. A mix of fear and generosity accumulated deep in Ike's chest. He knew the boy sought the same help he'd sought for himself years ago, but the prospect of exhuming that pain warned him to stay away.

Still, yielding to a magnetic force that had no regard for his own protection, Ike stood, smiled, and walked to the boy, ignoring the condemning stares from the people eyeing Jack. Reaching into his jacket pocket, he pulled out a small Rubik's Cube he carried to amuse distressed kids on long flights to distant oil provinces.

He stopped in front of the pair and asked the woman, "May I?" while he showed her the toy. The dried streaks down her cheeks told him she shared the boy's pain. He recognized her from the news reports but didn't want to remind her that millions of people were now witness to her custody battle with Jack's mother's family—and the progression of her devastating pretrial defeats at the hands of the district attorney.

"Oh, that's so kind of you," she said, nodding gently.

Ike gave Jack the toy and sat beside him. Jack's smallish build and timid posture made it hard to believe he was ten—and he'd killed someone.

Jack sniffled and wiped his nose with the back of his arm.

"Here, honey," the woman said as she handed him a Kleenex. Jack wiped his nose and immediately began twisting the cube, ignoring Ike.

"I'm Lauren Bottaro," the woman said. "This is Jack. I'm his aunt."

Ike reached out. "Ike Rossi."

Her eyes flamed with familiarity. She seemed stunned. "You're Ike Rossi?"

Jack handed the cube back to Ike. "Done!"

Ike wasn't sure what startled him more, the look on Lauren's face or the fact that Jack had solved the cube in less than a minute. "That's great, Jack." Ike offered Jack a high-five, but Jack awkwardly hesitated. Finally, he slapped it and Ike returned the toy. The tears were gone, replaced by a proud smile. Ike looked back at Lauren, who'd apparently caught herself staring at him.

She seemed to regain some composure, and a serious expression swept across her face.

"Mr. Rossi, can I ask what you do, now?"

Ike hesitated, hearing more than just that question in her voice.

He looked up and saw Mac Machowski, grinning.

"I'll tell you what he does."

Ike could have kissed Mac for the timely rescue.

Mac counted on his thick gnarled fingers. "He fixes things that can't be fixed. He keeps fat cats from getting kidnapped—or killed if they do—and he's the best damn investigator I've ever seen."

Ike noticed Jack had stopped playing with the Rubik's Cube and was listening intently to Mac, along with Lauren.

Ike smiled. "Mac, I'd like you to meet Lauren and Jack."

Mac tipped the bill of his Pirates cap to Lauren. "Ma'am." Then, extending his meaty paw, he knelt painfully and came face-to-face with Jack. "Nice to meet you, young man."

Jack nervously looked away but reached for Mac's hand and shook it.

"Jack. What do you say?" Lauren said.

Jack faced Mac. "Nice to meet you, sir."

Mac's joints creaked as he reached to the floor and pushed himself up. "You ready there, partner?" he said to Ike. "We gotta catch him before he leaves the courthouse at nine."

As Ike stood, Lauren rose with him. "So you're a detective?"

Ike threw a nod toward Mac. "He is—a retired homicide detective. I'm a private security and investigative services consultant in the oil and gas business."

Lauren tipped her head back, as if enlightened. "That makes sense now."

"What makes sense?" Ike said.

"I saw your name written on my brother's day planner."

The claim jolted Ike. "My name?"

Lauren nodded again. "Did you speak to him?"

"No, I've never talked to your brother." Ike was sure investigators would have checked the planner, but he'd never been questioned.

Jack reached up and tugged on Ike's forearm. "Can you help me?"

Those eyes were begging again.

Lauren gently pulled Jack's hand from Ike's arm. "I'm sorry," she said. "He's been through a lot."

Jack kept his eyes, now wet again, locked on Ike. "My dad wouldn't do that to me. He wouldn't kill himself."

Ike was frozen by Jack's stare. It was as innocent as any ten-year-old's. A primal desire to protect Jack stirred in Ike's heart. He didn't want to believe the kid—but he did.

Lauren hugged Jack. "It's okay, honey." She looked back at Ike and Mac. "We have no right to ask you th—"

A thick, towering woman with dark brown hair and a stone-cold stare wedged into the space between Mac and Lauren. She studied Mac, then Ike. "What's going on here, Lauren?"

Ike immediately recognized her from the news reports. Jenna Price represented Jack. For the last two months, she'd been billed as a hopeless underdog, and the string of losses so far—other than prevailing at the bail hearing—supported that label. A basketball player-turned-lawyer, she was battling a DA who so far showed little mercy. She worked with her father in their tiny firm, and every talking head said she didn't stand a chance.

Lauren said, "Jenna, this is Ike Rossi and Mac… I'm sorry?"

"Machowski," Mac said as he shook Jenna's hand.

Jenna gripped Ike's hand and held it as she spoke. "My dad said you were the greatest quarterback ever to come out of western Pennsylvania."

Ike always had one answer to that comment to quell any further discussion of his accolades. "That was a long time ago."

"What are you doing now?" she asked.

Jack leaned around Lauren and nearly shouted, "He's a detective. He can help us!"

Lauren hugged him tight again. "Shhh."

"A detective?" Jenna said.

"A private security and investigative services consultant."

Jenna nodded and held her gaze but said nothing.

"We gotta go now," Mac said, looking at his watch.

Ike stepped back from Jenna. "Stay strong, Counselor." He

nodded to Lauren. "Ms. Bottaro." Then Ike offered a handshake to Jack.

Jack sheepishly held out the Rubik's Cube for Ike. Immediately, Ike felt Jack's awkwardness.

"You keep that, Jack." Ike raised his hand for another high-five. Jack took the cue this time and slapped it. "Ladies," he said, turning with Mac and walking down the hall.

As they reached the stairs at the end of the corridor, Ike glanced over his shoulder. He could see Jack edging around the two women to keep his eyes on Ike, with the Rubik's Cube clutched in his hand. Ike turned back to the stairs.

"You okay?" Mac said. Ike nodded and started up the stairs to meet a man he despised. A man who might finally deliver the key to *his* parents' murder.

If you enjoyed the excerpt, you can buy your copy of *The Victim of the System* here:

https://www.amazon.com/Victim-System-Steve-Hadden-ebook/dp/B0D8L62HQ5

ABOUT THE AUTHOR

Steve Hadden is the author of *The Sunset Conspiracy, Genetic Imperfections, The Swimming Monkeys Trilogy, The Victim of the System, The Dark Side of Angels, The Secret That Killed You,* and *The Mentor's Daughter.* Steve writes intriguing thrillers with **heart**—stories that show memorable characters making their way through life's dilemmas and adversities to discover life-changing answers about themselves and the world around them.

Visit his website at *http://www.stevehadden.com*

www.ingramcontent.com/pod-product-compliance
Lightning Source LLC
LaVergne TN
LVHW041113080826
845145LV00007B/1800

* 9 7 8 1 9 6 3 5 8 4 0 7 3 *